Knights of the Magical Realm

Shadow Warrior

By

Layla Chase
Delilah Devlin
Betty Hanawa
Myla Jackson

Triskelion Publishing
15327 W. Becker Lane
Surprise, AZ 85379 USA

Printing History
First e Published by Triskelion Publishing
First e publishing June 2006
First printing by Triskelion Publishing
First paperback printing July 2006
ISBN 1-933471-99-9

Cover design Triskelion Publishing
Cover model: Andrei Claude

Cougar

By
Layla Chase

Chapter 1

A breeze whispered through the branches of tall pines and cedars. An owl screeched, its eerie cry echoing through the moonlit forest. The man jerked and dragged an elbow on the weathered planking. With slow movements, he stretched, moving his legs, and his calf scraped on a nail head.

Aw, shit.

He cracked open an eyelid, scanned the immediate area and confirmed what he'd dreaded. He lay sprawled on the cabin's porch, naked.

Not again.

Kol Thorstein shivered in the chilly night air, rolled to one side and rose up up on his hands and knees. Pain shot through his muscles and he pushed himself to stand, gritting his teeth against the stiffness in his joints. With one hand braced against the wall, he dragged himself to the door and opened it. The clothes he'd worn earlier lay strewn in a line across the room where he'd obviously stripped and dropped them in his haste to get outside.

Why? What had been the trigger this time?

Fuck, he had to figure out what was happening. Living sequestered in the Rocky Mountains wasn't getting him back to his unit any time soon. His CO would boot his butt out of the squad if he learned about Kol's blackouts.

A soldier who couldn't maintain control was a soldier who couldn't be trusted.

A black tee shirt lay on the woven rug and he snatched it up. With jerky moves, he pulled it over his head, aware of the cloth grazing sensitive skin. He flexed his shoulders, and the sting of fresh scrapes zipped along nerve endings like heat lightning. With a hiss of inhaled breath, he pulled off the shirt and wrapped it around his neck. Better to let the scratches scab over.

His stomach rumbled and he glanced at his wrist. Damn, where the hell was his watch? He moved toward the kitchen to read the clock on the microwave. 8:52. Well past dinner. Had he eaten?

No pans on the stove, no dishes in the sink.

He yanked open the refrigerator door and pulled out the closest milk jug, lifting it to his mouth and drinking hungrily. The cold liquid settled in his stomach, driving away the immediate hunger.

Next, he had to add this incident to the log. With measured steps, he moved across the rug, down the hallway and into his office. Nervous energy still ran through his system and he remained standing at the computer station. A two-second press of his thumb on the ID pad and the notelink whirred to life.

"Ready for data," a modulated voice announced.

Whatever entries he made into his symptom log had to be logical without the emotion he currently felt. "Read last entry."

"4:48 p.m., 8 April 2020."

Four hours missing this time. He paced to the opposite side of the room and back, trying to remember where he'd been before the blackout.

"Feeling lightheaded. Tingling starting in feet...affecting han−" The databank voice clicked, paused, and clicked again.   "Entry incorrect in grammatical formation."

More than just grammar was wrong here. Shoving a hand through his hair, he knew he had to solve this problem and fast.

Moonlight streaming through the window lured him and he stepped into the silvery square. The light enveloped him and he forced himself to relax, widening his stance on the carpet and flexing his hips.   Through the screen wafted an earthy scent — musk and an element undefined but familiar.

"New entry. Databank, note time. Scenting musk on the wind. Sexual awareness heightened." A different ache ran through him and settled low in his gut. His cock flexed. A feeling that always followed close on the heels of these damn blackouts.   Adrenaline ran through his system, pumping his blood so only echoes sounded in his ears. His hands fisted and he set his jaw.

He needed a distraction. Something to keep his body from focusing on his primal urge. He shifted his gaze to the window and concentrated. The view outside showed a few rangy pines silhouetted against the dark masses of the forest. Above the trees, Culebra Peak formed a jagged outline against the star-studded black sky.

A breeze blew the musky scent deeper into the room.   He inhaled deeply, and his cock lengthened in response. With an absent movement, he rubbed a hand over his stomach wondering at the strange pull in his chest. His blood raced and the urge to conquer and claim filled him.

Then his hand moved lower and he stroked his cock, running a thumb along the top, smiling when the organ beneath his fingers surged and thickened.

Tension spiraled in his gut and his balls tightened.

Maybe a distraction wouldn't work this time.

A cloud slid past the half-moon and a shaft of moonlight filtered through the evergreens to the forest floor. Zoia Stavros winced at the flash and ducked her head, then leaned a shoulder against a tree trunk. She flipped up her night-vision goggles but left them strapped on. Better to keep them handy in case the cloud cover moved again.

She slipped a GPS unit from its hook on her utility belt. Careful to shield the screen with her free hand, she tilted it toward the light and took a reading. 37°08′56.66″ N 105°17′02.68″ W. With a flick of a couple buttons, she rechecked the distance from her hidden transport.

Close. Her quarry was within range.

From above, wings fluttered and a hoot faded on the night air.

What the hell was that? Zoia gasped and pressed harder against the tree, ignoring the bite of the rough bark. To the count of ten, she breathed in the cold night air, straining to hear any sound of movement on the ground. She hated being surprised by animals that moved fast.

Why hadn't she assigned this job to Antonia? Her assistant loved the wilderness, loved hiking and cooking over an open fire. Zoia barely tolerated the wild outdoors with gritted teeth and pure determination.

If Eagle Investigations' budget could have accommodated the overtime pay, she might have considered that possibility. Until her fledgling business registered a profit, she'd be pulling the long assignments.

With the tip of her boot, she gently scooted aside twigs and needles so she could step on damp earth. Her footfalls were whisper quiet as she progressed through the thick stand of conifers. Scents of fragrant pine and musty vegetation rose to tickle her nostrils. Another check of her GPS unit showed less than 300 yards to go. Her nerves kicked in—her stomach pinched and perspiration gathered at the base of her hairline.

Up ahead, a rustle in the underbrush sounded, paused then rustled again. She steadied herself with a hand on a nearby tree, hoping to pinpoint the direction. But her heartbeat thumped in her eardrums, pushing away all other sounds.

Not good.

A good private investigator wasn't scared off by a few noises in nature. Rats and cockroaches she could handle, but she was not ready to face down snakes. She closed her eyes and took a couple of relaxing breaths. Keep it together, city girl. Tonight, visual confirmation. Tomorrow, apprehension.

A few more steps and the trees thinned into a clearing. Moonlight spotlighted the granite rocks and matted grass like a museum exhibit. A breeze rustled the branches above her and a soft sigh filtered over the area. Staying hidden in the shadows, she reached into the pouch strapped to her thigh and pulled out a small set of binoculars.

At the far side of the clearing sat a modest building. She scanned the exterior of the structure, disbelieving her first impression. With the binocs on 300% zoom, she traced the outline of the two-story structure. An honest-to-the-Spirit log cabin.

The first one she'd seen outside the archived files from the late twentieth century. Behind it, she spotted the roof of a small outbuilding, maybe a barn. At the far end, muted light shone through several curtained windows.

Her heartbeat kicked up. The cabin was definitely occupied and she could catch a break. The hours of travel and adrenaline of the hunt were catching up. She just wanted to identify the subject and find a bed for the night..

Five minutes later, she'd circled the house and now had a clear view through the inches-wide gap in the curtains. If she leaned a bit, she could see the side of a dark desk with an open notelink spotlighted by a lamp out of her line of sight. By leaning in the other direction, she saw the foot of a bed with rumpled--

Oh, hello!

The patch of light on the grass spread as the curtains were drawn apart.

Instinct pushed Zoia deeper into the shadows. She eased off her goggles and lowered them to the ground beside her. Curiosity kept her gaze riveted on the window. Was this her chance to verify the whereabouts of the Army Special Forces soldier who'd gone missing?

The illuminated rectangle darkened then lightened. The cycle repeated. And again. As if a person paced just out of her range of sight.

Then a tall figure appeared at the window and braced his forearms on the glass above his head. The man's silhouette was fabulous—wide shoulders, lats with definite bulges, tight waist. A lean and fit male—and every muscled inch gloriously naked.

Ooowee—she sucked in a breath and held

it. This guy was hot. Zoia's fingers itched to use the binocs but couldn't risk a reflection off the lenses. Searching her memory, she ticked off her quarry's vital statistics—6'2"--check, athletic build—that and then some, blond hair—maybe, hazel eyes—she'd have to confirm that later.

Her gaze trailed along his physique, registering muscles that looked sculpted from marble and hours of disciplined exercise. She spotted the tattoo proclaiming his blood type and evidence of his last anti-fertility inoculation, but was too far away to confirm the data. A cloth hung around his neck. She couldn't call herself a red-blooded female, especially one of lusty Greek heritage, if she didn't take note of his cock. Yep, it was as solid and strong as the rest of him.

Her breath quickened and her nipples tightened. She wondered what had him so turned on. Her pussy clenched in response, dampness wetting her female curls. What was she thinking? Forget that they were probably the only two people for miles around. Forget that the chance of anyone finding out was next to nil.

He was the target and she couldn't forget that.

The subject disappeared from the window.

Her body sagged. Damn. Just when she started to relish her new role as *voyeur*. She shook herself and peeled back the sleeve of her neoprene jumpsuit, revealing a photo of Kol Thorstein, rank - captain. A definite possibility.

She might have found her man. After a glance back at the house, she gasped, "Oh."

The man had returned but this time his stance was different. One hand braced against the window, and the other rubbed circles on his chest, straying across his rippled abdomen and lowering to stroke his beautiful cock.

Her womb clenched and she pressed her thighs together. Get real, girl. You are on the job. Worry about getting laid when you're back in civilization.

Maybe this was more up-close-and-personal than she wanted. With effort, she tore her gaze away from his hand's intoxicating movements and looked at his face.

By the tilt of his head, he appeared to look right at her. If she moved now, he might notice. And she couldn't risk giving herself away.

Instead, her gaze moved back to where he caressed himself, fingers alternately cradling, rubbing, and circling his cock. A couple of times, his hand lowered to cup his balls but quickly returned to stroke the length of his rigid erection. His fingers encircled its girth and pumped, his forearm pistoning with increasing rhythm.

Her breaths grew shallow and a flush bloomed over her skin, moisture oozing in her pussy.

With a jerk, he pulled the cloth from his neck and held it under his cock. His hips flexed, his hand pumped and then his body went rigid. Only his hips rocked.

Zoia exhaled and willed her heart rate to return to normal. One final look at her quarry— eyes closed, head tilted back—told her he was occupied for a few moments. Perfect opportunity to check for a vehicle. She skirted the closest tree and crouched low, jogging around the house. Pausing again, she sucked in deep breaths. Damn altitude.

With a gaze that bounced between the

house and the pickup parked at the edge of the gravel road, she reached for the binocs. If the plates matched the identification data she'd researched, she'd confirm the sighting and exit the area. For now.

Leave the man to his private entertainment.

Careful to angle the lenses to avoid reflecting the moonlight, she focused on the license plate and pressed the button to record a digital image.

A cloud obscured the moon and the digits on the license plate blurred in shadow. Crap!

Glancing over her shoulder at the house, she moved in a direct line, intending to input the data in her palm computer. When she was within ten feet of the truck, a siren whooped and the truck lights flashed.

Her stomach sank. Busted! Who the hell set a perimeter alarm out in the middle of nowhere? She dashed for the protective cover of the truck and waited.

The alarm whoops were so loud she had no hope of hearing a response from her quarry. Her hands drew into fists. She had to get away. With stealthy moves, she backed into the darkness of the forest, positioned herself behind a tree, and stuffed her fingers in her ears to block out the blaring.

Finally, the alarm stopped. She unplugged her ears and the echoes faded into the distance.

A chuff of breath not her own sounded. And an earthy scent reached her nose—a mixture of musky pine, dampness and crisp night air. A gasp froze in her throat, and she stilled, senses alert in every direction. This was the part she hated even more—losing the quarry's location.

The swish of shifting needles sounded from

her left side.

Tilting her head, she hoped to spot movement through the darkness. To plan her escape, she needed to know which path was clear. The breeze blew the clouds past the moon and the trees became distinct shapes. Her gaze was snared by a pair of luminous amber eyes peering from the shadow of a tree. If her mouth hadn't suddenly gone bone dry, she would have screamed.

Inch by inch, his head emerged into view as he prowled toward her. No emotion showed on his face. The tanned muscles of his chest gleamed in the pale light, while navy fleece pants hung loose on his hips. His feet picking a path on the forest floor were bare.

Hair blond—confirmed. At least part of her brain was still on the job. Hazel eyes—maybe a really light shade. At his approach, she pressed back against the tree, wanting to reduce her exposure.

He came within four feet, never blinking, and then circled the tree, his movements liquid, but controlled.

She bit her lip. Why hadn't he confronted her? Demanded to know her purpose? Was he putting her through some kind of psychological test? If so, he was good. A few more minutes and she'd surrender. He entered her peripheral vision on her left and she tracked his movements, unable to drag her gaze from the fluid rhythm of his body in motion. Kol Thorstein was a commanding presence, power radiating from him in waves. Excitement spiraled low in her belly and her nipples tightened into diamond-hard points.

Not good, Zoia. Forget that you just witnessed the man in an intimate act. Treat him like the object of the hunt.

Kol stopped. His gaze finally broke from her face to scan her body from head to toe. He leaned his weight on the balls of his feet and sniffed, his narrowed gaze shooting straight to her pussy.

Could he detect her arousal? Not possible. She shifted her stance and reflexively squeezed her thighs together.

With one step, his chest was against hers and his forearms bracketed her head.

Caught off guard, she stiffened and sucked in a breath. Her gaze shot to his face but he appeared to be inspecting her hair. What was —

He leaned forward and nuzzled the tendrils of hair that escaped her tieback. His forehead pressed against her head, his hair scraping her temple, and a rumble sounded deep in his chest.

The knot in her stomach loosened. Her body betrayed her even though her head still screamed she was in a dangerous situation. What form of interrogation was this? She didn't know how to defend herself against his total assault on her senses. His nuzzles broke through to something basic inside and she relaxed, her fingers itching to touch his taut skin.

Warmth trailed along the rim of her ear and was gone, followed by a tingly chill.

Had he just *licked* her? No.

The skin along her neck heated then cooled. Well, maybe.

He shifted his stance and leaned close, rubbing his nose on hers then touching his forehead briefly against hers before feathering kisses over her eyebrows.

Zoia closed her eyes and sagged against the

tree, a sigh puffing through her lips. Everything about this situation screamed danger. But she couldn't deny the fact he was the kind of danger she craved. For a moment longer, she relished the sensation of his lips against her skin. Then she kicked out a foot, wrapped it around his ankle, and pulled to the side.

He went down, flat on his back and started to roll.

She followed him down, trapping his knees with her thighs and stretching to grab his forearms. With him pinned beneath her, she could question him.

A growl ripped through the air. He bucked his hips and levered against her grip.

She shimmied up his legs and squeezed with her thighs while struggling to keep hold of his arms. This wasn't how the hold worked in martial arts class. Her center of power wasn't balanced. Her back ached from the strain of the odd angle. He was too damn tall.

He raised his arms over his head and dragged her right along. Her legs straddled his hips and he flexed upwards, rubbing his hard cock against her *mons*. His gaze bore into hers and the side of his mouth curled upwards, exposing perfect white teeth.

Eons of feminine instinct guided her response to an alpha male, and she lowered her pussy against him, moving in a sensuous circle. Her nipples pebbled and she leaned down to rub them across his bare chest, a moan escaping at the delicious friction.

Kol rolled hard to the side, knocking her off his body, and landed in a crouch.

She landed on hands and knees, and shook

her head. Her muscles ached and her too-rapid breaths showed she'd exerted more effort than he in their little tussle. How could she still be aroused? This was crazy.

He sprang and landed behind her, clamping an arm around her middle, wrestler-style, and trapping her legs with his muscular thighs. Ducking her shoulder, she moved to roll out of his grasp, but he was too strong. She tried to fall flat, but his grip held her in a hands-and-knees position.

His hand on her stomach inched upward and teased her nipples. The ridge of his cock pressed into the back of her thigh. His free hand ran along her side from chest to thigh, heating her skin though her clothing. Then his fingers inched inside her waistband, loosened the folded-seam fastening and yanked down her pants. She gasped, the chilly air wafting over her flushed skin.

His hand now caressed her bare thigh, his touch as glorious as she'd imagined earlier. For an instant, her mind reeled at what was happening and then her body took over, relaxing into his touch. A feather light slide of his fingers up her leg, tickled the sensitive inner thigh, and glided along her pussy lips. A finger plunged inside, pressing along her walls in rhythm with his thumb circling her clit.

A guttural moan sounded. Was that from her? She moved her hips, circling against his hand, enjoying the spiraling urgency in her womb. A second finger joined the first and the thrusts increased. She pressed her knees into the ground and resisted the pressure of his movements, the friction deliciously increasing the tingles in her pussy.

His hand eased away, his knuckles grazing

her ass.

She bit back a whimper. He wouldn't leave her wanting, would he? Was this still a test? Then the head of his hard cock pressed against her pussy, probing, retreating, probing deeper. Her skin stretched deliciously around his girth and she rocked back her weight, in ecstasy over the fullness. For too long, she'd gone without this exciting feeling. For too long, she'd used only clit stimulators.

He pumped into her, faster, harder, deeper, his thighs slapping the back of hers.

She dug her palms into the dirt and needles, grasping for an anchor, but his powerful thrusts scooted her forward. His grip on her middle tightened, and a deep rumble sounded in her ear. She rocked backward and circled her hips, moving in sync to the rhythmic purr, in sync to the rush of sensation flooding her pussy.

"Ahhhh." Her satisfied cry rang into the night's silence and her shaking elbows gave way. Breathing hard, she slumped forward and rested her head on her forearms.

That was glorious.

Strong hands clamped her hips and pulled her body upright, her thighs resting on his, her calves tucked beneath him. She braced her hands on her knees and let him move her sated body. He raised her slowly so her pussy barely held the tip of his cock and then plunged her down to his lap, his rock-hard length sliding deep inside her channel. This time when he raised her, his cock sprang free and he rubbed her clit against its slippery head.

Instinct drove her hips into a circle. Electric tingles shot from her clit to her nipples, hardening them to bullets, and back, causing her juices to flow. Again, her climax spiraled close. "Oh, Spirit above. Do that again."

His grip tightened and his cock plunged inside her, thrusting fast, hard and deep. His breath huffed out between clenched teeth. The pace slowed and he slammed her into his lap once, twice, and then he stiffened, hot jets of cum pumping into her pussy. An eerie, strangled cry erupted from his mouth.

His body sagged, knocking her back to her hands and knees. His rapid breathing fluffed the hair on the side of her face. She welcomed his warmth and the fleeting feeling of closeness following such an animalistic act. She'd never had sex outdoors, never without talking, and never with a stranger. A night for firsts.

Her arms and legs trembled at the strain of holding up his considerable weight. She squirmed, thinking to rouse him enough that he'd move off.

His breathing had slowed.

She shoved her arms upright and jostled him to the side.

He scrambled to his knees, facing her. His gaze darted at the surroundings, down at his now bared body, then narrowed as he stared at her disheveled clothing and partial nudity. "What the hell did you do to me?"

Chapter 2

Kol stared at the wide-eyed woman sprawled five feet away. The dark-haired stranger whose delectable pale ass stood out against the dark forest surroundings. From the chilly sensation along the length of his still-engorged cock, he'd conclude they'd just had sex.

The last thing he remembered was— What? He squeezed his eyes shut, fighting for a memory.

A hollowness invaded his chest. That was the problem, he couldn't remember. With a shake of his head, he looked back at the woman.

"You're kidding, right?" She scooted backward, one hand tugging on the waistband of her pants. "You think I did this?" Her dark gaze flashed between their bodies.

"Who are you?" And how in the hell did she get this close without him knowing? His skills were deteriorating since his release from his Special Forces squad.

She scowled and pointed a finger at him. "Stay there. Give me a couple seconds."

He narrowed his gaze then nodded.

She flopped onto her back, levered her hips off the ground and yanked up her pants. In a quick movement, she twisted then rose onto the balls of her feet. "Now we talk."

A breeze wafted her scent—musky female mixed with the earthy aroma of their fucking—to him and his groin clenched. He stood, yanking his pants over his lengthening cock. This time he'd deal with the stranger using his bigger brain. "So, talk!"

"I got lost in the woods and stumbled onto your cabin."

He crossed his arms over his chest. "Lady, this is a forest."

A smile flickered across her lips. "Zoia."

"What's that mean?" His gaze strayed to her mouth, to her full lips and straight white teeth.

"It's my name, Zoia Stavros. I'm a research photographer."

"Where's your equipment?" He watched her expression for any sign of subterfuge. From the day of his release, he'd been expecting someone to arrive. He just hadn't expected such an enticing package.

She rested a hand on a hip and jerked it away, wincing. "Oo, my hands are cut."

A faint memory of a struggle niggled at his thoughts. His gaze ran her length, noting how she balanced her weight. Surely, this short bit of a female hadn't tried to subdue him. He flexed his legs and the skin around his knees pulled. A stab of guilt ran through him. Maybe she had.

"Not much of a talker, are you?" She pivoted and started toward the cabin. "That's okay, I'm used to it. My four brothers say I talk enough for the rest of them combined. I'm sure you've got water and first aid supplies inside."

The chit meant to invade his space! He stole a glance at the glorious movement of her hips. His hands itched to grasp her firm ass cheeks shaped by snug pants. "Hey." He jogged up behind her, his senses immediately overloaded by her musky scent. He gritted his teeth and backed away a step.

With a hand resting on the porch railing, she looked over a shoulder and arched a dark eyebrow.

"Thorstein, Kol." When her expression didn't change, he brushed past her and held open the screen door. "Thought you'd want to know whose cabin you're invading."

She hesitated then strode past him, wavy hair bouncing with each step. The tang of citrus followed in her wake.

He gripped the door handle and huffed out deep breaths. A little soap, a little water, a couple of adhesive strips—and she'd be on her way. Self-imposed seclusion would be his again.

Only a few steps into the room and panic hit. Where the hell was she? Had he left his notelink open to a page containing sensitive material? "Ah, Zoia? What can I help you find?"

"I'm doing great." Her voice carried from down the hall, over the sound of running water. "I found what I need in here."

Kol moved across the living room to his bedroom. With the click of a couple buttons, he closed down the active link, his gaze scanning the room for evidence she'd been in here first. He sniffed the air but detected no citrus. Or female musk.

An itch tingled between his shoulders. He'd become used to being alone and having her here made him nervous. Stifling the urge to pace, he braced a shoulder against the doorjamb across from the bathroom. Waiting. Unwilling to allow her to venture deeper into his space.

"Hey, Kol. Do you mind—" She poked her head around the open door and stiffened at seeing him. "Oh, you're here. Would you mind if I showered?"

The image of her entire body naked flashed through his thoughts. Would her skin be creamy white all over? He swallowed hard, willing his cock to behave.

"I've got scrapes on my knees, too, and..." Her gaze faltered as her words trailed off.

He had a good idea what else she'd wash away. "Be my guest."

"Thanks." She flashed him a wide smile before disappearing behind the wooden door.

His chest tightened and his stance went rigid. Her smile did him in. He hadn't felt a simple human connection like that in so long. Do not cave over a friendly smile, Thorstein. A smile is just lips and teeth. What if she were the forward scout for an invading party?

Water ran in the pipes and a feminine voice raised in muffled song sounded from the room across the hall. She'd be naked about now. His gaze centered on the brass doorknob. Two steps and a quick twist might satisfy his curiosity. He straightened and strode down the hall and out of the cabin. Throwing back his head, he jammed his hands on his hips and stared at the star-filled sky.

He dragged the cool Colorado air into his lungs and his blood rate slowed. He glanced ruefully at the receding bulge in the front of his pants. Maybe now he could think straight. Something about that woman's scent rattled him. Since his release, his sense of smell worked in hyper-drive. He'd adjusted to most scents but not hers. Wouldn't his squad members laugh at the normally unflappable Captain Thorstein getting a hard-on within a ten-foot radius of this particular female? Kol prided himself on his proven record of carrying out a mission, no matter what surprises were thrown in his path. This lady shot that record all to hell.

Might as well check from which direction she'd come and if he could locate her transport. He stepped back toward the porch and grabbed a genlight from its hook on the cabin wall, squeezing the handle until the greenish light strengthened enough to discern footprints in the dirt.

Kol walked slowly toward his truck, panning the light in arcs across the ground. He retraced their criss-crossed paths from the spot where they'd wrestled and followed her tracks back toward the truck.

Ten minutes later, he stopped at a spot along the tree line where her tracks first entered the clearing. He glanced over his shoulder to verify the cabin's position and noticed the direct sight line to his bedroom window. Light glowed through the window onto the ground outside. How long had she been in the area? Had she seen him at the window? Taking a closer look at the ground, he discovered two rounded indentions where some person sat and faced his cabin.

He prowled deeper into the forest, looking for a second set of prints but found only hers, although in places the trail nearly disappeared at the base of trees. Not exactly the type of trail he'd expect from someone who was lost.

*****

Zoia stepped out of the shower, feeling refreshed after hiking through the woods and that strange wrestling match that turned into a first-class fuck. She glanced at the pile of her clothes and couldn't bear to pull on the muddy garments. From a hook on the back of the door hung a flannel plaid robe.   She convinced herself the captain would understand if she borrowed it just until her clothes dried. She ran a sink full of water, squirted in some shampoo and swished around her clothes.

With a quick look at the mirror to make sure no leaves clung to her curls, she opened the bathroom door and peered out.   "Hello?" No imposing blond man stared from across the hall. On the desk in that room sat a silver and black notelink. Her fingers itched to tap the keys and make a connection with her assistant.

Silence greeted her.

With a tug on the robe's belt, she stepped into the hall and quickly walked to the end, peeking around the wall into the living area. "So, are you cooking us something?" This part of the house was empty. She wandered into the small kitchen and opened random cupboards. Assorted ceramic dishes and cooking utensils in one. Another held a few cans of food and a towering stack of foil pouches—survival rations.   She grimaced. "Some host you are."

Hand resting on the refrigerator door, she bent over and looked inside.   Peanut butter, mustard, salsa, wilted lettuce, a few eggs and a moldy orange. And four gallons of milk.

Interesting diet.

She grabbed the opened milk jug and pulled down a glass.

"Help yourself."

At the male voice, she gasped and whirled, slinging milk across the floor. "Don't do that."

"Don't enter my own home?" He closed the door and walked toward her.

"No, don't come up behind me. You scared me." She exhaled and looked at the shiny puddles on the floor. "Where's your robotic?"

"These still work." He opened a lower cupboard and pulled out a couple cloth rags. Moving to the middle of the floor, he knelt to wipe up the spill.

She stepped forward and held out her hand. "Pass them over. I can do that."

"I've got it." He squinted up at her, a flash in his hazel eyes. "Nice robe."

Oh yeah, the robe. Her hands rose to pull the lapels closer. "I hope you don't mind. My clothes are soaking in the sink."

His brows lowered then he ducked his chin, seeming intent on swiping at every drop. "You washed your clothes?"

"They were muddy..." The change in his behavior was subtle, but she spotted a muscle jumping in his jaw. "You wouldn't have wanted me sitting on your furni—" Oh blessed spirits, she'd put her foot right in her great big mouth. He hadn't intended to let her sit—the man wanted her gone. Long gone.

He stood and dropped the rags into a nearby plastic basket then turned and leaned against the counter. His hands rested next to his hips. "Who buys your photos?"

She tried to ignore how his stance pulled the t-shirt taut over his muscled chest. "My what?" His manner changed again, back to conversational. How much had she told him earlier?

His eyes narrowed. "You said you photographed animals. For a science institute or a nature group?"

All her rehearsed details fell into place in her mind. She took a moment to put the milk back in the refrigerator and turned to face him, imitating his pose. "I have a modest grant from a private research facility." Only a small stretch of the truth. The Halcyon Institute had given her a money card preauthorized for three thousand dollars. Payment in advance for the identification. Of this man. Her conscience twinged.

He crossed his arms. "Tell me the premise of the research."

Ooo, he was sharp! "I'm documenting the populations of several species following the absence of large predators in this sector." Zoia thought exposure to the athletic friends of her five brothers would have made her immune to sculpted arms, a ridged stomach and rock-hard thighs.

But no. A part of her wanted to stare gape-mouthed at his hard body. Probably because she knew exactly what he felt like up close. She clenched her legs together and struggled to keep her gaze on his face.

"Which ones?" His stare intensified.

"Which animals? I mean mammals." Crap. When she'd invented this phony job, she hadn't expected to be interviewed. Mountain nocturnals? "Let's see. I'm looking for raccoons."

"Elevation's too high."

Oops. Her stomach knotted. "Foxes."

"Seen a few."

What else? Her mind raced for a sure-fire species. "Bats!"

"Got plenty of those."

A sigh escaped. She'd gotten over that hurdle.

He pushed away from the counter and put his hands on his hips. "Where's your camera?"

"Why?" The knot was back and twisting this time.

"I can point out some nesting places."

"Now?" Her idea of a perfect nesting place involved a warm blanket and a fluffy pillow. His comment didn't sound like he was following the same thought wave. "You want to go along with me?"

"Sure." He shrugged. "I've got insomnia and you're used to staying up all night. Right?"

"Oh yeah." She waved a dismissive hand and forced out a laugh. "At this time of night, I'm just getting going."

He pointed at a bundle on the floor next to the sofa. "That your gear? May I?"

"Uh huh." They sounded more like grunts than words. Back in her office when she'd invented this cover, she'd had no idea she'd have to enact the part. This man expected her to go out into the wilderness, the dark and scary wilderness, and search for the very creatures that she'd heard skittering through the underbrush on her hike here.

A shudder ran through her and she tightened the belt on the robe. The borrowed robe she wore. "You know, we can't go out right now." She plopped down on the sofa, extended her legs over the cushion and heaved an overloud sigh.

From where he squatted and dug the camera from her backpack, he looked up, his gaze skittering the length of her body. "We can't?"

She raised her hands palms up and shrugged. "My clothes are soaking wet."

A scowl wrinkled his face then he stood. "So, I'll find you something to wear.."

Zoia watched him stride from the room and fell back into the sofa. Wasn't he Mr. Resourceful? Knowing where to look for the nests and offering to get her cam— She bolted upright, her breath catching in her throat. Had he been searched her pack? Maybe she should make contact with Halcyon, confirm his identity and take her chances on finding her transport in the dark.

She unzipped an outside pocket and dug for her satphone, relief running through her when she grasped its familiar shape. With a peek over her shoulder, she checked to see if Kol was returning. She twisted her body to block her actions and bent to punch in the numbers then stopped. The screen was blank. On closer inspection, she saw the casing was split along one side. That could have happened when she jumped against that last tree. Or when she'd tossed down the pack in the scurry to avoid the blaring pickup.

Cut off. Her skin chilled. No direct communication with her assistant. Anything could happen here in this isolated location and no one would know she was in danger. What was she thinking?

"Ready?"

She jumped at the unexpected sound of his deep voice and she dropped the satphone into her open bag. "Sure." She stood and turned to see him holding out a fistful of clothes. "For me? You really shouldn't have." When he didn't react to her sarcasm, she grabbed the items and stomped down the hallway to the bathroom.

A long-sleeved thermal shirt and sweat pants with a drawstring. She pulled on the clothes and looked at herself in the mirror. Great, the shirt was so tight it could double as a sports bra and the pants made her ankles look like the face on a Shar Pei. A double knot in the drawstring would keep the pants in place. She leaned against the wall to pull on her running shoes without socks. A yucky sensation but not to be helped.

A knock sounded on the door. "Do they fit?"

She yanked the door open and glared. "Of course they don't, but they'll suffice."

His gaze zeroed in on her breasts and heated. He swallowed hard and jerked his head toward the door. "Let's go."

The discomfiture she'd seen in his expression fueled her as she walked through the house and while she gathered her gear. He obviously didn't want to be affected by her, just as she didn't welcome the heat she felt. Well, fine. They were even. Until she contacted her assistant and checked for further instructions, she had to keep playing the game. The research photographer who got lost at night.

Zoia hitched the straps of her backpack onto her shoulders and walked in front, genlight ready. Her mind raced with the research she'd done on this sector. No worries about encountering large predators—wolves, cougars, bears—those had been gone for a decade or more. Logic stated she should be searching for bats and owls in the trees and foxes, rabbits and wild pigs on the ground. She figured they'd make too much noise to cross paths with any deer.

Maybe if she made *enough* noise all the animals would stay away.

Why had she thought a photographer was a good cover? And for nocturnal animals? She'd never been comfortable in the wilderness. And now she needed to appear competent.

"Which way shall we go?" His voice came close to her ear.

She jumped, her heart rate increasing.

"Quit doing that."

"What?"

The guy didn't make any noise when he walked. "Do you like seeing me jump?"

He frowned and swept his hand toward the clearing. "Lead on."

She scanned the ground still lit by moonlight. Okay, which was the least scary animal? A rabbit? And rabbits lived in burrows at the base of trees. At least that's what she remembered from nursery rhymes. Trees ringed the area around the cabin so she had her choice. Might as well do this in organized fashion. She turned hard left and set off to the closest one from the back of the house, her boots crunching twigs and needles as she walked. From behind came the faint swish of needles shifting. How did he do that?

At the edge of the trees, she bent and studied the ground looking for footprints. For what evidence, she didn't exactly know. Would the mark be long or short with points where the claws had touched?

Kol leaned close on her left. "See anything?"

Her whole side warmed and she fought from swaying closer to this man's heat. She could swear he was sniffing the ground. *Why* would he do that? "Not yet, but I will." She stood and set off, squeezing her genlight until a pale green circle appeared in front of where she walked.

Two hours later, they'd spotted tracks for rabbit, mole, and wild pig. Well, Kol found and pointed them out to her, explaining the differences in the marks each animal left behind. On her own, she'd snapped images of two bats and an owl, and picked out the sticks atop a cliff that indicated an eagle's aerie. Now her energy was gone and her chest ached with the effort of drawing in enough of the thin mountain air.

They were on the trail of a pair of foxes and she lifted a leg to cross a log. Her other leg trembled and she sat heavily on the rough bark.

"What's wrong?" Kol dropped into a crouch in front of her. As his head moved slowly to check out each direction, he reached back and circled her ankle with a hand.

The protective gesture went straight to her heart and she almost started blubbering. "I just tripped."

He turned to look at her, squinted, and then rummaged in his pack. "Have a drink. You look exhausted. If you needed to rest, we could have stopped." He held out a water bottle.

"Thanks." She unscrewed the top and sipped at the cool liquid before handing it back. No matter what, she couldn't let on how tired she really was. "My body is adjusting to the altitude. Give me a minute or so."

Kol eased up from his crouch and sat beside her. "Is this one of your normal nights?"

Oh, yeah. Locating a log cabin in an isolated forest, being seduced — no taken — by a stranger, then having to wear his clothes while chasing after wild creatures was all part of her daily routine. She wasn't sure what to say that wouldn't blow the lid off her frustration. Not to mention her cover. She cut him a sideways glance, trying to determine if he was laughing at her.

"Or do you normally follow just one animal?" He inhaled then braced his hands on his knees and scooted a few inches away.

Ah, that kind of normal. Logic told her a researcher was similar to a private investigator. "I follow where the clues lead me." A yawn stretched her mouth before she could bite it back and her shoulders slumped. "Sorry."

"Which way? More tracking or back to the cabin?"

He was giving her a choice so he must believe her cover. If only she could gloat over passing his little test. Better keep the fact she'd known his intent to herself. "I'm happy with the night's findings. But I'm ready for more photos." She pushed off the log and her leg muscles tightened in protest. A groan escaped.

He chuckled and reached a hand under her elbow. "Definitely time to head back."

The skin he touched heated and tingled. Zoia didn't know how, but the man was too quickly getting under her skin. An unusual occurrence. The guys she'd dated had been casual acquaintances for a while before sex entered the relationship. With this guy, the tension simmered with every look, breath and touch.

She squeezed her genlight and stepped into its circle, hoping to put some distance between them.

"Zoia."

Hearing her name in that deep voice gave her goose bumps and tightened her nipples. She looked over her shoulder, willing her heart rate to return to normal.

He cocked his head to the left. "This way."

Heat flushed her cheeks and she gritted her teeth before nodding. "I'll follow you." And maybe her body would be calm by the time they reached the cabin.

Kol set out and she trailed him, knowing he'd shortened his normal stride to make the walk easier. From her position, she could watch the flexing of his shoulder muscles as he walked, the clenching of his ass when he stepped onto a boulder. Maybe her body would take a bit longer to calm.

Near the edge of the clearing, she heard a rustle in the needles to her right. She gasped then bit her lip and flashed the light over the floor of the forest. Can't blow her cover now! By stepping to the left, she hoped to pass Kol and get to the open area faster. But a foot or so inside the treeline, the genlight picked up a strange pile of leaves and twigs behind an unfamiliar track.

Round, about four inches wide, with four toes.

With one hand fumbling for her camera, she stopped and lowered to a crouch. "Kol, look at this." Disbelief ran through her at what she saw.

"What?" His boots tramped up to where she waited. "Another animal?"

From behind the camera, she spoke and then pressed the image button. "This can't be. My research concluded animals of this size were hunted out of existence a decade ago."

He leaned over. "What are you looking at?"

She pointed and adjusted the light sensor on the camera. "A cougar print."

Hand on her elbow, he pulled her upright. "Let's get back." He stepped on the track, twisted his boot and continued walking.

"Hey, wait a minute." She tugged against his hold but couldn't break free. "I wanted more photos."

He kept walking. "You're mistaken."

Chapter 3

Kol moved across the clearing with purpose, but Zoia fought him every step of the way. He counted on the fact she hadn't fully acclimated to this elevation to work in his favor. His mind ran over the past few minutes and he struggled to figure out his actions. Why had he moved on pure instinct to destroy the animal track?

"You know, I can walk by myself." She tugged against his hold, leaning her weight backwards.

They'd reached the porch so he released his grip. "After your stumble at the log, I figured you'd appreciate some assistance."

Her dark brows drew down over a questioning gaze. "Really? Do people you know show their appreciation by resisting your grasp?"

Okay, so he felt like enough of an ass without her rubbing it in. "Uneven ground makes walking together tough."

"Right." With a shake of her head, she stomped up the steps, scraping her shoes on the sisal mat.

The smell of citrus and her tangy perspiration assaulted Kol's senses and his groin grew heavy. He wondered how he'd cope until daybreak when he could send her off in the right direction. A thought niggled at the back of his mind, but he refused to admit he should have done exactly that hours ago. His rationale was sound—

he'd had to determine she was the researcher she claimed to be.

Not someone who meant him harm.

Uneasy about how to provide an explanation for something he couldn't explain, he entered the cabin and stooped to untie his boots. Lately, he hated the confined feeling shoes created and relished the sensation of going barefoot. Curious...he'd never really cared to before.

Zoia stood at the sink, washing her hands. "I hate to impose but I'm hungry..." She turned as she briskly dried her hands.

Her breasts jiggling with the movements of the towel caught his gaze. "What do you want?" That's it, keep the situation low key.

"Look at the time. It's so late.. Maybe some soup?" She tilted her head and smiled. A hesitant crooked smile.

He loved crooked smiles. In the kitchen light, he thought he spotted the outline of her aureoles through the tee shirt. God, help him. He needed a task to focus on. "Let me check what my sister left in the pantry."

"Oh, is this her house?"

"It belongs to the whole Thorstein family. We gather here mostly for vacations." He shot her a sideways glace and shrugged. "Her family used it last."

She pulled on the sleeve of her shirt. "So, this is her shirt?"

He glanced at how the fabric caressed her body and felt his heart rate kick up a notch. "Hers or my niece's."

"Good, because I wanted to scream when I thought I'd fit into one of yours. Frankly, I didn't see how that was possible." Her dark-eyed gaze assessed his body.

So, the lady could give back as well. He moved to the far side of the room and pulled open a long cabinet door. Inside were rows of shelves packed with food. He glanced at the right hand section of the third shelf and read labels aloud, "Beef vegetable, minestrone, clam chowder, tomato."

She moved next to him and leaned forward. "And they're not self-heating cans. This really is roughing it."

"How hard is heating up a pan of soup?" He shrugged and reached for the cans in back. "Bean with bacon, chicken and stars—"

"Wow, I haven't had chicken with stars since I was little." She leaned forward and her breast brushed his arm.

Almost overpowered by the fresh smell of soap, her scent was less potent but an undercurrent remained. His arm heated where her breast touched, no, branded him. A task—he needed to focus on a task. He grabbed two cans and moved toward the stove. "My nephew's four and he loves this stuff."

"Hey, are you insinuating my choice is childish?" She pressed a hand to her hip and tossed her head. "That's not true for all my tastes."

Before he could stop himself, his gaze raked her athletic body and his cock twitched. A solid reminder of the skin-on-skin tussle they'd had earlier. Not the best interaction to remember. "I meant nothing by --"

She laid a hand on his arm and smiled. "Sorry. I'm always getting needled by my brothers and their friends. I guess I overreacted to your teasing." She winked before moving away.

Her wink weakened his resistance even more than her touch. Teasing? Had he really done that?

By focusing on the menial tasks—popping off the lids, dumping the contents and lighting the stove—he pushed his thoughts away from the sensation when her soft skin rested on his arm. A click of the sparker and the fuel cell lit under the burner. After a little food, maybe she'd settle herself in one of the beds and he could retreat to his room. With a solid door between them, he'd have hopes of escaping her scent.

He remained at the stove, stirring soup that didn't really need his attention. Definitely a more productive task than trying to determine where she was by the location of the clatter and swish of sounds she made behind him. Within minutes, he pulled the pan off the heat and headed for the bar counter where he usually ate.

"Oh, is that where you wanted this?"

He turned toward her surprised voice and saw she sat at the small table at the far end of the room. A table set for two. With placemats. The scene was too domestic for his tastes and he was about to tell her he wasn't hungry. Until he looked into her dark eyes, eyes the color of sable.

Where the hell had that thought come from?

"This is fine." Unable to ignore her hopeful expression, he set the pan on the pad in the middle of the table then sat. "Appreciate your help."

"Do you have any crackers?" Her gaze skittered away and she shrugged. "I didn't want to search the cupboards."

For fear over offending him? Irritation ran through him. "I didn't mean to—" The woman probably thought he was the worst host on record.

He stood and walked to the pantry, reaching to the top shelf for the metal tin. "While you're here, share what's available. Wouldn't want you thinking badly about wilderness hospitality."

"I appreciate that." She smiled and a dimple appeared in her left cheek. "I may take you up on that after we eat."

What the hell did she mean by that? His offer was for what was found in the kitchen and the pantry. Why did it sound like she meant something else? Give him a set of plans, a time frame and a team and he'd figure a way into any type of camp, building or vault. But deciphering the hidden meaning of a woman's words left him stranded on the outside every time.

As he served himself, the metal ladle clinked against his bowl and the aroma of chicken broth filled the air. He couldn't remember when he'd sat at this table last. No moonlight shone through the dark windows beside the table, creating a closed-in feeling. Almost intimate. His breathing hitched and he shifted in his chair so he looked at the inside of the cabin instead. So why was he here now? Why hadn't he taken his bowl to the counter?

For several minutes, they ate in silence.

After a few spoonfuls, his appetite was gone. One leg bounced as he worked on the reason behind his actions.

She reached across the table for the metal tin and the whiff of citrus hit his nostrils.

Need crashed through his blood and his muscles screamed for movement. He had to put some distance between them. "Do you want something to drink?" He stood and shoved the chair away from the table, wincing at the scrape he'd probably etched into the wooden floor.

Brows pulled into a frown, her gaze moved to the center of the table. "Besides water?"

On each placemat sat a glass of water. Oh, she'd thought of that. "Yeah, I meant a beer...or maybe milk."

Her head shook and dark curls bobbed around her face. "No, thanks. I had some earlier."

Curls bobbed? When had he started thinking in those terms? What about this woman drove him nuts? He stalked to the refrigerator, grabbed the closest plastic jug, and yanked off the cap. Stretching to the cupboard, he reached down a glass and filled it. Maybe the refreshing liquid would cool his thoughts like it did his throat. He upended the glass and drained it. When he reached for the jug again, he was suddenly aware she watched his movements. "Can't seem to get enough of this stuff."

Zoia stood and carried her dishes toward the kitchen. "Yeah, I noticed all the jugs in the refrigerator. Always been a milk lover?"

Actually no. Milk hadn't been part of his regular diet since boot camp. How had that fact slipped his notice? He leaned a hip against the counter. "Since being on...uh, this is a recent craving."

"Interesting." She cleared the table and carried the rest of the items to the sink. With hand on the cabinet knob, she angled her head sideways and smiled. "You cooked, so I'll clean. Family rules from my upbringing. Will I find what I need under here?"

The overhead light reflected in her dark eyes and he smelled oranges and woman. "Yep." He pushed himself away and walked to the table, telling himself he was clearing away the placemats and not running from her sexy allure. Movement caught his eye and he watched her reflection in the dark window, letting his gaze slide over her.

As the water rushed into the sink, she swayed to music that only she could hear. A throaty hum filled the air.

The sound washed over him and he paused, wondering at his lack of irritation. Since starting his leave, he'd guarded his privacy, even discouraging a visit from his sister's family the previous weekend. Although he itched to connect his notelink, he couldn't pull away from this room, from this vital woman.

"Of course, you could always help by drying these." She muffled a yawn against her shoulder. "Sorry, it's late."

He glanced at his wrist and read 0330. "I see that."

"I'm about to fall on my face." She wiped her hands on a towel. "Aren't you tired?"

"Don't sleep much." He shook his head.

She walked toward him, tapping her fingers. "You don't hardly eat or sleep. You can't sit still. You're distrustful. I suspect you had a memory blackout when we first," she hesitated and cleared her throat, "met outside the cabin."

She'd noticed. He narrowed his eyes. "Is there more to your statement?"

She flopped onto the couch and pulled her legs up under her body. "Those four brothers I mentioned earlier...they're in police work. Last year, my oldest brother Gregos was involved in a hostage crisis that went bad. His symptoms were like yours and his diagnosis was post-traumatic stress disorder."

A direct hit. If the woman only knew the files of information saved on his notelink on PTSD. "And you're insinuating…what?"

"Have you thought about what put you here?" She yawned and covered her mouth. Her eyelids drooped. "Sorry."

He started to cross his arms over his chest then reached them over his head in an exaggerated stretch. No use in telegraphing his emotions. "Put me here?"

A frown creased her brow. "Alone in an isolated cabin?"

Her ability to read him rankled. One of his particular skills on the force had been maintaining an unreadable expression. "Tell me why you think I'm here because of something bad."

She lowered her head and ran a hand over her neck. "In my line of work, I have a knack for reading people."

The hair on the back of his neck prickled. Her line of work? "You read *people*? As a research photographer."

Her eyes widened. "Did I say work? Actually, I meant my volunteer job. I spend a couple Saturdays a month interviewing teens at a crisis center."

He forced a yawn. "On second thought, I am tired. I'm headed to my room."

"Can you point me toward an extra blanket and pillow? I'll camp out right here on the couch."

"Beds are available." He waved a hand at the far end of the house. "A bedroom there and a dormitory setup in both of the upstairs rooms."

She stood and stretched then grimaced. "I'm too tired to think about climbing any stairs." She grabbed her pack and slung it over her shoulder then shook her head. "Probably won't use anything in here for the rest of the night. I don't want to be a worse imposition by leaving my stuff lying around. Night, Kol."

He watched her disappear into the master bedroom and tried not to picture how many articles of clothing she might remove before crawling between the sheets. An awareness of how quiet the room seemed without her settled over him.

That was the craziest thought ever! He'd known the woman less than 12 hours.

For her to pinpoint what he suspected was his problem, his behavior must be unraveling. He pivoted and stalked to his room, shoving up the top to his notelink and swiping his thumb across the ID pad. Might as well get some work done. He maneuvered the cursor through his research folder, hunting for a specific article. Letting his gaze skim over the list of symptoms, he mentally checked off the ones he'd experienced. Damn near 100%.

He stood and paced to the window. A thin cloud layer had moved in and the forest was lit with intermittent patches of silvery light. His breath hit the window and immediately condensed into frost. Temperature must be dropping. The last thing he needed was snow. Tomorrow, he wanted no reason to keep her from hiking out to her vehicle.

Shoving away from the desk he strode down the hall and around the living room. The walls were closing in on him and he fought to keep his thoughts focused. No lightheadedness affected his balance but his chest was tight and his breath was coming in shallow gazes. He walked back to his room. Were these new symptoms?

*****

Zoia sat upright, listening to Kol's footsteps pad across the room outside her door. Halfway down the hall was a floorboard that creaked every time he paced. She doubted he even heard it, but she had. Every one of the eleven times he'd passed over it.

Creak. Make that twelve times.

She threw back the blankets and dragged on her pants again. This could not continue all night. Her hand grabbed the knob at the same time she flipped on the overhead light. Squinting against the brightness, she yanked open the door and stomped into the hallway. "Kol, why are you pacing the house?"

He stuck his head out of his doorway. "I woke you?"

She walked a few steps toward him, wondering why this seemed more intimate than before she headed to bed for the night. "Well, I could hardly fall asleep with the multiple creaks of the floorboard and your nervous footsteps."

"Sorry. I'm just restless."

"I know just what you need." She covered the remaining space and grabbed his elbow, steering him into his room. "And I'm going to give it to you." The muscles under her hand stiffened.

Kol stopped and pulled against her hold, reaching out to shut the top of his notelink. "What do you mean?"

"Lie flat on the bed, facedown, and don't use the pillow. I'm giving you a back massage." She rubbed her hands together. When he didn't move, she nudged his back with her elbow. "Go on. I'll grab the lotion I saw in the bathroom earlier and be right back." Within a minute, she'd returned and found him sitting on the edge of the bed, hands braced on his knees.

"I don't want to keep you up."

She bent her knees and looked him in the eyes. "My only hope of getting to sleep is to get you contained." Her smile was one she hoped instilled confidence. "Assume the position."

"Bossy, aren't you?" He tossed the pillow to the side and pulled his tee shirt over his head before lying down like she'd instructed.

"I can be." At the display of his toned muscles, she swallowed a gasp and flexed fingers that itched to touch his skin. "Get comfortable, because I've been told my hands create magic." She dribbled a small puddle of lotion into one hand and cupped her other hand over it for several seconds. Easing her weight onto the mattress, she scooted her hip against his. "What I found was lime-and-coconut lotion. I hope you don't mind."

"Probably my sister's. If it's too girly, I'll shower it off."

She spread the lotion on her palms and lowered her hands to the middle of his back, applying pressure and moving them toward his sides. The skin beneath her fingers rippled as she moved but the muscles underneath remained tight. She closed her eyes and willed him to loosen his rigid control—for his own good. "Take deep breaths and try to relax. That way, you'll get the maximum benefit."

He breathed in and his back rose a couple inches. "Um, you are good."

Her eyes opened and she couldn't suppress a smile. "I took classes." Using the heels of her hands, she walked from his shoulders downward toward his hips. Warm and smooth—his skin felt so good. "At one time, I thought I wanted to be a massage therapist."

"What changed?"

His voice rasped and the words were slower, more drawn out. She felt the difference in his body. He was relaxing. "I still liked what I was learning, but I couldn't handle the laboratory practical exercises." As her fingers worked small circles down his left arm, she gazed at his body. Several scars marred the tanned expanse of his skin—some small, others jagged and a few that looked recently healed. She moved her fingertips over the raised skin and immediately her heart ached for what injury he must have endured. Tears welled in her eyes and she swallowed against the burning at the back of her throat. "I couldn't handle the emotional intensity that's part of a thorough massage. Go figure."

"Ummm."

Her hands moved to his upper back and brushed over a pink line that looked too straight to be an injury. Strange. She leaned forward to get a better look.

A low rumble sounded from the head of the bed.

A snore? She pressed a hand in the middle of the mattress and leaned to the side to check Kol's face. His normally stern expression had softened into one that was quite handsome. Not sure if he really slept, she kept running her hands over his back and curving them around his sides. Her nipples tightened and peaked against the tee shirt.

The sound deepened. Now he was almost purring.

Her hands continued the last light caressing touches to finish the massage, but her gaze already centered on the notelink. This was the opportunity she'd wanted. With slow movements, Zoia lifted her weight off the bed until she stood next to it.

Kol's breathing didn't change.

She moved to the desk and flipped up the lid on the notelink. The fan whirred and the screen lightened. A blinking cursor awaited her. Good, he'd left it connected. The document open on the screen listed the symptoms she'd been discussing with him earlier. So maybe he'd listened to her story about Gregos.

With a few taps on the keys, she'd connected to her web server and dashed off a quick email to let Antonia know she'd arrived. She typed in "quarry located and identified" then hesitated, a knot tightening her stomach. That statement ended the assignment. She highlighted those four words and deleted them. For reasons she couldn't explain, she wanted to keep this information to herself. Enough to let her assistant know she was safe.

She tapped "goodbye" and then lowered the cover on the small notelink. Maybe she'd get a chance to use it later.

The sound of Kol's snore filled the room.

The sound was soothing and her eyelids drooped. She stood and moved to the bed, pulling a blanket over his body. As she did so, she let her fingers trail along his form and fought her body's impulse to climb in beside him. Sheer force of will made her step backwards. At the doorway, she leaned a temple against the smooth wood and just gazed at the large man who had become special so quickly.

Probably only a handful of people ever saw him in such an unprotected state.

Chapter 4

The click of a door latch, the quiet padding of footsteps, the sounds of snuffling breaths, the pressure of a furry limb rubbing her leg, a warm rasp on her thighs, a delicious chuffing of warm air on her pussy. A sense of being watched and protected settled over her.

The images in her dream brought a smile to Zoia's lips and she rolled her head on her pillow. Light jabbed her eyes and she groaned then squeezed them shut. Goose bumps rose on her arms. Where was her blanket? Without opening her eyes, she stretched out a hand to grab it and met resistance. Her arm wouldn't move. Had she slept on it wrong? She pulled again and a restraint chafed her wrist.

Her eyes shot open. For a moment, she was blinded by a shaft of sunlight coming through the split in the curtains. Squinting, she turned her head to look at her arms. Plastic ropes bound her wrists to the iron bedstead. She moved her legs and discovered she was spreadeagled, clad in only the thermal shirt. Annoyance fueled her struggles against her bindings. "Hey, what is this?"

"Who the hell are you?" The lethal voice came from the far side of the room.

By hunching her shoulders, her head raised so she could see him lounging in a chair in the shadowed corner near the door. "Quit kidding around, Kol."

"How do you know my name?" The man leaned forward and braced his elbows on bare knees.

"Oh, I know so much more than your name." The instant the smart-ass retort was out of her mouth, she regretted it.

His body snapped upright into a rigid posture that was definitely soldier-trained. "You invaded my perimeter. Why are you in my cabin?"

His voice demanded and was so cold. She shivered, which did all the wrong things to her exposed body. Nerves tickled in her stomach and she strained to push her knees together. No luck — Captain Kol Thorstein was not a slacker at knot tying. "Kol, this isn't funny."

"What do you want here?" He stood and approached the bed, his narrowed gaze focusing on the tight buds poking against her tee shirt.

He was gloriously naked and aroused, his cock thick and full between his legs. Her pussy tingled in response to the sight. Maybe he was enacting a Dom/sub game. Ooo, she'd heard about these. If she just played along, they could have some fun and a good laugh afterwards.

With a pang of regret, she stopped gawking at his sculpted body and dipped her chin. "I have come to fulfill your wishes." Although how she'd accomplish that from this confined position, she didn't have a clue.

"Who'd send me a whore?" His hand clamped onto her thigh and squeezed.

She stiffened but forced herself not to look up. Had he discovered her purpose for seeking him out? So far, nothing he'd said pointed in that direction. Using all her self-control, she forced a light, breathy tone into her words. "Not a whore, sir, a playmate."

"A playmate?" The mattress sagged as he

stretched out along her side and ran his hand up the inside of her leg. "Then I choose the game."

Her skin responded to the heat radiating from the hard planes of his body. His cock pressed against her hip, an urgent reminder of rewards yet to come. Although her arms felt heavy from being held in one position so long, she shivered at his touch, nerves tingling at the circles he traced on her thigh. The need to touch him grew. Her request to be released was on the tip of her tongue, and she couldn't resist raising her head.

Amber eyes with elongated pupils glared with a gaze icier than she'd seen before.

A gaze that held no recognition.

Real fear grabbed her throat. She swallowed hard and told herself to breathe in then out.

He didn't know her, he really didn't know who she was.

His PTSD condition was nothing like her brother's. Her thoughts whirled, but she focused on the training she'd taken for her volunteer service at the crisis center. In particular, she remembered the psychology lecture on dealing with teens unhappy with their reality.

Don't deny what they're feeling. Find something in common. Create a bond. "Okay, what are the rules of the game?"

"You lie real still..." With a quick twist, he rolled on top of her and braced his hands below her raised arms, his cock settling between her legs. "While I question you. If I like the answers, I'll untie you."

The looming stranger scared the ever-loving crap out of her. If she let him know that, it was over. She was already in some serious trouble but if he found out the real reason... She lifted her chin and met his stony gaze. "I can do that. Fire away."

"I searched your pack. Where are the rest of your clothes?"

Her thoughts reeled at what he learned from the search, especially if he got to the numbers in her satphone. Oh, that's right. No battery. "Drying in the bathroom. They got dirty when we...um, fought and I washed them, but that was before I knew there's no—"

He pushed down hard and jolted the bed. "Enough."

She sucked in a breath and her nose filled with Kol's scent—pine forest and male musk. At least that part was familiar, she had to hold onto that.

"Answer just the question."

How could she establish a bond that way? She nodded and waited.

"Who sent you?"

Careful thought went into her answer. She couldn't reveal anything they hadn't already discussed. Had she told him a name of a university? "I'm on assignment."

"To do what?"

"Gather research on nocturnal mammals in the region." She watched his face for any sign this information was familiar.

His gaze flicked to the side and he frowned.

A sign of uncertainty. "If you searched my pack, you must have seen my camera."

"The pack has a camera." He leaned close, his gaze scrutinizing her face. "I could remove the memory chip and view them on my notelink."

Was he starting to believe her? She nodded. "Let's do that."

"No." With a subtle movement of his hips, he pushed his cock against her pussy. "Your agreement came too quickly."

Her insides chilled. Oh, please don't let him do something they'd both regret. "Kol, for just a minute, listen. I arrived here last night. Your truck alarm went off and I hid. You stalked me into the forest. We wrestled and had down-and-dirty sex—a wild and exciting introduction not soon to be forgotten." She watched a flicker in his eyes, an awareness that hadn't been there before.

He tightened his jaw and extended his arms until they were straight again. "No, you aren't supposed to be here."

She was losing him. Come on, Stavros just go for broke. "I got lost, took the wrong road, remember? Today I was going to find my transport and continue to my research camp."

"What camp?"

Crap, she hadn't gotten that far in her story. "Farther into the mountains." The words sounded vague even to her ears. "You helped me get those photos, Kol."

"No one should be here."

The flat tone of his voice scared her almost as much as his blank gaze. Find the emotional bond. Keep your voice calm. "We hiked all over last night. You led me to the nesting places of several species. Did I tell you how much I appreciated the safety of a guide?"

He snorted. "The fuck with safety! Danger surrounds me." He shook his head and grabbed a fistful of her hair. "How did you find me?"

She sucked in a breath through clenched teeth but didn't cry out. Danger surrounds him? Why would he think that? Forcing a soothing tone, she scrambled to remember every detail from the previous evening. "After we finished outside, we shared crackers and soup. Chicken with stars. Remember, you said it's your nephew's favorite. Mine, too, but you never mentioned his name so I can't corroborate that fact." She willed his memory to connect to something she'd rattled off, because she was running out of details. "But you did say he was four."

The tension on her scalp eased, but his fingers remained entangled. "His name is Garth."

She barely heard what he muttered, but drew hope from this piece of information. Something in him was responding to her voice, was reaching out to her. "Um, then I cleaned the dishes and we went to our separate bedrooms. Only you didn't. You paced, making the floorboards creak, and kept me awake. So I went to your room and gave you a back massage. I bet you can still smell the lime-and-coconut lotion on your skin."

He turned his head enough to raise a shoulder toward his nose and inhaled. His grip released another fraction.

The lotion. Scent. If her fingers weren't numb, she'd snap them in discovery. Of course, the sense of smell is the strongest link to a memory. She turned her head, wincing at the tug of her hair, and waited until he met her gaze. "Kol, listen hard to this. After I finished showering last night, you seemed affected by the shampoo I used. By a particular scent. I recall hearing you sniff near me, and then you'd move away like you were fighting a reaction. It happened once in the cabin and then again when we were outdoors on the log."

His chin dipped and his eyes lit with a hazel fire. "Citrus. Tangy."

This might be working. Hope flooded her and she couldn't keep a smile from her lips. "Smell my hair, Kol. Then you'll know I'm Zoia and I'm not a threat."

A pang ran through her at the fib. Her entire reason for being in this state, on this mountain and tied half-naked on this bed posed a threat to the exact man who held her prisoner. Right now, she couldn't bring herself to meet his gaze, afraid of what he'd see there.

He shifted his weight to her right side and draped his arm over her chest, ruffling the curls away from her forehead. As he sniffed at her hair, he nuzzled her temple with his forehead. "My Zoia. I remember you."

Thank the Spirit. She pressed her head back against his. Tears stung her eyes and she stared straight at the ceiling, not wanting him to see the depth of her relief. "I'm so glad." She could feel him winding her hair around his finger then releasing it to spring back into place.

A nice comforting gesture.

His hand slipped from her head to her shoulder then trailed to her breast, a finger idly drawing circles around her nipple until it pebbled.

Another nice gesture and one she would love to reciprocate. She sighed and her pussy clenched. "That's nice, Kol, but could you untie me?"

"Untie?" He lifted his head and his wide-eyed gaze ran the length of the bed. "What the--?" He sat up, turned his back toward her and ran a hand through his hair. "Did I do this?"

She stifled a laugh. "Earlier I said that my hands created magic. But I couldn't possibly have tied the last knot."

He shifted on the bed and looked at her, his eyes focusing on her chin, his mouth drawn in to a tight line.

Okay, wrong response. "Sorry for the sassy mouth. I bet this looks bad. I know it wasn't my favorite experience of all time. But, Kol, I'm okay." She waited for his gaze to meet hers, worry fluttering in her belly. "Look at me, please."

His body tensed, he raised a haunted gaze to hers.

"I'm not hurt. Really and truly. Please untie me." Later, we'll talk about what this all means.

"I'm sorry, Zoia." He stood and stepped toward the pillow. With quick movements, he untied her wrists. "How do they feel?"

When her hands dropped to the surface of the mattress, she groaned at the different strain on her muscles. They were like lead and she couldn't imagine them ever moving on their own again. "They feel dead. Could you move them into a more normal position?"

"I can't believe you want me to touch you again."

Knowing he wasn't ready for another sassy remark, she kept her looks focused above his neck. "Kol, we have to talk."

With gentle touches, he rotated her arms to lie along her sides. "Shhh." He leaned over her and gently massaged at the tightness in her shoulders, rubbing away the soreness with strong thumb movements. "Let my hands create some magic."

A sigh escaped and she closed her eyes to enjoy his pampering. All thoughts of telling him about his behavior dissolved. She floated on a cloud of caresses and strokes. Until the needle-like prickling set in. She shifted her shoulders, trying to pull away. "Ow. The sensations are returning."

His caresses stopped. "Let me distract you." His lips pressed kisses from her shoulder down to her fingertips. "Like this." His warm tongue lapped at the sensitive spaces between her fingers. "Or like this." Then he turned over her hand and nibbled at her palm.

She gasped and all her thoughts zeroed in on enjoying those bites. Her nipples tightened under the shirt. "Oh, that's nice." When she writhed, the scrape of the fabric shot zingers to the pit of her stomach and lower. To her pussy lips moistening with creamy juices.

The mattress dipped from his added weight and she felt him crawl over her outstretched leg. A tickle of leg hair against her knee followed by a silky graze of his erect cock on her shin. A finger traced the pink double helix tattoo on her abdomen. Pink, not the original vibrant purple. Her eyes popped open to tell him another month remained on this ovulation inhibitor injection.

He knelt between her legs, a finger pressed to his grinning lips. He pointed to the royal blue tat on the inside of his bicep and winked. Non-verbal confirmation they were both disease free and protected. In anticipation, she shivered.

"Cold?"

Her tongue was stuck to the roof of her suddenly dry mouth and she could only shake her head.

"Good. How are your arms? Do they work?"

She tried lifting them a few inches off the mattress. They moved without pain but felt heavier and slower than usual.

"Toss me that pillow." His gaze smoldered with intent and he winked.

Without turning her head, she reached to her side, grabbed the end of the pillowcase and shoved the pillow toward her feet. Her still bound feet.

With a flourish, he lifted her hips with one hand and jammed the doubled-over pillow under them with the other.

She could barely take her gaze from the rippling muscles in his arms to watch his golden head descend between her legs. "What about untying my feet?"

He hesitated, a glint in his eyes. "Do they hurt?"

A wiggle of her hips provided the answer. "No."

A negative shake of his head. "Then this is how I want you." He scooted toward the end of the bed and lowered his head.

A stream of warm air circled her pussy and she quit worrying about her feet.

His warm tongue lapped at her opening, delving inside then retreating to circle her clit. The tip of his tongue probed the rim of her lips and edged inside her channel. Vibrations ran deep inside.

She heard his hum at the same time the pressure hit her clit. A new variation that worked wonders. Her hands shoved up her shirt and fingered her already hard nipples, rolling and pinching them to heighten the spiraling heaviness in her womb. She moaned and pressed against his mouth. Sensation built on sensation, but she missed being filled. A hand dropped to his head and rubbed through his short hair.

He nuzzled her hand, but kept his tongue working on her pussy.

"Inside me." She tugged on the rim of his ear. "Fill me with your cock."

With a resounding smack, he kissed her clit then sat up. "Will do, boss lady." He twisted first to the right then to the left to untie her ropes, rubbing each ankle in turn. "Take off your shirt."

Using slow movements, she bent her knees and dragged her feet toward her ass. Digging in her heels, she arched her back off the mattress and shimmied out of her shirt, tossing it to the floor. Muscles ached in protest but at least she still had feeling in the limbs.

"Nice dance." Kol hooked an arm behind her knees and twisted her sideways in the bed, dragging the pillow under her hips. "I want you here. Rest your legs on my chest." With his left hand braced on the headboard, he pressed into her pussy and threw back his head. "That feels fucking good." This pose resembled the one when she'd first seen him highlighted in the bedroom window. His hands roved over her breasts, tweaking her nipples. "Damn, baby, your pussy is tight."

She grabbed handfuls of bed sheets, trying for leverage to press against his thrusts. The friction was delicious and heat spiraled everywhere their bodies touched. "Kol."

"Don't be shy, let me hear you." He thrust into her and groaned in satisfaction. "Oh, yeah."

So, the guy's a talker in bed. This wasn't close enough. She scooted a leg down to wrap around his hip and the sensation of his cock sliding in and out intensified. The other leg slid around his hip and she arched her back to improve the angle.

"Looking for the rub, huh? You like this?"

The instant his thumb circled her clit, she was lost, her pussy pulsing with the waves of her orgasm.

He grabbed her hips and held her steady while he pumped several more times before groaning. "Oh baby, that did it." Two last thrusts and he exhaled on a long breath. "Ahhhh." Leaning forward, he lay on the mattress and rolled her onto her side. Gasping breaths filled the room, as did the rich aroma of sex.

Zoia untangled her hand from the sheets and raised it to his chest, stroking his pecs, enjoying the human connection. She felt drained from the emotional roller coaster of the past day, especially this past hour, and pressed her forehead to his shoulder.

His arm spanned her back and pulled her close. "That was awesome." He leaned across her and grabbed a sheet and pulled it over them. "Just let me sleep twenty minutes and I promise a second go-around."

Third go-around, she mentally corrected him. Zoia snuggled close, her thoughts spinning about his behavior in the two interactions. In the woods, silent — in the bed, vocal. Something about the difference should...if only she could keep her eyes open.

Chapter 5

Zoia awoke slowly, stretching an arm out to touch Kol. But her hand tapped only the cool mattress. She shoved curls off her face and glanced around the room. The fact the man had insomnia explained his absence.

One peek at the window told her she'd slept for several hours. There was defused light coming in, so the direct rays must be hitting the other side of the cabin. She scurried down the hall to use the bathroom, taking only a moment to glance into his room.

Ten minutes later, she pulled on her clean, if stiff, clothes and wrapped a towel around her freshly shampooed hair. "Kol, are you back yet?" She crossed to the window and looked out toward the forest but didn't see him. Before she invaded his computer, she walked to the door and went out on the porch. "Kol? Can you hear me?" A faint echo bounced back.

His truck was still parked at the edge of the clearing so he hadn't driven to town. This was his turf and he was a big, strapping guy so she shouldn't worry. She removed the towel, spreading it over the porch railing and shook her head to loosen the tangle of curls. How did the guy live this far away from the activities of the normal world? Within a few minutes, she'd accessed the hard drive of her personal notelink and sorted out the PTSD research she wanted. What were the chances she could get him to submit to tests? Or get him to talk to a professional?

When she clicked to create a folder on Kol's desktop, the screen blanked and then brought up a simple table. What button had she pushed? She scanned the first couple of entries and recognized a log of Kol's physical symptoms.

Was reading this an invasion of his privacy? The mental debate raged for all of five seconds. Not if her intention was to help him. As she read his words, she gained a sense of the man's confusion and isolation. Compassion welled up in her throat and softened her conviction about getting him to a doctor. Now she'd settle for an honest discussion. No wonder he'd been so suspicious about her presence. Guilt nipped at her conscience, knowing he had valid reasons for his suspicions.

She glanced at the notelink's clock and concern settled over her thoughts. Where was Kol?

As she always did, she initiated the spyware program on her computer. A familiar icon—green H superimposed over an inverted yellow triangle--caught her eye. Was that--? Oh, crap. The Halcyon Institute was tracking her, and that stupid icon served as proof. With rapid strokes, she eliminated the trackers and disconnected from her computer, hoping the bug hadn't infiltrated Kol's system.

She shoved away from the desk and paced, arms wrapped around a churning stomach. Why would the organization that hired her to locate a missing soldier be trailing her movements? She'd been on the job less than a week. Had they kept watch from the beginning or had something triggered this interest? Her mind reeled at what information they might have already obtained.

Fuel and restaurant purchases, the motel in west Texas, the flat tire in New Mexico. And since arriving here the purchases stopped.

Her breath caught in her throat. Using that money card created a trail that pointed to this region.

When had she last used it? She tried to remember the location of the last fuel stop—Country Road something. Although she dreaded his reaction, she'd have to reveal her identity and warn Kol about The Institute. Just when they'd established a tentative trust.

The outside door banged against the wall.

She jumped at the sudden sound then turned to head out of the room. Time for revelations. "About time you showed up for our little talk." She walked the length of the hallway and rounded the wall, ready to greet him with a morning hug.

In the middle of the living room stood Kol. Stark naked. And breathing heavily.

The sight of his taut body set her heart racing. "Hey, you didn't tell me you were a nudist."

At the sound of her voice, he turned his head and stared, no recognition in his eyes.

"Although this location would be great..." The words caught in her throat and she stopped.

He lifted his head and sniffed then frowned. With precise steps, he covered the distance between them, stopped in front of her and sniffed again. The impassive expression on his face didn't change.

This was the stranger who'd tied her to the bed. The Kol she knew was in the middle of another PTSD episode. Her revelation would have to wait. Now she had to do what she could to help him.

He circled her, touching his shoulder to hers and rubbing it along her back.

This quiet, sensual approach was arousing and she closed her eyes to concentrate on the emotions. While at her back, he buried his nose in her hair and inhaled deeply then a groan rumbled from his throat. He moved to her side, nuzzling her neck and blowing chuffs of breath along her hairline.

The caress of those breaths sent sparks along her skin. The heat radiating from his body permeated her skin. She inhaled and smelled forest and sunshine and the musk that was his alone. Using senses other than sight was intoxicating, and instinctively her body reacted, her juices wetting her curls.

At the touch of his lips on her neck, she tilted her head. She was suddenly hungry for a kiss they'd never shared. Would that be shared with the brooding Kol or the talkative one? She reached out a hand to stroke his chest, reveling in the hard muscles under her fingertips.

Waiting for his next move.

His lips traced her neck to her ear and a warm tongue lapped the rim then circled the shell. He cupped his hands around her neck and ran his thumbs along her jaw.

Every inch of skin he traced came alive and her body relaxed with a sigh. The feeling of being cherished ran through her and she turned herself over to his touch.

He answered with a moan and a rubbing of his forehead against hers.

She raised her hands to touch his face but he'd moved again. Padding footsteps sounded to her right.   She started to open her eyes, but hesitated, following what her heart told her.   By trusting in the relationship they'd built and enjoying this other part of Kol Thorstein.

A large hand squeezed her ass then slid along the hip of her neoprene pants to cup her *mons* and pull her back against his body.   His rigid erection pressed against her lower back.

A moan escaped her lips and she reached back to run her hands along the outside of his rock-hard thighs.   This time, she needed a physical connection, needed him to know she was sharing. When his hand grappled with the pants fastener, she opened her eyes and stepped away, holding out a staying hand.

He snarled, his gaze watchful.

As quickly as she could, she stripped off her clothes.   Glancing around the room, she tried to find the place that met both their needs—his for a quick coupling, hers to be able to see his face. Suddenly that was important for her to be able to understand what was happening with him.   Aware of his approach on quiet footsteps, she backed away, sucking in a breath when she encountered the wall's cold surface.

Her stomach fluttered with uncertainty as she waited.   Should she have let him control the situation?   She watched his nostrils flare as he stared at her in this new position.   Her natural inclination would be to use words to draw him near.   Not the time for words, but for action. Without letting her gaze meet his, she smiled and lifted her arms in a welcoming gesture.   And waited for him to step into her embrace.

The crush of his body pressed her hard against the wall and his nose burrowed into her hair. A hand traced her side, his thumb drawing circles and swirls as it descended. Then his fingers petted and combed the thatch of curly hair between her legs.

She remembered that odd gesture from the first time. What did that mean?

His fingers slid along her pussy lips, tickling her clit and pressed inside.

Abandoning all logical thoughts, she focused only on his touch and rubbed a foot along his leg.

He grabbed her waist and lifted her, stepping between the legs she wrapped around his hips. With one thrust, he entered her and flexed his hips, pumping hard.

She grabbed his shoulders and held tight, riding his cock, her pebbled nipples brushing his chest with each stroke. From deep within, the spirals started and she bit her lip to keep from crying out.

His grip on her hips tightened, his thrusts increased and he groaned.

She tightened her legs around him and angled her hips. Heat enveloped her pussy and her release throbbed. She pressed her mouth against his chest but couldn't hold back any longer. "Ahh!"

*****

Her satisfied cry was all he'd been waiting for. "Let me hear you." He tightened his hold on her back and pumped fast, his balls aching for release. At his climax, he kissed a trail of nibbling bites along her damp neck to her shoulder. Her orgasm milked his cock, squeezing out every bit of his hot seed. When his breathing slowed, he pressed his head against hers and raised a hand to draw circles on her nipple.   "Damn, that was good."

She stilled and lifted her head. "Kol?"

"Expecting someone else between your legs?"   Heart racing, he leaned a forearm against the wall and worked hard to get enough air into his lungs. Let the wall hold him up for the next couple of minutes.

"You're back?"

The sound of Zoia's hesitant voice forced him to move. He turned to look at her and froze. "What the hell happened?"

Her body stiffened and her eyes widened. "What's wrong?"

"Where are you hurt?" His gaze took in the blood streaks staining her neck and jaw. "Why didn't you say anything?"

A frown wrinkled her brown and she shook her head. "I'm not hurt."

He wrapped his arms around her back and raised her off his cock then carried her to the couch. Once she was seated, he knelt in front of her, brushed back her hair, his gaze scanning her jaw and neck.

"Kol, you're scaring me.   Tell me what you're doing."

"I'm looking for where you're cut. There's blood on your neck."

"I told you, I'm not hurt." She leaned away from his touch, her gaze riveted on his hands. "But..."

He held out his hands, looking at his palms and turned them over. Reddish stains marked the skin between his fingers and trails ran down the back of them. His stomach clenched and bile rose in the back of his throat. "Tell me I haven't left the cabin today."

Zoia crossed her arms over her chest and blinked rapidly. "You were gone when I woke."

Oh, God, had his worst nightmare come true? Had he hurt someone while in one of his blackouts? His chest tightened and the edges of his vision blurred. "How long?"

"How long have I been awake?"

He nodded, unwilling to meet her gaze.

"An hour, maybe longer."

"Fuck." He rose to his feet and stalked across the room, aware of the air on his naked skin. He looked over his shoulder. "I returned buck naked, right?"

She chewed her lip for a moment before nodding.

"Shit." He returned his gaze to the forest out the window, knowing he couldn't look at her and say what he had to. "Zoia, pack your stuff and head out."

"What? Kol, you can't mean that." She shot off the couch and started across the room.

He fisted his hands. "Stop where you are."

"I don't understand."

"You're in danger here. I want you to leave."

"Sorry, can't do that."

He turned and took two steps toward the feisty woman who stood in all her naked glory with fisted hands on her hips. Didn't she understand what he just said? "Why not?"

"Because you're in danger, too. Since I'm the one responsible," she shrugged and shot him a weak grin, "I have to stick around to explain."

"What the hell are you talking about?"

"I'm not having this conversation stark

naked. Ten-minute time out while we clean up and get dressed then meet back here. Agreed?"

Determination radiated from the woman, in the thrust of her jaw and the glint in her dark eyes. After answering her with a nod, he watched as she grabbed her clothes and headed toward the bathroom. Anger did wonderful things to a woman's walk. He went to the kitchen and braced his hands on the edge of the sink. She took this new twist a hell of a lot better than he was. What happened out in the forest he might never know. But he would do everything possible to keep her safe.

He ran a sink of water to soak off the blood. A quick swipe at the rest of his body with a towel and he headed toward his room, pausing outside the bathroom door to listen.

From inside came the sound of water running and singing. Did she sing when she was happy or nervous? After their talk, after he told her about the weird conditions he'd been going through, he probably wouldn't get the chance to find out.

And that would hurt. More than he could imagine.

As he pulled on cargo pants and a tee shirt, he evaluated that thought. Deep down, he didn't want to send her away. She'd brought light and laughter into his isolation.

Her safety was more important than what he wanted. He stalked into the living room and paced, as if he could walk away from what had to happen.

"I see you're working out your frustration on the floor again."

Forcing himself to look calm, he flopped

onto the end of the couch and waved a hand at the other end. "Tell me why you *have* to stick around. Then I'll tell you why you must go."

She dropped onto the couch sideways and drew one leg close to her body. Her dark gaze was direct and serious. "You may be in danger. And I caused it."

A repeat of what she'd said earlier and it still made no sense. "What could you have caused? Before yesterday, you'd never heard of me and you haven't been outside this compound."

Her gaze flicked down and she picked at the couch fabric.

Shit. His hands dug into the back of the couch. Her body language gave her away. "You weren't lost last night, were you?"

Her head lifted and shook. "I wasn't lost." She took a deep breath and squared her shoulders. "I'm not really a research photographer. I'm a private investigator and I was--"

At the words "private investigator", he quit listening. The government wasn't hunting him. They wouldn't put someone from the private sector on his tail. But her investigation had to be tied to his recent release. If not the government, then who? This unknown danger could be worse.

"--the stupid truck alarm gave me away," she waved her hands in the air, "I had to play out my backup plan."

What was she talking about? He scooted closer and grabbed one of her hands. "Zoia, I need short answers. Who hired you?"

"The Halcyon Institute."

The name didn't mean anything, and he shrugged. "What did the person you talked to look like?"

"I never met anyone. The interview happened over the phone."

"Does that happen often?"

"Not really, but let me explain. My business—"

"Short answers." He breathed in through his mouth. "What was your assignment?"

"Track down a missing soldier and report his location."

"Didn't you think that should be the government's job?"

She shook her head and laughed. "Kol, in my business, you wouldn't believe..."

He tightened his grip over her trembling hand. Shit, he was scaring her and all he needed were answers.

"Sorry. No, the situation wasn't so odd."

"What's your method for reporting in? And have you done so?"

"I hate being interrogated like this. Let me tell it in my own way."

He released her hand and leaned back but watched her face, judging if she was spinning a story or not. "Go ahead."

"I was supposed to use my satphone because it would have registered your global position. But it got damaged. So I logged on to your notelink and sent my assistant an email. This was last night, but I just told her I was safe." She reached out a hand to touch his arm but withdrew it. "I swear I didn't confirm the quarry located."

"Then after this morning, after our..." She jumped up and walked to the door and back. "When you weren't here this afternoon, I used your notelink to retrieve the research I had on PTSD. You remember I told you about my brother, the policeman, because that's definitely what I think you're experiencing." She sucked in a breath. "That's when I discovered my computer had a tracking bug placed by Halcyon and that's why you're in danger."

His thoughts jumped from statement to statement, trying to follow her leaps of logic. "Quarry? I'm in danger because your computer is bugged? How?"

"Not because of the bug. But the fact they bugged my computer means they're probably tracking the money card."

The muddy explanation was clearing. "They gave you a money card as payment? And you've been using it?"

"Well, yeah." Her eyebrows shot up. "I have to cover my expenses. But I haven't used it in almost 24 hours, so I'm worried they'll be converging on this region."

His buddy, Evan, had enough computer savvy to get them out of this problem. "So are you going to report that you found me?"

She sucked in a breath and jammed her hands on her hips. "Of course not."

"And that's the extent of the danger?"

"That's all I discovered." She sank onto the couch. "I'm so sorry for bringing this problem to your door. Aren't you mad?"

He shook his head. "A single phone call will throw them off the track. But you still need to leave."

"I know I lied about who I was." She pressed her lips tight before continuing. "I can understand why you'd want me gone."

"This is not about a professional fib." He leaned his arm along the back of the couch. "You can't have forgotten how I returned to the cabin? Weren't you scared at what you saw?"

"What I saw?" Her eyes shone and a smile crept across her lips. "A sexy man in his prime intent on having sex with me. Nope, not scary at all."

He gritted his teeth. "Zoia, I meant the blood."

"I know." She scooted along the couch until she rested her head against his shoulder. "I'm telling you I was never afraid, Kol."

"Why not? I must have looked like a raging bull."

"You did, but I kinda stumbled onto the log of your blackouts."

Vulnerability wasn't a comfortable fit. He twisted to glare. "That was—"

"Private, I know." She sighed and rested a hand on his chest. "Calm down. I apologize for invading your privacy, but I can help."

"I've been chewing this over for weeks and haven't made any progress. You've been here less than one day." He raised a hand and let it drop to his thigh. "How are you going to help?"

"Exactly. You've been working solo, but this is a job for a team." She sat forward and touched her pointer to her chest. "I'm a professional observer. Who better to track you when the weird sensations start and you decide to play nudist?"

"This is serious." He hated involving her but damned if her idea didn't make sense.

"Believe me, I know how serious PTSD is. Working together, I'm positive we can figure this out."

He laid a hand on her shoulder. "Tracking

me could be dangerous."

She shrugged and rubbed her cheek against his hand. "So we confine you."

"You got an answer for everything?"

"To help you...I'll find the answer we need. Can I stay?"

He couldn't ensure her safety and that fact rankled the hell out of him. But the need to identify his problem prevailed. His fingers trailed over her cheek. "You're on the team."

Layla Chase   73

Chapter 6

Zoia didn't know when she'd heard words more beautiful. "What's our first step?"

"Figure out how to confine me." He dropped his head to the back of the couch.

She hated his haunted look. "The ropes on the four-poster bed sure kept me in one place." She winked, hoping to lighten the mood.

He shuddered. "Don't remind me."

She rested a hand on his arm. "Sorry, I know this will be easier with two."

"I don't want to do this in the cabin."

"You don't want your family's things around."

"No." He hooked a finger under her chin and turned her head so he could look deep into her eyes. "For you to have a safe place to run. If things go bad."

A lump clogged her throat. "I appreciate that, but I'm not leaving until we figure this out."

"Yeah? I anticipated that answer. I'm hanging the storm window outside my window and installing a throwbolt on my bedroom door. Just in case."

His concern for her safety made her heart sing. "I'm handy with a screwdriver."

"You'll stock the room with water and food for twenty-four hours. Find something in the barn to serve as a portable toilet."

"You're serious."

"Better ready than surprised." He stood

and pulled her to her feet. "Gather your supplies then meet me in the barn."

Twenty minutes later, she stood next to him in the musty barn, surveying two empty stalls and one containing an exercise contraption. The scene of leather and manure was faint but still discernible. "What's the plan?" She turned to look at his face as he scowled at nothing in particular.

"We have to secure a stall. I found a couple old cattle guards to lay on top of the rails. I—we'll tie them down with baling wire." He hesitated, clenched his jaw then met her gaze before finishing. "You'll nail the gate shut."

"Okay, but that's later. What can I do now?"

He pulled gloves from his back pocket and handed her the pair. "Grab that roll of wire and carry it to the middle stall." With a grunt, he hefted a rusty metal grate over his head and walked into the stall.

She yanked on the gloves, grabbed the metal wheel of wire and followed him. Slap a pair of Levis, a denim shirt and a Stetson on Kol and he'd be one fine cowboy.

As they worked, they talked about inconsequential things—their childhoods, his summer vacations here at the cabin, her crazy, smothering Greek family—anything except the reason behind the need for the pen.

Finally, after rechecking each fastening, he pulled off his gloves. "It's ready."

With tears burning the back of her eyes, she nodded and slipped her hand into his. "Looks strong."

He squeezed her hand once and headed out of the barn into the dusk. "I'll update the log.

Have you got what you need? Pens, paper?"

"In my pack." She tried to match his stride but he moved out too fast. "Do you have a voice recorder? I left mine in the transport."

He hesitated at the base of the porch steps and glanced over his shoulder. "No recorder, sorry."

"That's okay." She watched him disappear into the cabin. He must need time alone. Lowering herself to the porch, she leaned back her head and scanned the evening sky, enjoying the deepening blues and purples. Off to one side, a star twinkled. Or was it a planet?

Since arriving on this mountain, she'd been all turned around. In more way than one. What would the night bring?

The flutter of wings overhead and the sight of a small darting creature at the edge of her vision convinced her Kol's alone time had now ended. She dashed up the steps and into the cabin. A quick check of her pack confirmed she had what she'd need. From the outside pocket, she extracted a plastic card then wandered down the hall to his room.

He sat in front of his notelink, a topographic map displayed on the screen. With each click of the mouse, he switched views from an aerial shot to a variety of lateral shots then to a realistic photo.

"A favorite spot?"

His shoulders stiffened then relaxed. "Never been there."

"That's a lot of images of a place you've never visited."

"Weird, huh? I can't explain it, but I have an urge to go there."

She leaned over his shoulder and focused

on the readout at the bottom of the screen. "Davis Mountains. Hey, those are in west Texas. I drove through them on my way here."

He turned and looked up, a frown creasing his brow. "They're not on the direct route from San Antonio."

"Yeah, well, I took a wrong turn somewhere outside of Fort Stockton. By the time I realized it, I'd driven too far to go back." She shrugged, tossing her curls. "So I just plotted a new route."

"Some investigator." He grinned.

"Hey, I got here, didn't I?"

His hand grazed her ass and grabbed her hip, tugging her against his side. "I'm glad you did. Have I thanked you for what you're doing?"

Do not cry like a baby. She swallowed hard. "It's nothing. Hey, you wanted to do something with the money card. Here it is."

He took and turned it over, scrutinizing the encoding strip. "Great, I'll email this data to a buddy of mine. He's an electronics whiz. I'll get him to order a pizza and rent a motel room in Colorado Springs." With swift movements, he tapped the keys and hit the send button.

Her stomach jumped with nerves. "I have one request."

"Computer hibernate." He waited until the screen saver appeared then scooted away from the desk. "Okay, ask."

"Before you enter that pen, I want a real kiss."

"A goodbye kiss?" His eyebrows rose. "What happened to looking at the positive?"

"No, our first one." She met his gaze, pushing aside the nervousness about what her request might reveal. "On the lips."

"Our first, huh? Gotta fix that." As he stood, he grinned and closed the distance. He smoothed a curl behind her ear and cupped her jaw. His arm came around her shoulders and he drew her against his chest.

Her arms circled his back and she waited, heart beating double-time. His breath brushed her waiting mouth an instant before his warm lips pressed to hers. His lips tasted hers, first gentle then with increasing pressure. She gripped him tighter and gave herself up to the sensation of breathing Kol's scent, of listening to his faster breathing, of learning the texture of his lips. When the tip of his tongue probed the seam of her lips, she was eager to open and taste more. His tongue teased hers, invading and retreating, enticing her to duplicate the play. Her nipples tightened against her sports bra and she couldn't resist grazing them against his chest.

He groaned and leaned away, cradling the back of her head and easing it to his chest. "Can't go too far here."

She nodded, knowing he spoke the truth. "I'm ready, if you are."

"No choice, it's what has to be done."

Gathering their supplies, they returned to the barn. Kol grabbed a couple of horse blankets from a chest and tossed them on the stable floor. "The box of nails and a hammer are on that bench. Make sure you use a half dozen." He stood before the opening of the pen, hands on hips. With a deep breath, he bent at the waist and walked inside, pulling the gate closed behind him.

Knowing this was for the best, she centered the first nail in the board and smacked it with the hammer. Out of the corner of her eye, she saw Kol flinch, an action repeated with every blow. Each thwack of the hammer tightened the knot in her stomach, and she blinked back hot tears. After the last stroke, she leaned a forearm against the stall and sucked in a deep breath.

"Put in a couple on the other side." His words were strangled and pitched low.

Five minutes later, she settled herself on a campstool next to the gate.

Kol stood with arms braced against the stall rails, his head drooping between hunched shoulders. A dark patch ran down the middle of his shirt.

"So, what shall we talk about?"

He turned and walked the inside of the pen, his head ducked several inches to avoid scraping the cow grates. "Talk about?"

"To distract you." She propped her chin in her hands and thought. "Okay, you've got twenty dollars for entertainment. Do you enjoy a single event or buy an item that can be enjoyed more than once?"

He moved to the far side and walked back and forth. "Zoia, I can't handle this. I hate being confined."

"My mom can't stand crowded elevators." She grabbed the pad and pen to record his admission. "Claustrophobia. Have you always had it?"

"No, the symptoms are recent." He held onto a rail, planted his feet at the bottom and pulled his chest close. "At times, I need to feel the fresh air on my skin."

"I've noticed." A wide grin spread across her lips, but he didn't look up from his exercise. "What other symptoms?"

He moved close to where she sat and squatted so he could see her between the slats. "Promise not to open that gate until I tell you."

"What if you need my help?" She strained to connect with his gaze but the dim barn lighting cast his face in shadow.

"You'll help by writing down everything I say. We'll sort out the clues later.' He reached a hand through the slats, palm up. "Take my hand, Zoia, and say the words."

She slipped her hand in his and squeezed, hoping the touch helped him in some small way. "I promise."

An hour passed. Playing a few games of Hangman kept him preoccupied for a while, until the restlessness returned. He'd gotten a crick in his neck from bending over while pacing so he relied on calisthenics when the walls started closing in.

Two hours passed. Zoia gave up on conversation because Kol quit responding. He alternated between pushups, sit-ups, and sitting with his back in a corner, a stormy expression on his face. On a prowl around the barn to help her stay awake, she found an old horse enthusiast magazine and started reading aloud.

"Zoia, stop. I don't care about the advantages of alfalfa over other grains."

She ignored the sharpness of his tone. "I know the subject isn't exciting, but I'm getting bored and sleepy. Just listen, and you'll know you're not alone."

Somewhere in the fourth article, she drifted off to sleep, a forearm propped against the gate cradling her head.

"No, let me rest."

Zoia jerked at the sound of his strangled

words and sat up, blinking against the light.

Scuffling sounds then a loud bang. "My turn again?"

She kneeled next to the stall and watched Kol, sweating and agitated, back himself into a corner. "What's wrong, Kol?"

"I'll answer your questions. No injection." He leaned forward and swiped a hand at the back of his neck. "Something hurts."

She grabbed her pad and a pen. "What do you see? Tell me what you hear."

"Taste sweat. Want water. Tall mountain to climb. Hell Hospital."

"Kol, look at me." She scooted opposite him but his eyes were unfocused.

"Voices of pain." He covered his ears and rocked back and forth. "Tormented pleas. Women screaming names, children crying."

"Kol, can you hear me?" Whatever he was remembering had taken him somewhere else. Somewhere she couldn't reach him. Her throat ached with frustration and she wished she could touch him. "I can't help you if you won't share. Where are you?"

He kneaded his hand at the back of his neck and shook his head. "Can't tell. Punishment." With teeth gritted, he groaned, eyes squeezed tight.

She scrambled to the far side of the stall and touched his shoulder. "Kol, I'm here."

He whirled, edging away. "Don't touch me." The overhead light caught his eyes and they glowed amber.

A shiver ran over her skin, but she didn't back away, she kept jotting notes.

"Argh. Pain." Kol grabbed at his body — his elbows, his hips, his knees. "Can't fucking stand it."

Was he sick? She gripped the edge of the rail. "Kol, what's wrong? What can I do?"

He writhed sweat running down his face. His yells turned guttural.

"I'm getting you out." She dashed to the tack room, grabbed the hammer and ran back to the row of stalls. With jerky movements, she tried to lever the claw under the nail heads. It wouldn't catch. "Kol, you're not alone and I'm going to help." When that didn't work, she stretched her hand inside the pen and clumsily pounded at the board.

Kol sprang at her on all fours and snarled. "Don't."

Instinct pushed her back, and the hammer fell from her hand. The sound was so guttural she couldn't tell if he'd really spoken a word. As she watched, he paced on hands and knees, his movements strangely rhythmic. She scurried to her pack and dug out her binocs, resting them on the middle rail.

He crawled past her position, threw back his head—a head that looked too round--and let out a strangled cry.

A cry like a woman dying. High pitched and eerie.

Big white teeth showed in his too-wide mouth. She gasped, but clicked a couple images. From her research, she'd learned only one animal made that sound. A predator that was supposed to be gone from this region. The memory of the footprint near the clearing flashed in her mind. The stack of twigs and leaves. "Can't be."

Kol started peeling off his clothes and resumed pacing, yowls emitting from deep in his throat. A strange shimmer covered his body.

As she clicked the magnification on the binocs, she saw fur sprouting on his skin, his ears growing points, and a tail curling from his ass. Her breathing ratcheted up and her chest tightened with fear. Her grip on the binocs tightened. The events happening before her eyes were unexplainable.

How could a man change into a cougar?

Whatever was happening was scaring the shit out of her.

In rapid succession, she remembered the details of her contact with Halcyon — the urgency of the request, the hints of his location, the fee prepaid in cash. Guilt at her involvement weighed heavily in her heart. She leaned an arm on the rail, her gaze tracking the ani — Kol's movements. He no longer seemed in pain, just nervous, as he walked the length of the stall turned and walked back.

Some time later, the binocs dropped to the floor with a thud and she jerked awake.

The cougar rested with his head on his paws, ears pricked and amber eyes watchful.

Her eyelids drooped but she forced herself to walk to the adjoining stall. Maybe a workout on the rowing machine would help her stay awake. "I'm here, Kol. I could talk so you have a human connection."

As she moved, one of her grandma's Greek songs came to mind. The words tumbled out and she closed her eyes, using the rhythmic pulls to work out her frustration. How could she be so stupid? To have taken a job solely for money. Why hadn't she thought of how her success might hurt him? When perspiration dripped into her mouth, she stopped and leaned her arms on her knees.

A shuffling sounded from the pen followed by a groan, and she turned.

Kol lay curled into a ball on the hard floor, naked and shivering.

"Oh, thank the Spirit, you're back." She rushed to the stall and stretched an arm through the slats. "Kol, look at me and let me know you're okay." When he didn't answer, she squeezed her body between the slats and approached him. "It's Zoia, I'm here with you." She grabbed one of the blankets and gently laid it on him.

He flinched but didn't turn his head.

Crouching, she rested a hand on his shoulder. "Kol, I'll keep talking and when you're ready, you can answer. I tried to write down everything you said. You can read over my notes and tell me what I left out." She tugged the blanket edge up to his shoulder. "You know, I don't mind keeping up more than my half of the conversation. My brothers—"

"The four cops, right?"

"Kol!" She threw herself on top of him and squealed. "Oh, I'm so glad to hear your voice."

He rolled to his back and grabbed her tight. "Didn't you promise to stay outside?"

She tossed her head and grinned. "I didn't open the gate."

"What did we learn?"

She drew back and ran her hand along his smooth chest, avoiding his gaze. "A few things."

He lifted up her chin until he could look into her eyes. "Tell me."

"I don't know how."

"Judging by the fact I'm buck naked again, I had another episode. I remembered details of my capture. That's a first. Did you get any notes on that?"

"Yes, but they are real brief. That was only part of what happened. Kol, somehow you transformed into a cougar."

He jerked and sat up, running a hand over his face. "What are you talking about?"

Entangling herself from his embrace, she walked to the side of the pen and scooped up the binocs. "Uploading these would give us better images, but click this. You'll see…"

He held them to his eyes and flicked the buttons.

She knew the minute he saw the transformation. Watching as the color drained from his face, her chest ached. What must he be thinking?

His body stiffened and he almost fumbled the instrument. His breathing grew labored before he shot to his feet.

"I think they implanted something in your back. You kept pulling at it, complaining it hurt."

He held out a hand, his body rigid. "Hand me the hammer and stand back."

*****

Twenty minutes later, they'd both showered and Kol tapped on the notelink's keys. "Evan took care of those transactions. I'm keeping him in the loop about what we've discovered."

Gazing at the lightening sky, Zoia rubbed a towel over her hair. "Do you want to talk about what's happened?"

"Plenty of time for talking on the drive."

She turned, a frown creasing her brow. "We're taking a trip?"

"Two seconds." He stared at the screen and then gave a short nod. "Computer shut down." He crossed the room and embraced her, tugging her against his chest and resting his chin on her head. "Remember I mentioned an urge about the Davis Mountains? Evan's been tracking chatter about unusual activities — too many vehicles and strangers traveling in that area."

Her body stiffened. "What about getting that thing in your back checked by a doctor?"

"Removing it will be your job." He tightened his arms and nuzzled her neck. "Can't trust anyone else."

She turned in his embrace, dark eyes shining. "Your trust means a lot."

Leaning forward, he touched her forehead with his. "I need to discover who did this and find Hell Hospital. I owe it to the others left behind."

"And you think I can help?"

"I'm heading back to civilization." He kissed her, tasting her tender lips, pulling the lower one between his and sucking. "You brought me out from the shadows. We're a team now and we'll see this through to the end."

Jaguarondi

By
Betty Hanawa

Chapter 1

Dylan Gomez's day sucked. As he swam into consciousness, he realized he was once again stark naked. He curled on his side practically in a fetal position inside a cage too small for him to stretch his aching limbs. The top of the cage banged his shoulder when he tried to lever himself up on one elbow. He felt the wire mesh squares against his back with the other side barely inches from his chest and knees. Yep, Dylan's brain foggily decided, his day definitely sucked.

Then he saw the black barrel of a gun pointed at him. His day just got worse.

"Who the hell are you?" Despite the shakiness in the woman's voice, the GLOCK she held didn't quiver. Dylan knew how much that gun weighed with a full load. He knew from experience her solid hold on the semi-automatic pistol took long, concentrated hours of practice at a firing range.

He used a GLOCK first in his part-time college job as a police officer in his town, then during his military stint. With World War Three raging, everyone under the age of forty-five served in some capacity in the military for a minimum of two years. Deferments belonged to his great-grandfather's generation of sixty years ago in the 1960's and 1970's. He was only able to complete his Ph.D. because he did it while being employed as a cop.

Weird how his mind drifted when he came out of those damn blackouts, Dylan thought to himself. He needed to figure a way out of this cage. He definitely didn't want to run the risk of ending up in Hell Hospital again.

Instead, he fixated on the short, clean fingernails of the tanned hands holding the gun with only a mesh wire cage door separating him from the barrel's eye.

Her hands mesmerized him. She had long, intensely feminine fingers on large hands attached to strong wrists. Nicks and scratches marred the rosy perfection of her skin. Her tanned skin was still shades lighter than his. She wore no rings, just a plain watch on a leather band peeked out from under the cuff of her long-sleeved uniform shirt.

He'd live in uniforms for years. From the khaki shade of the uniform, he thought she could be in Wildlife Control.

His thoughts floated to the snow-kissed queens of the Norse myths and legends he used in his theses, both for his Masters and Ph.D. Christened Dylan Thomas Gomez, he ate up poetry with his pabulum. He already had a Doctorate in European Literature before he realized it didn't do him any good in the law enforcement job he'd taken to postpone his military service. He loved the job enough to make it his life's work. But all the memorized stories from college brought him comfort in the evil world he'd existed in for several months.

His dick reminded him the nurses in the Hell Hospital weren't as good-looking as Brunhilde holding the gun on him. As usual after one of his blackouts, his muscles and joints acted like they were stretching after being tied tightly and he had an aching hard-on, making him want a woman more badly than any teenage hormonal fantasy.

His dick wanted those lovely hands wrapped around it. It pulsed with exquisite pain. What it wanted, it wanted now.

With sheer will, he overrode his blind eye and forced blood to his brain. He needed to think. "I asked you a question. Who are you? *Como se llamas?*" Her Spanish held the accent of classroom lessons, unlike his bilingual skills that came with his mother's milk.

He cleared his throat. "Water? Please?" The gun and the pretty hands disappeared from view.

The cage sat near the edge of the back of a van. The van's doors were open. An aluminum ramp extended downward. Its bright metal reflected the sun with the heat of summer into the van and through the mesh wire cage. South Texas didn't care the calendar said mid-May.

Dylan checked his internal clock. This blackout lasted barely two days.

Hell Hospital put him through sleep deprivation and tried to mess up his concept of days and nights by keeping him in windowless rooms with lights and meals at odd intervals. They even placed him in complete sensory deprivation. Despite their best efforts, his internal clock took the licking and kept on ticking. His *culendero* uncle told him it was because he was in tune with Mother Earth. Because he always knew *when* he was, he always kept a kernel of *who* he was. He was grateful his clock kept him sane.

He cringed away from the jumbled memories since the last time he'd been fully aware of himself. This waking up naked with no idea where he was had to stop soon. He wanted to go back to being a cop since his military service was now *kaput*. The damn blackouts got him invalided out of his military duty and Special Forces, despite his protests.

The lovely hands came back into view, set a bottle of water and pile of clothes beside the cage. On top of them, she placed a digital camera, and then efficiently unsnapped the clasp on the cage. Damn, he hadn't realized it wasn't locked. Of course, he didn't exactly have the strength to cut and run.

He heard the subtle click of a double-barrel rifle being cocked into ready position. Shit, even if he tried to run, Brunhilde would probably shoot his balls off before he got three feet away. The woman had a freaking arsenal. In addition to the GLOCK and the rifle, he spotted a second, smaller gun.

Slowly, feeling joints creak and pop with strain, Dylan squirmed from the cage far enough to grab the water bottle. He gulped it down, easing the dryness and being absorbed into his system almost immediately. He took a deep breath, then emptied the bottle down his throat.

The nice hands exchanged a second bottle for the first one. Dylan was falling in love with those hands. He drank the second bottle more slowly, but still finished it quickly.

"More?" The feminine voice circled around his head. Her light scent held no perfumes, just the pleasant odor of sun-warmed woman in starched clothes. His dick assured him he was still alive and it was fully functional.

"Maybe in a minute. Thanks."

"You're not an illegal. Your accent is South

Texas, not Mexican. Who the hell are you and where is the jaguarondi? Did you have a falling out with your poacher buddies?"

Dylan propped himself up on an elbow and tilted his head up to see his captor who sounded more confused than he was. "What are you talking about? I just regained consciousness. Who the hell are you and where do you think you're going to take me?"

Now he could see that she wore the Wildlife Control Management uniform. His correct guess pleased him. The name badge read "Lundberg." To his surprise, Ms. Lundberg's face drained of color as he watched. She tightened her grip on the rifle until her knuckles whitened. The barrel never left his face while she sank onto the dirt.

"Ma'am?" Dylan pushed on the back of the cage with his feet. The cage rolled backward allowing him to further slither from it without falling face first on the hot metal ramp. "Are you okay?"

He got out of the van and knelt in front of Brunhilde, wincing at the rocks and stickers under his bare feet. He shrugged off the slight pain and focused on her.

He didn't try to take the gun. She might decide to blow his head off if he touched her rifle.

Her pale blue eyes looked a little wild. She didn't look at his engorged dick, which kind of surprised him. While he didn't think he was any more of an egotist than most men, women did tend to view his package with appreciation.

She looked at his left ear as though it were a snake about to bite.

Dylan reached up to touch his ear, suddenly aware of it throbbing with its own sharp pain. His fingers rubbed on a chunk of plastic embedded in his upper cartilage.

"What the hell?" He tugged at it, but wasn't able to dislodge it. "What is this?"

The Norse goddess shook her head as though she were rearranging her thoughts. Her dark blonde hair gleamed like the late afternoon sun itself was trapped in it. Her color began to come back into her face. She stood up in one swift movement and poked Dylan in the chest with her rifle. Her full lips thinned white and her jaw hardened. "It's an endangered wildlife tag. I put it on a jaguarondi. Now where is the cat and how did you get it on? As a matter of fact, how did you get it off the cat? Those things have a locking mechanism that only Wildlife Control personnel can remove."

What kind of trap had he fallen into *this* time? Dylan stood up. No way in hell was he going to give her the psychological advantage of standing over him, not that it helped much. In her boots, she stood several inches taller than he. Plus she had bigger bones, a rifle, and clothes on. Granted at 5'8" he was on the short side for a man, but no one ever made him feel like a shrimp. Hell Hospital taught him not to let being naked rattle him. So far she hadn't shot him. He wanted to know what was going on.

"What jaguarondi? Lady, I don't have a clue what the hell you're talking about."

"You poachers are getting damn brazen. I was out of sight of the van a grand total of five minutes. How did they manage to get the cat out and you in while I was gone?"

"You know more than I do," Dylan snarled back. "I've been unconscious. I don't know what happened to your damn jaguarondi. I just woke up naked and squashed in that cage. I'm not a poacher. Why'd you leave the van anyway?"

"I went in the convenience store to pee after I filled the van. Got a problem with that?"

"No, Ms. Lundberg, I don't. I do have a problem with waking up naked in a too small cage and no idea where I am."

"How do you know my name?"

Dylan grinned, then drawled, "Forget you're wearing your name tag?"

She blushed lightly with a sheepish look of having swallowed a stupid pill. She dropped her eyes from his face, then even more quickly returned her attention to his face. Her blush flashed scarlet.

Dylan crossed his arms over his chest, well aware his dick still proudly commanded attention. He now held the upper hand in their subtle battle for control. He began to relax. Even though they never broke him, the participants at Hell Hospital never got rattled. Since Ms. Lundberg's composure was slightly shaken, he tentatively thought she might not be part of that organization. Maybe she really was a Wildlife Control officer. Time for him to go on the attack and press his advantage.

"I am damn tired of people trying to mess with my mind. I don't know what kind of drugs were in that gun *your* friends shot me with," Dylan rubbed his thigh feeling the adhesive roughness of temporary skin where someone had patched him. The bullet must have gone cleanly through. "But I know damn well I'm not going to be held prisoner again."

He watched her blush fade to pale again, almost as if she were trying not to faint.

"Where were you a prisoner? Mexico?" Her white face registered confusion. Her innocence became more convincing for Dylan when her hands fractionally relaxed around her rifle.

She acted like she was hoping he'd been in one of the God-forsaken Mexican jails. If he had been, he might have been able to bribe his way out, unlike the Hell Hospital.

"In a circle of hell." Dylan stepped into her personal space for the satisfaction of watching her back up against one of the open doors of the van. Her hands tightened again. When he moved backward, she remained against the door, but her hands relaxed. Maybe if he put on the clothes, she'd relax more and he might be able to grab the gun. He plucked at the clothes. "May I put these on?"

"Yes, just put the camera on the van floor. When you get dressed, I want to show you some pictures."

Dylan shook out the material to discover a one-piece jump suit. He shrugged off the lack of shoes. If he had to, he'd run barefoot. He pulled up the pants, then got his arms covered. He lifted his dick to press against his stomach for room to zip up the jumpsuit. It jumped painfully in his hand, begging for relief.

"What's the matter? Can't you get your pickle in?"

Dylan stared at Brunhilde. How the hell did this woman know his long time nickname? His older brother and cousins had corrupted Dylan to Dill, which promptly became a family joke. Fortunately, it hadn't followed him into the cops or the Army.

She looked away from him and shifted the

rifle to her arm. Her cheeks flamed red.

"I apologize," she formally told the dirt. "I have a younger brother. When he was born, I asked why he looked different from me and my older sister said it was his pickle."

A bit more tension eased in Dylan. Why, he didn't know. It just made him relax to hear her explanation. With her remorseful and not paying attention, he had his chance.

He lunged forward and got his hands around the rifle stock.

She promptly kneed him in his groin.

Dylan dropped to the ground, clutching his poor dick and balls.

The gun barrel pressed against his belly.

"Do I shoot you now? Or later?" Brunhilde sounded cool and dispassionate as though she were trying to decide what to order in a restaurant.

"Shoot me now, please," Dylan managed to say. "Put me out of my misery."

Pain radiated from his groin, even making his hands tingle.

He managed to jerk his attention from his painful dick to his hands. The tingling grew to aching, then burning. His fingers curled inward and his fingernails began to grow. The pain moved to his feet, making his toes curl inward. The jumpsuit seemed looser.

"Help me," he tried to say, but his tongue didn't work right. The words came out as a growl.

Her face turned the gray of dirty concrete.

His butt flashed with pain, making him forget aching groin.

He saw the Norse goddess set down her rifle. But instead of helping him, the sadist was using the camera to film him like a sick-o wanting snuff pictures to post on the Internet.

When she set the camera down, he was panting with exhaustion. He saw her load an odd looking cartridge into the smaller rifle, and then take aim.

No one was going to shoot him while he had a spark of life in him. He leapt from his prone position and hurled himself at her jugular.

A burning thump hit him in the chest at the same time he heard the rifle boom.

He dropped back to the ground and tried to pull a plastic dart from his chest.

Brunhilde set the rifle back in the van. Even though she knelt, she loomed over him.

Her pale blue eyes filled with tears. "I'm sorry if it hurts. It'll be better soon."

Yeah, right. It'll be better soon because he was dying. She's sorry she shot him. Dylan wanted to laugh at the irony.

She reached a hand to his chest, but he batted her hand away.

She jerked back with a gasp and stared at her bleeding hand.

Just before the blackness swallowed him, he saw her taking pictures again while the blood dripped down her hand from three ragged scratches.

Chapter 2

No matter how many times she watched what she recorded, her stomach still crawled up her throat when she watched the man she met this afternoon turn into a jaguarondi. Part of her didn't know why she hadn't shot him.

Then she remembered the green-gold frightened eyes. Even when he completely turned into a jaguarondi, she didn't have the heart to shoot him.

Instead, she smuggled the wildcat home and left him in her bedroom. Throughout the evening, she periodically took pictures of the sleeping jaguarondi. Eventually, she watched and controlled her nausea while she recorded his body converting back into human.

Her phone warbled the opening bars of the Beatles' classic "Hard Day's Night," her personalized ring for the station.

Took them long enough to make a decision, she thought in exasperation while she touched the ear bug to activate it.

"Lundberg," she said into the vocal tab.

"Hey, Haley," responded the clear baritone of the sole officer on night duty. "Chief says it's okay for you to take your two week leave starting tomorrow."

"You'll have enough staff?"

"Joe will be back tomorrow."

"Oh, good. His family is feeling better

then?" Haley heard the bidet activate, then the shower start. Relief made her shoulders eased. Her guest had stayed in human form and hadn't changed into the jaguarondi again. She hated to think what a scared, enraged wildcat might have done to her bedroom, but she didn't want to leave the person trapped inside the cat in the cage.

"Yes, and he said to tell you he really appreciated you giving up your vacation time so he was able to take care of the family."

"Tell him he's welcome. I was happy to help, but I really want to visit my sister. She has this virus that's going around." Her sister was actually busy trying to find a vaccine to fight this damn virus. Haley hoped her sister and colleagues at the biomed lab that employed them were going to be able to carve out a little bit of time to test the blood Haley had drawn from the man, both in his human body and the jaguarondi body.

"Chief says to stay in contact. With this gawdawful virus around, he might need to recall you. No problems releasing the cat?"

"Not a bit," Haley lied yet again. As if anyone was going to believe the truth anyway. "I'll be in touch and you can always call me."

"Got "cha. Have a good trip. Night, Haley."

"Night. Thanks, Fred. Thank the Chief and Joe for me."

"Will do. See you in a couple of weeks."

"Bye." Even as she toggled the closure switch on the phone, she headed to the kitchen, then switched direction to the bathroom. She wanted to find out his *name* before she fed him.

She heard the shower click off before the efficiency unit stopped it. Like others who lived in

South Texas, he knew how to shower quickly to save water. The desalination plants at the coast helped, but everyone knew how precious fresh water was.

She knocked on the bathroom door. "Hey."

The door opened and Mr. Lean-and-Gorgeous with green-golden eyes stood in front of her. His shoulders, chest, and abs still gleamed with water, making him glimmer like a bronze statue in the rain. Dark stubble covered a strong jaw and partway up flat slabs of cheeks that ended in sharp cheek bones. Above lips made for kissing, the stubble made Haley think of a soft mustache tickling her clit while a tongue laved deeply.

He had skimmed his wet hair back into a short ponytail at the nape of his neck. Her pink rubber band didn't detract from his confident masculinity any more than the rose decorated towel slung low around his hips. His chest had a smattering of dark hair and thickened into a trail that led from just below his navel to hide under the towel, which tented enticingly.

No, she told herself, don't *go there. You don't even know his name. Okay, time to rectify that.*

"Hi." Haley swallowed hard. "I, uh, didn't catch your name earlier."

He leaned one shoulder against the door jam and folded his arms in front of his chest above those tight abs. "I didn't give it, Ms. Lundberg. I don't introduce myself to people who want to shoot me."

"Well, excuse me, but as far as I was concerned you were a part of a poacher pack. As the old saying goes, 'The best defense is a quick offense.' I wasn't going to risk getting hurt."

"And yet you brought me where? Into your

house?"

"Yes. My house."

"Why?" He stepped forward and tilted his head upward to look straight into her eyes.

Barefooted, he stood at least three inches shorter than she. Yet for some reason, Haley felt as though she were the smaller of the two of them. She took a step backward.

"I felt sorry for you," her mouth said before she thought.

"Sorry for me?" His jaw dropped, then his eyes narrowed. "You're the one who kicked me in the nuts. You're the one who held two different guns on me, then shot me with a dart. What the hell was that anyway?"

"I shot a tranquillizer dart into you to trank you."

"Why the hell did you do it?"

He pressed forward again until her back pressed on the hallway wall. His towel-covered, jutting cock brushed against her.

Her body jumped with electricity. She wore a summer skirt and panties, but her muff wept with hot fire as though his naked skin had rubbed against hers.

His voice deepened and grew rougher. "Did you bring me to your house to be your sex slave?"

His voice vibrated across her skin like a cat's purr. He stepped even closer to her. She smelled the mint tang of toothpaste. His heavy cock pressed against her belly.

She held herself rigid, not trusting herself to not rub against his whiskered cheek.

"I must say. Being your sex slave beats the hell out of the last prison I was in."

Haley stepped sideways from him. To her surprise, disappointment sank through her that he didn't pursue her. His eyes gleamed with a smug look of being a superior being.

Annoyance flashed through her. *Jerk with a cock, he needed to go jack off.*

"You're not my sex slave. You can leave anytime. You have no money. No I.D. You won't get far. Or you can tell me your name and I'll fix you something to eat, then drive you where you need to go. Your choice."

"First tell me why the hell you tranked me." He stepped into her space again. This time he held himself with the tenseness of a trained fighter ready to do damage if he didn't get answers.

"I didn't trank *you*. Well, I did, but you weren't exactly yourself at the time."

Dylan realized she wasn't intimidated despite him standing next to her body with his tell-me-or-get-hurt stance. Her winter blue eyes held his without flinching.

She rubbed her lovely left hand across her right palm as if massaging away pain. Dylan took her hand as carefully as he would take his baby niece's. On her palm he saw the dark color of artificial skin covering three long parallel lines.

He remembered her reaching for the trank dart embedded in his chest and himself knocking her hand away. Why did he remember her blood dripping into the dirt while she took pictures of him?

"I wasn't myself? Then what was I?"

She took her hand out of his. "I tranked the jaguarondi that was attacking me."

"Riii-ggghhtt, lady. Sure, you tranked a jaguarondi, not me. What the fuck is it with you and this jaguarondi obsession?" As he talked, another memory tumbled through him. This time his mind's eye gave him a picture of himself launching his body up at her, determined to rip out her throat before she could shoot him. He saw paws where his hands should be, claws outstretched. He ran his tongue around his teeth reassuring himself he didn't have the fangs he'd felt when he'd tried to grab the gun, just before the thud hit his chest. He looked at his chest and saw a small scab of a puncture wound.

He shook his head. *No. He wasn't going crazy. He wasn't going to let her mess with his mind.*

"Do you want something to eat?" Her gentle voice smoothed the confusion eating at his gut from the muddled memories.

He didn't think they were his memories, but his internal clock counted the time for him. He remembered the pain. Maybe if he ate something, he'd be able to think more clearly.

"Yeah. Okay. Thanks. I'll," he gestured at his lower body with his towel-covered dick insisting on making its presence known, "get some clothes on."

Belatedly it occurred to him. "Thank you for the clothes and shaving stuff."

"You're welcome. I worked in uniform supply for awhile when I first did my compulsory service. I'm used to eyeballing a person and guesstimating the sizes."

"What else did you do in service?" He didn't think she learned that self-defense and her ease with armaments by passing out uniforms and skivvies.

Her mouth lifted in a grin. Dylan found himself enchanted by a dimple that popped into view by the corner of her mouth.

"The Hellcats."

Hot damn. He knew this woman embodied the spirit of the Norse goddess Brunhilde. Dylan bowed. "This Special Forces mud foot is honored to meet one of the goddesses of the First Amazon Division. I no longer bear the humiliation of being smacked down by a girl. You ladies sure wrecked havoc in the Middle East."

She shrugged. "It's easy to infiltrate wearing a *hijab*. Plus the men aren't expecting a woman to fight them, even though numerous women in their culture have been used for human bombs. Cultural prejudices work both ways. Food?"

"Please." Dylan turned to go back into the bathroom to shave and finish removing the tags from the clothes she'd purchased.

"Hey, Mud Foot."

"Yes, Hildy?"

"Hildy?"

Oh, shit. His nickname for his goddess just slipped out.

"Sorry. Um," *Now how to extract his foot? Might as well be honest.* "This afternoon, I thought of you as Brunhilde the Norse Goddess. Hildy just kind of fits you."

"Interesting. My name's Haley."

"Thank you, Haley. I'll try not to call you Hildy again."

"As you wish." She shrugged. "And will you be Mud Foot or Pickle?"

Dylan flinched at Pickle. He sure didn't want to be called by his despised kid nickname. "Dylan. Dylan Thomas Gomez." He held out his hand.

Her palm slid into his. Her handshake was just as firm as his. He felt the ridges of the artificial skin again. He turned her palm upward and traced the lines with his index finger.

"How did this happen? And don't give any guff about a jaguarondi."

She pulled her hand from his. "We'll discuss it after you've eaten. Bacon and eggs? Or do you want something more substantial like a steak?"

"A steak?" His mouth watered at the thought of a steak, cooked to perfection, the juices running on the plate.

"Steak it is then," she said with a laugh.

Dylan ran his tongue over his lips to make sure he wasn't drooling.

"How do you want it?"

"Rare." He barely stopped himself from licking his mouth again. He thought for half a second he felt his canine teeth lengthening to fangs. *Oh, joy. Bad enough Hildy kept talking about a jaguarondi. All he needed to completely lose his mind was to imagine himself turning into a vampire. Just put a stake through him right now. On second thought, he'd wait on that until he had a steak in his belly. Maybe then the world would make sense.*

"You've got it. See you in a few."

Smearing on shaving cream, Dylan looked at himself in the mirror and saw the chunk of plastic had been removed from the top of his ear. He shaved, being careful not to leave any wicked bristles.

"Stupid ass. You're just hoping to get lucky," he told his reflection while he rinsed the pink disposable razor. He closed his eyes telling himself he didn't want any of the last of the unscented shaving cream to get in them while he rinsed his face, but he knew he didn't want to look at the hungry lust in his eyes.

Dylan looked around the room while he dried his face. Nothing in the room indicated even a casual male presence. From a mirrored tray filled with bottles of various shapes and sizes to the thick flowered towels, fruity scented shampoo and liquid soap, the bathroom was definitely a girly-girl's haven. She obviously bought the guy type bar soap and unscented shaving cream for him when she bought the jeans, tee shirt, and other things. He tore off tags and ripped opened packages of socks and his choice of boxers or briefs. A quick check proved even the tennis shoes were the right size.

What a woman. She knew how to coddle a man in addition to being sexier than a real-life pin-up. From the look he saw in her eyes, he knew sex with her was more a matter of "when" rather than "if." As much as he wanted Haley, he didn't think sex with her was something he needed to pursue when he didn't know what the hell was happening to him.

He held the briefs in one hand while he checked the aching place in his thigh. He didn't know if Haley had treated him, but he was pleased the bullet hole seemed to be healing cleanly.

His hand drifted to his dick.

"Goddamn it," he told his yet again hard dick. He tossed the briefs back on the floor and sat on the toilet. His dick didn't care he'd jacked off in the shower. It wanted satisfaction again.

He rubbed it more vigorously. He smelled food cooking. His stomach growled, but his dick screamed its importance. Still stroking himself, he dug through Haley's laundry basket and found a nightgown. Deeply inhaling her scent on the soft cotton, he looked through the cabinet drawers.

Hot damn! He smiled at her collection of vibrators and butt plugs. What a woman!

After helping himself to a generous supply of her personal lubricant, he sat on the toilet and laid a towel across his thighs. He stuffed the sweet nightgown into his mouth to stifle his moans at how good the gel felt while he rubbed his dick and his balls. He thought of her hands and breathed in Hildy's scent. The gel warmed his dick and balls, but not as sweetly hot as a woman's – Hildy's – slick folds and juices.

His balls constricted, then exploded. His cum drenched the towel and he sagged against the toilet tank.

Damn, he wanted a woman badly, but tonight he had to keep his mind focused on stopping the damn blackouts. He had no business letting himself be distracted by a girly-girl who knew how to kick ass. Resignedly, he cleaned himself and the bathroom, then got dressed.

He walked into the kitchen to see Hildy – Haley, he had to remember her name –lifting a steak from the oven's broiler. She dropped the tongs she used in the sink, then carried a steak-filled plate to the table where a smaller plate held a baked potato and a shallow bowl held a large, crisp salad.

"Hi, Dylan. Help yourself." This time instead of soothing him, her voice made his dick twitch.

He thought how great she'd sound moaning his name, inviting him to help himself to her body. *Stop it. You're more than a dick.*

Dylan managed to pick up the knife and fork. "Thanks. It smells and looks great."

The knife slid through the steak like butter. The juices spilled from it. He took strong control over himself to not bury his mouth in the meat, but be civilized and carry the bite to his mouth on the fork. He ignored the weird way his teeth felt and concentrated on not biting his tongue.

When he finished the meal, his stomach had settled down although his dick once again took on a life of its own.

"Feeling better?"

"Yes, thank you. Oh, and thank you for taking that chunk of plastic out of my ear. I assume you did it?"

"Yes. You're welcome. Now," she turned the laptop she'd been looking at while he ate to face him, "I need you to watch this." She started a video program on her laptop.

Dylan watched himself writhing with pain tas he changed into a jaguarondi with a dart in its chest. The video showed the jaguarondi sleeping on her bed then morphed into him sleeping there.

"Interesting pictures. Nice morphing software you have on your computer. It almost looks like I changed into the wildcat and back."

"You did," she said.

"Yeah, sure. You're good, lady. Thanks for the meal. Now can you drive me someplace?"

"Wait just a minute." Haley left the room and returned with a mirror before Dylan did more than put his dishes in the dishwasher.

"Look in the mirror." She held a hand mirror to his face.

When he saw his face, he jerked the mirror from her hand and drew his lips away from his teeth.

"That's right." This time her voice held the

coldness of a woman pissed off because her word had been doubted. "I've been watching you eat. As soon as you cut the steak, your teeth sharpened to those of a predatory cat."

Chapter 3

Not only did he have pointed teeth, but now long, black, stiff hairs sprouted from his carefully shaved cheeks. His cheeks hung slightly over his mouth and his nostrils flared on a flat nose.

"Look at your ears."

Because Hildy – Haley, Dylan reminded himself – sounded like a dispassionate scientist observing a interesting phenomenon, Dylan managed to control his panic.

He moved the mirror to see one ear. It rode high on his head and turned forward with the top of it in a sharp peak. When he touched the peak, he realized tufts of hair covered it, not his regular hair.

He checked the other ear. The peak on it showed, but it almost sat where human ears were supposed to be.

"You're changing back."

Dylan used Hildy's calmness to anchor his own. He watched the fangs and pointed teeth become the rounder and flatter shapes of the omnivore instead of a carnivore.

The flat nose, whiskers, and dewlaps morphed back into his own familiar nose and clean-shaven cheeks. His mouth and face stung and tickled, then quit. His ears shaped back into their normal shells. He ran his tongue over his teeth reassuring himself everything was back to normal.

"Are you okay?"

"What the fuck do you think?" Dylan slammed the mirror on the table. The mirror shattered into dozens of glittering shards that flew across the table and to the floor. "What the hell happened to me?"

"Damned if I know," Hildy yelled back while she brushed shards of glass from her t-shirt with trembling hands. The sane part of him didn't want to contemplate the consequences if one of those shards had hit her face instead of her shirt and skirt. Her shrieking voice shook slightly, "I picked up a jaguarondi and ended up with a naked man in the same cage. A naked man who changed back into a jaguarondi in front of me. You're damn lucky I used my trank gun instead of my rifle."

Dylan stood, knocking his chair backward. A piece of glass from the shattered mirror crunched under his foot. He stamped it to dust. "My life is screwed and you tranked me!"

Hildy rounded the table to him. With her quick steps, the calf-length gauze skirt she wore swirled above her knees.

In the bright kitchen light, Dylan saw her red lace bra pressing against her pink t-shirt. His vision sharpened as he focused on her nipples peaking against the lace and consequently the t-shirt.

Dylan clamped down on the flash of lust tightening his groin.

Hildy got right into his face. "Screw you, bud! Like I said, you're lucky to be alive. Most people would have seen you change from man to animal and killed you rather than deal with a monster that belonged in a Hollywood Special Effects movie."

He knew, in a logical part of his mind, his

rage came from the terror of seeing his face being cat-shaped, then watching it change back to normal along with the nauseating thought of his entire body changing into a wildcat. He didn't want to think about it. Instead, he distracted himself from his fear by yelling at this woman who was responsible for the very clothes on his back.

"If I'm such a monster, why didn't you just shoot me!" Dylan tilted his head slightly to look into her eyes.

Her lips pressed into an angry straight line that Dylan resisted, just barely, tracing with his finger. Pale blue eyes narrowed above sharp cheekbones covered by smooth skin slightly flushed with pink. Honey-blonde eyebrows furrowed together making small puckers at the top of her long nose. Dylan wanted to ease the creases with kisses just like he wanted to tuck the strands of hair framing her face behind her ears.

"I don't kill innocent people." She screamed. She took a deep breath, which had an interesting effect on her tits hidden by the t-shirt and lace bra.

More calmly, she continued, "Under the jaguarondi, I knew an innocent man was trapped in something beyond his control." Her breath wafted sweetly to his nose and held the scent of the green tea and sugar cookies she ate while he devoured the steak and other accompaniments she'd given him.

Dylan stepped away from her before his lust turned him into a caveman who wanted to take her here, now.

He knelt and began to pick up pieces of broken mirror. In each small sliver he saw his face holding thirty years of growing from child to teen to man. He saw the faint lines brought by studying long hours, by concentrating on skills to save his life and others, by joyously loving family, friends, and incredible women. His anger dissolved and left him tasting the bile of force-swallowed fear. "I suppose I should thank you for sparing my life, but…"

"But maybe I didn't do you any favors considering what you just saw happen to you?"

Thank God, she didn't sound sorry for him. He wanted his own pity party and he didn't want to invite anybody except Jim Beam or Jose Cuervo.

She knelt on the floor beside him. Her lovely fingers began to gather glass fragments.

The silence they worked in broke with a gasp of pain from Hildy.

Dylan looked up to see her sit back on her heels and jerk a sliver from the gauze skirt. A blotchy red flower of blood bloomed in the pastel floral material.

"Crap." Haley snatched the stained skirt above her knees to see blood trickling down her shin. She blinked back quick tears. The tears came more from her long denied reaction to the stressful day rather than the dying pain of the small cut and the blood leaching her favorite skirt. "I love this skirt. I bet I never get the blood out."

"Hydrogen peroxide and cold water." Dylan's voice sent hot shivers through her to tighten her nipples unbearably and make her muff wet with longing.

"Oh, please, all-knowing male," Haley grumbled while held her skirt away from the gore leaking down her leg.

Crunching glass, Dylan walked to the sink, bits of glass sparkling on his jeans' shins like tiny diamonds. He unrolled some paper towels and ran water over them.

Haley managed to struggle to her feet, "I'm such an innocent female. Please tell me something else I've known since before you were old enough to slap your sausage."

Dylan's gush of laughter surprised her. The change in his face from solid world-weary fighter to easy joy twisted her heart with tenderness. He knelt at her feet and pressed the sopping paper towel against the small cut.

Rivulets of cool water slid down her leg. His touch made her so hot she found it amazing the water didn't turn to steam immediately.

"First you call my dick a pickle. Now it's a sausage. Is this some kind of food fetish with you?"

"Everything's always better coated with chocolate," Haley's mouth said before her lust filled brain had time to think.

Dylan stopped cleaning her leg, but continued to apply pressure to the cut. He leaned back and looked up at her.

"Got any?"

His voice held the challenge of man-in-full-sexual-rut-wanting-a-piece-right-now. Underneath the alpha male command that appealed to her inner take-me-take-me cavewoman, the gentle hint of invitation beguiled the romantic in her. Part of her felt assured if she decided not to go further in this, her choice would be accepted without rancor.

"In the frig," she said, her mouth wanting his tongue in it to ease its sudden dryness.

Be practical, Haley. Always inspect the merchandise first. Her mother's advice for everything from apples to sex rang in her memory.

Haley worked salvia in her mouth and asked, "Your sexid?"

Dylan wiped the last of the water and blood from her leg, then set the wet, pink paper towel on the table as he rose to his full height.

Haley had the giddy feeling of being an in-love twelve-year-old again. It took one rapid heartbeat to realize the impression came because Dylan was shorter than she, the way the first loves in her life had been before they finally got their adolescent growth spurts.

Dylan rolled up his sleeve. Haley touched the tat of deep royal blue indicating that within the past month his blood had tested free of communicable diseases.

She traced it with her fingers, relishing the rock hard biceps under his skin. Underneath his blood type and clearance, a clear dark green date indicated his fertility was inhibited.

Her tanned fingers looked white against his toasted wheat bread covered with honey skin. She laughed at her food fetish. She did want to eat this delicious looking man.

"And yours?" His hand slid up her arm to move her shirtsleeve with a sensual deftness that further inflamed Haley. She almost felt that heated touch taking off her bra and thong, and then feeling her the way he thumbed her own sexid.

Her tat had begun to turn the more purple of the mid-term test. When the type blaze turned fully red, the blood needed to be retested.

Like his, her fertility inhibition showed deep green. She never let it lapse even to a grass green. She wanted a baby, but on her terms, not because she neglected to stay up-to-date with free and easy protection. Why run the risk of having a baby during schooling and job skill years when the situation was avoided with a visit to the local Population Planning Council?

She stepped closer to him. At the scrunching sound under her sandals, she stopped, looked at him again, then headed to the broom closet. "We'd better finish clearing up the glass first.

"It's not that I'm a tease," she told his frowning face. "There is a problem."

"How much of a problem is it to finish cleaning up the glass? I don't want any glass to stab your cute ass when I take you on the floor. Program your floor cleaner and let's get down to it."

"These are my floor cleaners." Haley opened the kitchen closet and pulled out a broom, a mop, and a bucket. "I don't have a robotic. Stay where you are," she ordered him.

She wanted to be taken here and now, on the floor, on the table, on a chair. She ached to take him. But she also needed to work out this wildcat business with him. She'd seen him change because of pain and then partially change while he ate the steak. She didn't want to suddenly have a jaguarondi on her just as she reached orgasm. What a turn-off. She probably would shoot him then.

"It's not just the glass." She laid a dish towel on the floor in front of his glass glittered jeans, then used the broom to sweep his jeans so the shards dropped into the towel. Her juices wept at the thought of sweeping her palms across his bulging crotch.

His voice deepened. "I can understand the glass, but both of us are healthy and temp infertile.

What's the problem?"

Haley tilted her head almost certain she heard a cat's growl in some his words. "The problem is I've seen you turn into a jaguarondi. After you ate the steak, you saw your face change back to normal. We need to find out why you change."

She swept the last of the glass into a dustpan, which she emptied onto the towel. She set the broom and dustpan away, then picked up the towel at Dylan's feet. When she stood, she looked into his face set in solid slabs of muscle and marveled at his self-control. If she were the one changing, she'd have the screaming jeebies.

Dylan's arm snaked out and caught her. He drew her to him, then took the towel from her and placed it on the table. He pressed her ass until her pelvis rubbed against the rigidity of his crotch.

He tilted her face down to his. His mouth nibbled her lips, coaxing, wordlessly pleading for her to open her mouth.

She forced herself not to rub herself against his body, but surely a single kiss would be all right.

When his tongue slid against her mouth, she let him in. His tongue dived between her lips as though she were the sweetest juice he ever drank. Their tongues played the game of chase and retreat, conquer and surrender.

Dylan felt her hands around his waist, then the tug of his shirt being pulled from the jeans. While her hands slid up his skin, he managed to get them turned around and her back against the wall. He got one hand down her t-shirt neck and pushed down the bra cup to capture one nipple in his palm. Dylan rolled his prize with his fingers while continuing to lick and suckle her mouth the way he wanted to do her muff.

He used his full body to press her against the wall. Her legs parted under the skirt. He lifted one of her strong legs to wrap around his waist.

Finally, he had access to the treasure he'd wanted to touch ever since he first saw her.

Dylan ran his hand across the smooth skin of her ass and traced the silk ribbon of the thong between her butt cheeks. He plundered her mouth and toyed with her nipple while he ran his fingers under the thong.

He dipped his finger across her folds judging how wet she already was. Her groan of pleasure encouraged him to slide the little bit of silk to one side to probe deeper and harder.

Her mouth grew frantic under his. She took her hands away from his chest long enough to tug her own t-shirt from the skirt's waistband.

Dylan pushed it up and freed her bra clasp with his teeth. She pressed her head against the wall and arched her back to give him access to her generous breasts.

He paused to enjoy the sight of strawberry red areoles and jutting nipples on the mounds of her creamy skin. When they got around to it, he wanted to use her chocolate to have himself some chocolate-covered strawberries and cream. In the meantime… Dylan suckled one nipple deep into his mouth and enjoyed its taut texture. He found her clitoris and tickled its tight knot with his fingers the way he tickled her tit with his tongue.

She undulated against him. Her hands dug under his jeans to grab his butt in both hands. Now she pressed him against her.

He flicked her again and drove two fingers deep inside her. Her inner walls clenched around his fingers and her entire body shuddered. Her gasps grew sharper and higher in pitch.

Bless her, even while she shook with her own pleasure, she unsnapped the jeans button and pulled down the zipper.

His engorged dick pushed its way through the opening in the briefs. Her hands wrapped around it and tugged.

Dylan pulled his fingers from Hildy's wet muff and ripped her thong on one side. He pressed her tighter against the wall while he lifted her other leg around his waist. The remaining bit of the silk thong slithered around her thigh.

His fingernails dug into her round ass while he positioned her to plunge into her welcoming wetness the way his tongue had been greeted by her mouth.

"Ouch!" Hildy screeched in his ear. "You scratched me!"

"What? Huh?"

"Get your fingernails out of my rear. You're hurting me! Let me down!" She pounded her fists against his chest and started squirming and kicking.

"What the fuck?" Dylan let go of her butt and set her legs on the floor before she wiggled loose and fell from his grasp.

Her pale blue eyes flashed angrily, then widened. "Oh, damn, damn, damn. Dylan, you're changing."

Dylan stepped away from Haley and looked at his tingling hands. Claws protruded from his fingertips.

Haley stroked across his face.

He jerked his head away when her fingertips touched his sensitive whiskers.

Whiskers?

Dylan reached his hand to his face. Yes, he still had a hand.   The claws curved over the fingertips. He brushed the stiff whiskers with the claws.

"Hildy?"

From someplace far away, he heard the command voice of his Valkyrie of the First Amazon Division. "Hang on, Dylan. Remember who you are. Concentrate on being you. There has to be some way for you to stop this. Think. Stay with me, Dylan."

Chapter 4

Dylan looked up at Hildy, not quite certain what she was saying. He understood his name, but the rest was garble. The calmness in her voice soothed him even if he didn't have a clue what she was babbling.

Her eyes worried him. She pressed against the wall as if she were afraid of him. He never wanted to hurt her. He didn't mean to stick her with his claws.

"Speak English," he told her, but his own voice didn't sound his.

He shook himself and the clothes around his backside slid off. He switched his tail to and fro, enjoying the freedom. Now he needed take off this shirt that clung to his neck. He got front paws freed from it easily, but he had trouble getting it off his neck.

"Dylan?"

He cocked his head at his Brunhilde enjoying the cadences in her voice even if she did persist in talking that weird foreign language. He learned several languages during his compulsory military service. Unfortunately, none of the ones he learned seemed even distantly related to whatever she was speaking. He wished she'd go back to English or her bad Spanish or something he knew.

She moved closer to him and the scent of her sex nearly overwhelmed him. She smelt of ripe, sexy woman cream, strawberry shampoo, lavender and oatmeal body wash, laundry detergent, fabric softener, the potato she baked for his supper, that wonderful steak.

Out of politeness, he had eaten the potato and salad she served with the steak. He wanted to devour the steak and maybe a second or a third one. He still smelled its juices hanging in the air.

"Dylan?"

His Brunhilde knelt in front of him. He smelled his own scent on her. He licked across his teeth, remembering the taste of her tongue in his mouth.

Every atom in his being wanted to take her and brand her his mate. He wanted to bury his teeth in her shoulder and drive himself into her, hard, fast, and deep.

He kept himself in tight control. Never in his life had he forced himself on a woman. He had no intention of ever doing so. As much as he wanted her, he didn't want to betray the trust she showed when she brought him into her house, gave him clothes, and fed him. He needed to build on her trust until she happily wanted him to enjoy her body.

She slowly stretched one hand out as though she wanted to touch him, but was afraid.

He quit struggling to take off the shirt and held himself still. He didn't want to do anything that might frighten her.

When she placed her palm against the side of his head, he rubbed against her. If he didn't mate with her right now, at least he wanted his scent on her. Other males might give her wide berth when they smelled him on Hildy's skin.

Haley, you fool, he told himself. *Her name is*

Haley, not Hildy. To hell with it.

For him, she was always going to be Hildy, his Brunhilde. For years he dreamed of meeting a living representative of the immortal Valkyries who determined which soldiers would be honored after death by being taken to Valhala and given the privilege of serving the god Odin.

Now one knelt in front of him, rubbing his ears, neck, and chin. She kept talking to him.

Dylan settled down into a rest position with his legs and paws tucked under him. Bread loaf, that's what his mom used to call the cats when they sat like that.

With Hildy stroking his head and talking to him, part of the tight tension in him unwound. He felt peaceful. For the first time since he had been captured trying to rescue people abused by the cartels, Dylan relaxed. His capture took a decidedly worse turn when he was imprisoned in the Hell Hospital for so many months. He'd never forget the battles he fought to stay sane in that place. The smell of puke and crap overrode the medicines and antiseptics. The cries and curses of other prisoners remained engraved on his psyche. Disjointed, anesthetic induced memories haunted his dreams. His purr rumbled from the soothed, calm place deep inside him.

A jerk snapped Dylan from his peaceful respite. He scrambled to all fours, puffed his fur into attack mode, and snarled at Hildy. "What the fuck did you do?"

Hildy jumped on the table

He glared up at her. The table's puny height offered no protection if he choose to go after her. Then he saw the t-shirt in her hand.

Oh, he realized, *she took the shirt from his*

neck. He shook himself, glad to be relieved of all the clothes.

"I'm sorry I yelled. You startled me. Warn a guy next time you want to strip him."

Strange. Hildy didn't act like she understood him. Okay. If she wanted to play stranger-in-a-strange-land games, he was willing to go along. If he convinced her to trust him, he might get lucky.

Damnation. The more he smelled her scent, especially her muff's natural perfume, the more he wanted her. Being horny hurt.

He needed to gain her trust by playing in her *I'm-a-scared-stranger scenario.* The first thing to do, he remembered from his training, when approaching someone who doesn't speak the language is to remain calm and don't make any sudden moves.

Nonchalantly, he scratched behind one ear with a hind paw. The healing bullet hole in his thigh muscle stung. He reminded himself it had only been a couple of days since he'd been shot trying to reconnect with his contacts fighting the human smuggling cartels. He was damn lucky it had been a stray bullet and gone cleanly through. Full use of his muscles with no hindrances was going to happen eventually, as long as it healed properly.

He gave the sore spot a couple of licks, but tasted the artificial skin. He groomed himself a bit more, both to look better and to get the nasty taste of the artificial skin from his tongue.

Dylan finally decided he was satisfied and settled back into his bread loaf. She still looked at him with wide eyes while in her hands she twisted the torn panties she'd taken off one ankle.

Dylan didn't have anything else to do, so he waited. Considering Hildy had the same tension as a cornered rat or rabbit, Dylan slid easily into the wait mode that deluded prey into thinking he'd fallen asleep.

Through half-closed eyes, Dylan watched Hildy climb down from the table. She approached him quietly and cautiously, then knelt in front of him.

Once again, her hand came in front of his nose. Her palm smelled like the covering on his sore, but it still smelled delightedly of her own scent.

Hildy fondled his ears, head, and neck for awhile, then stood. She picked up his unnecessary clothes and shoes, then looked at him.

"Com, Dylan." She held one hand out then pulled it palm first to her body.

Com? Hmmm, Dylan thought, *that sounded kind of close to 'come.'* He stood up, stretched, then followed her from the kitchen. While she walked, he strutted around her lovely legs and twisted his tail around them to further mark his scent on her. He wanted all males to know she belonged to him.

"Dylan," Hildy spoke a mouthful of garbles, dumped his clothes on a chair, the shoes on the floor, turned on a small Tiffany-style lamp, then sat on the bed, and patted the section beside her.

Hot damn. Dylan jumped on the bed, happy to have the invitation. He walked all around Hildy managing to rub his tail and scent on her. She lightly swatted his tail out of her face. Her laughter started his purr again.

When she got off the bed, he moved to follow. She placed the palm of her hand against his nose. "Say, Dylan."

Say? Say? With her hand in his face, it dawned on him she meant 'stay.' If that meant he didn't have to leave her bed, it was okay with him. Dylan curled into a warm circle and watched her take some pink flowered, flowing clothes from a drawer, then go into the toilet area off the bedroom, shutting the door behind her.

Dylan looked at the moonlight spilling across the bedroom floor from the window. Dust motes danced in the moonlight like silver fireflies. He heard an owl's hunting call and her mate's answer. A mouse's squeal died a sudden death. The owls' fledglings' supper was ready. Water ran in the bathroom. Dylan stretched out in pure contentment. His muscles tingled and ached. He forced his arms and legs out further despite their pangs and discomfort.

He stacked the frothy lace-covered pillows onto the bench at the foot of the bed. Two thick pillows, encased in covers that matched the flowered sheets, remained.

Tempted to remain on top of the comforter in all his erect, hard glory, Dylan nevertheless tossed the comforter to the end of the bed and crawled between the sheets. He wanted to give her the chance to back away.

If she wasn't interested, he needed to jack himself off again. Dylan looked at his pole holding up the sheet and cotton blanket and decided to lie on his side so his favorite asset wasn't on full display. If they just talked for awhile maybe she'd calm down enough to be interested in playing set-up-the-tent with him.

"Oh, you're back." Haley marveled at the complacent, smiling man waiting with his head propped on one hand and her yellow flower-splattered sheets bunched around his waist.

His naked shoulders glowed burnished bronze in the lamplight. The dim light and shadows delineated the dips and curves of his biceps and abs. His loose, dark hair framed chiseled cheeks and hung down to brush his collarbones. She itched to run her fingers through it, then across the smattering of chest hair, and trace the thicker trail down his abdomen.

"I've never been anywhere." His eyebrows lifted in puzzlement. "And you're speaking English again. Tired of playing games? I like the pajamas, by the way. Quite fetching."

Haley pirouetted so the wide pants legs swirled like individual skirts. "I love being a girly-girl. After years of plain, practical clothes, uniforms in various shades of cam, or wrapping up in the depressing clothes of a suppressed Muslim, I love wearing flounces. My mother always insisted I was too big for girly-girl clothes."

"You are the perfect size."

"Thank you," Haley pulled out the sides of her pajama pants and dropped a curtsy. "I'm happy with my size, too. Since Mom doesn't pay for my clothes, I wear what I want. My only regret at joining Wildlife Management is wearing a uniform. I make up for it by wearing lace undies."

Dylan gave her an exaggerated leer. "Yeah? You want to show me?"

"Not right now." Haley sat on the bed tailor fashion, well aware she didn't have on any undies beneath her flowing pajamas. Sex energy began to flow when she caught a whiff of his male musk. She wanted to rub herself all over him, but forced herself to sound calm.

"By the way, I've been speaking English.

You've been a jaguarondi for the past half hour."

Dylan twisted his kissable lips into a grimace. "I have not. I've been waiting for you to calm down. You were scared when I accidentally clawed you, lifting you up against the wall in the kitchen. I wish I knew how that was happening to me and why."

"You remember being in the kitchen?"

"Of course. You jerked the t-shirt off my head and then jumped on the table when I yelled at you." He slid his thumb and index finger along the pleat he made of a fold of her pajama leg.

Haley shivered with increased sex heat as though he were stroking her. Her breath hitched, but she refocused on the situation about his changes.

It gave her hope that he had memories of being a jaguarondi, even if he thought he was in human form at the time. For his own sake, he had to accept he changed.

"Why don't you describe what you were doing?"

"I told you, waiting for you to calm down." Dylan's smile disappeared into an annoyed scowl.

Haley didn't let his scowl bother her, but persisted, "No, I meant, tell me, how you were sitting."

He rolled his eyes at her, blew out air, and said, "I was in rest position. Waiting."

"Where were your arms and legs?"

Dylan started to say something, then stopped. His face twisted with puzzlement. "Why am I thinking I had them under my body like a cat making a bread loaf?"

Haley nodded. "And your tail?"

"Wrapped around my body."

The words hung in the air.

Dylan looked stunned as though he didn't believe the words came from his mouth.

"Dylan, it's going to be alright. We can work this out."

"I turned into a fucking cat and you have the gall to say 'It's alright' and 'we can work it out'? Why the hell is this happening to me?" He sat up and swung his legs over the side of the bed. "I'm going to kill the people who did this to me!"

Haley lunged across the bed and grabbed his shoulders. She leaned all her weight against his tense back and slid her arms around his chest holding him to her.

"Dylan, listen to me. I don't know how this is happening or who did it to you."

"I do," Dylan said. "And I'm going to hunt them down and kill them."

Haley shuddered to hear the cold, bleak determination in his voice.

"Dylan, right now, as much as you want to hurt whoever did this to you, you have to first accept what's happening."

"I don't have to accept it. I want to be me. Not some wildcat."

"Dylan," Haley leaned over one rock hard shoulder and literally got in his face.

Now her shudders came from pure sexual energy. Her breasts pressed against his bare back, her nipples ached to feel his skin instead of her silk pajama top.

His mouth set in a tight line she wanted to ease with her mouth and tongue, but she continued to try to persuade him to see some logic. "If you accept it, maybe you'll be able to learn to control it. Once you learn how to keep from changing, then we'll be better equipped to hunt down the why, how, and who were responsible for this mess in the first place."

"'We'll be better equipped?'" Dylan repeated her words back to her.

"Yes," she agreed. "We. You're not in this alone. I can help. What's been done to you is wrong. If you don't let me come with you, I'll track you on my own anyway. But whether you take me with you voluntarily or I follow you, I'll be your backup. If you wanted the ability to change species at will, that would have been your choice. But the way it is now, they've taken your freedom from you. I joined the Amazons because I wanted to be able to fight those who take away others' freedoms. Personal freedom for all is still my goal. If you know who's responsible, I'll help you hunt them down and hurt them for taking away your freedom."

Dylan's half smile warmed her. A little bit of her heart gave itself to him, willingly and happily.

"What's in it for you personally, not just fighting for freedoms?"

He twisted his body to face her. Haley saw the tip of his cock peeking from under the sheets. A drop of cum on its tip gleamed in the silver moonlight flowing through the window.

Haley slowly stroked around his cock with one finger. It jerked at her touch. She caught the drop of cum on her fingertip and licked her finger. She looked at his face. His golden-green eyes gleamed at her. Their hot lust inflamed her that she nearly came without even a touch from him.

She sat back against the pillows and told him, "Personally? I want to get laid. I want you to learn to control this because I absolutely have no desire to be in the midst of things to discover you changing. Bestiality is so not my thing."

Dylan placed one hand on her stomach and weighed one breast in his other hand. His thumb stroked her puckered nipple.

Her words came in gasps between breaths. "Kinky is okay. I can do kinky for a change of pace. I like an occasional light bondage, both as Dom and as sub. Once in a while, I even enjoy participating when my sister and her ménage partners have an orgy."

"Your sister's part of a ménage? F-M-F?"

"Mmhhh." She sighed as his hand dipped from her stomach to massage the silk pajama crotch. "No, M-F-M. Very stable threesome for several years now. Huge bed for them and their occasional guests. Takes up most of the bedroom."

Dylan felt the silk dampening under his fingers. He slid his hand back up her soft stomach, then untied the pajama bottoms ribbon, ran his hand between the silk material and her silken skin.

She spread her knees further apart as he parted the slick folds covered by her silky muff hair.

He took his hand away from her breast long enough push the silk and lace top up above her breasts. He held one in his hand, played with the nipple, while he placed his mouth on the other to feast on the full bounty.

"Now as for me,"

What the hell was it with women who chattered during sex? Damn it, if she didn't willingly put her hands on his dick in half a minute, he was going to come from just the feel of the sheets, her wet juices on his fingers, and the taste of her breast in his mouth. Everything had more texture as if his nerve endings had been enhanced to feel each molecule separately.

Scents grew sharper. He separated out the chemicals in the soaps she washed the sheets and herself. Then he concentrated on the natural scents – the grass outside, the smell of her skin, the flowing musk between her legs.

Colors and shapes came into crisp focus. The room no longer was the dim cave of seduction. He watched the interplay of light and shadows dance across her glowing skin. Between the lamp and the moonlight, the room was lit as bright as daylight.

Dylan knew if he lifted his head from his succulent feast of Hildy's breast, he would be able to see the mouse he smelled and heard rustling in the grass outside the window. He heard the male owl's hunting scream, then the whoosh, flap of wings. The mouse didn't have time to squeak its death call.

"But as for me." Her voice broke into Dylan's study of all the different tastes, textures, smells, and shapes created by his Brunhilde's lush body. "I prefer a single male at a time. And while I occasionally like my human males to act like animals, I do *not* want animal-animals as lovers. As much as I love your tongue on my breast, it's now starting to scratch. I think you're changing again. And if those damn claws come out while you're playing with my muff, I will break your cock in two."

Chapter 5

Dylan jerked his fingers from Hildy's muff. "Damn it all to hell!"

He looked at his hand, four fingers and a thumb – no claws, just fingernails. He breathed a sigh of relief that the changing hadn't occurred yet.

Tentatively, he ran his tongue across his teeth. His teeth hadn't turned into points. He rubbed his tongue against the roof of his mouth

"Are you sure I was changing? My tongue feels smooth."

"You were shifting into the jaguarondi." She narrowed her eyes at him.

Well, damn, he knew better than to doubt a woman's word, but still.

"My tongue feels normal to me."

She jerked down her pajama top and crossed her arms under the lovely breasts he'd been holding and eating. "How exactly do you know how *normal* feels? You spent half an hour in the jaguarondi shape and didn't even realize you'd shifted until I made you face facts."

Dylan flinched at the reality Haley once again forced at him.

"Want to feel it?" Dylan stuck his tongue out at her.

Haley leaned forward, her fingers extended. He hoped his First Amazon Division soldier didn't rip his tongue out in her anger. She swiped her own tongue across his, then sat back before he had a chance to grab her.

His dick pulsed angrily. He froze. If he moved across the soft sheets he'd come all over the bed.

"Dylan?"

"Just wait," he said between gritted teeth. Silently, sweat popping in beads on his forehead, he fought the battle for dominance with his almost out-of-control no-brains favorite body part.

The scent of her body on sheets, the aroma of her wet muff next to his head, the still slick feel of her juices on his fingers made it difficult to gain control over his dick. Damn it all to hell and back. His self-worth encompassed more than a nearly out-of-control cock.

His hard-on finally eased off enough he didn't think he was going to come at the moment. He made no promises to himself that the next time he'd win the battle or even want to. He hated not being in control of his body.

"You okay now?" Haley asked.

"*Absolutely just fine and dandy.*" How the hell did she think he felt? He had no control of this changing shit and his dick kept wanting to take full charge.

"I'm so glad you're feeling better." Her sweet, sugary, sarcastic voice flayed guilt across him for snapping at her. "I had nothing to do with this crap about you turning into a jaguarondi. Don't get snitty with me, you pickle head."

"Now I'm a pickle head?"

"Substitute dick for pickle, pickle head."

Dylan didn't know whether to laugh or groan. "I might as well confess. My older brother and cousins used to call me Pickle."

One look at her fighting back giggles and he

found himself grinning, too. "Yeah, yeah. Laugh. Dylan became Dill, which ended up being Pickle. They quit when I finally got big enough and mean enough to beat the crap out of them."

Their shared laughter eased some of Dylan's tension.

"Families suck."

"Yes," Dylan nodded, "and what would we do without them?"

"Good question. Okay, as long as we talking about siblings and confessions, I have a confession."

"You beat up your sister to steal her ruffles and laces?"

"I sure wanted to when we were kids. But no, this is different. My sister works in a biomedical lab in Houston. I took blood samples of you when you were in your jaguarondi shape and in your human shape. With your permission, I want to send the samples to her. Maybe she and her colleagues can discover what is triggering the DNA to change and help you to stop it."

"Why DNA?"

"This has to be happening to you on a sub-molecular level because the change is too perfect. You know, like The Incredible Hulk."

"Not an incredible hunk?"

She grinned at him and swatted him. "Behave. You do have your moments, but we'll get into that later. You said you knew who did this to you?"

"Yeah, I think so. It's not like I was born in a litter and have been doing this my whole life."

Her chuckle at his feeble joke soothed like a balm across his ragged nerves. He again slid his fingers up and down a fold of the loose silk pajama bottom. He wanted to rub her skin, but for the moment settled for the material.

"Do you know what happened to you? And who did it?"

"Specifically who? No. The area where it happened? Possibly. Why? And how? Not a clue." Dylan concentrated on the silk between his thumb and forefinger. "It has to do with my former job in Special Forces. I'd tell you what I did, but..."

"Yeah, yeah, then you'd have to kill me. My security clearance is pretty high. I'll have you know I came into Reserves as a First Sergeant."

"No, kidding? You outrank me. I was invalided out as a Master Sergeant. Should I salute you?"

"Your pickle has been doing so all evening."

Dylan shifted on his stomach, trying to find a soft place for his hard dick. "I have no control over it. Not only are you a toothsome wench, but one of the side effects of the damn blackouts...."

"Not blackouts," she corrected him. "Changing back to human form after being a jaguarondi. My personal opinion is you have trouble adjusting to the differences in your senses from human to jaguarondi, so you try not to remember the experiences and consider them as blackouts. I'll point out that you do remember what happened in the kitchen, even though you were a jaguarondi at the time."

Dylan thought back through what he considered blackouts. His internal clock ticked rhythmically. With it to remind him when he was and who he was, he forced himself through his memories beyond the confusion, the pain, the strange sights, sounds, scents. He compared his vague remembrances to his experience in Haley's kitchen. He realized his vision, hearing, and smell sharpened just before Haley made him aware he was changing while he was enjoying the preliminaries leading to finally getting some sex, which didn't happen, unfortunately. "You might be right. Maybe I'm adjusting since I can remember what happened in the kitchen and moving to the bedroom?"

"You remember all of that?"

"Yes. I remember walking with you and rubbing against you."

The gleam in Haley's eye gave him pause.

"What?"

"Do you know why cats rub against things? And stroke things with their tails?"

"I'm not a moron. To mark the things with the cat's scent. For the cat to mark whatever it wants as belonging to it."

"And since you were in a jaguarondi body, rubbing all over me, stroking me with your tail. Well," Haley paused for a heartbeat, "it gives a whole different meaning to the old term of pussy-whipped."

Dylan groaned at her gawdawful joke. He never understood why a woman's thatch was often called a 'pussy.' Eating a muffin made so much more sense. Having a muff warm his cock had some logic. But pussy? Weird.

At this point, he really didn't care what it was called. He just wanted his dick pounding hard and deep inside his Brunhilde's muff, its warm slickness taking away the ache. He shifted again on the bed, well aware he was close to losing control.

"You act like you're uncomfortable on your stomach. Why don't you lie on your back?"

"There's a side effect to regaining consciousness from the blackout." At her glare, Dylan corrected himself. "A side effect to shifting back to human."

"Besides ending up naked?"

"Yeah. Besides being naked, I end up horny. Very, very horny."

"Must be the animal part of you." Haley shrugged her pretty shoulders. One of the straps holding up the pajama top slid down her upper arm. "Lie on your back. You'll be more comfortable."

Her calm practicality amazed him.

"Um, it's a bit of a tent pole."

"Oooooh," her blue eyes widened with mock innocence and sparkling humor, "and you're afraid of frightening the sweet little lady?"

"Actually, you might be so turned on by its size you might force yourself on me." Dylan rolled onto his back, then scooted up so the bedstead braced his shoulders. He arranged the sheet and lightweight blanket, but his shaft still made itself known.

His Brunhilde eyed the pole holding up the sheet and blanket. She licked her lips, then frowned at him. "We have got to get this changing stuff under control. I really want to force myself on you. But not at the moment. Tell me what you think happened. The how and why will have to wait, until we find the specific whos and beat the shit out of them."

Dylan didn't want to think about his time in captivity, much less talk about it. But he also didn't want to spend the rest of his life changing into a wildcat at inopportune moments.

"It has to start with my Special Forces job that involved infiltrating the cartels across the border that smuggle people and drugs. For all the good it does to stem the tide. And the Wall across the Southern border is worthless. Amazing the damn ground underneath it doesn't collapse considering the way it's riddled with tunnels."

"Yeah, big old waste of taxpayer money. More people and infrared equipment works better. Even so, we spend a lot of our time in Wildlife Management rescuing people who've been abandoned in the brush and tracking down caches of drugs. So what happened with your spy job in the smuggling cartel?"

He grasped her silk pajama leg again and rubbed it. If he touched her naked skin, he might go completely animalistic. "One group I'd been working with got busted by a rival cartel. All of us ended up in one of the competitor's prison camp."

"Not fun."

"It gets worse. One night, a bunch of us were taken to a hospital straight from hell. You remember those psych tests we got subjected to when we signed up for our compulsory terms?"

Haley's full lips thinned. She nodded, her face set in hard, grim planes.

"Those were cakewalks compared to what we were put through. They also did tests for physical endurance. I have memory gaps during which I think they did medical things because I woke up with anesthetic hangovers."

"You keep saying 'us.'" Haley's fingers grasped his shoulder and kneaded it.

"Definitely more people were being experimented on. I caught glimpses of other people, plus I heard them. I want to find that Hell Hospital again. The place needs to be razed. They're not only experimenting on adults, they're using children." Dylan closed his eyes and swallowed hard. Once he found it again, he'd alert his former squad members and they'd pull the strings to close it down.

"It's in Mexico?"

Dylan shook his head and looked into Brunhilde's eyes. Her winter blue-sky eyes looked back at him with silent encouragement to continue. "I caught a glimpse of the area at night a couple of times. I have this strong urge to go to the Davis Mountains here in Texas. Maybe it was the star pattern I saw. I know I saw we were in mountains, but it didn't feel like Colorado or Mexico. I just have this insistent thought that it's in the Davis Mountains and I have to go there. I think it's The Halcyon Institute."

Haley's eyes widen. "That can't be right. The Halcyon Institute is a very respected research and development hospital for helping people with massive injuries and body trauma."

"I know their reputation," Dylan snapped. "They get appropriated a lot of government funding for their help with war injuries. I've been there to visit injured buddies. I was drugged a lot of the time I was held there, but I think the star pattern and mountain range is the same. I want to be positive before I start blowing any whistles. Besides, I have this extremely strong urge that I have to be in the Davis Mountains and soon."

"But how did you get out?"

Dylan knew by the skeptical look on her face she didn't believe him about The Halcyon Institute. Hell, he still didn't believe it either. But he was going to make sure. For now, it was enough that she wasn't calling the cops on him. Maybe if he finished his story, it might make more sense to both of them.

"Someone took us back to a prison camp in Mexico. At least, I woke up from a drug-induced stupor there. A coalition force of Special Forces broke into the cartel prison. The S.F. people said it was too easy, no more than a token resistance, as though whoever was in charge wanted us out of there. Everyone was suspicious as hell, but we were damn glad to be out."

"Then you came back and were invalided out because of your so-called blackouts?"

"Hard to stay S.F. when I kept waking up with no idea how I got places."

"I'm sure the naked raised a few eyebrows, too." Haley grinned at him.

One thing he loved already about Haley was that she was wacky enough to find something funny in everything. Her joy in life eased the shadows threatening him.

"The stand-up dick didn't help much either. I was actually worried I'd get busted out for being a pervert."

"Poor Pickle."

Dylan barred his teeth at her. "If my teeth were pointed right now, I'd rip your throat out."

Haley ran her hand down his chest. "I have an experiment I want to try. I want to see if we can learn to control this changing bit."

Dylan's blood heated at her touch. His dick jerked under the sheet. "Oh, yeah? Does it involve you getting naked and an exchange of body fluids, I hope?"

"However did you guess?"

Dylan lunged at her, but she pushed him back against the bed.

"Let me explain first."

"Talk, talk, talk. Yap, yap, yap. Ever heard of 'shut up and kiss me'?"

"Shut up and let me talk. I have a Master's in Biology."

"Big whoop. I have a Ph.D. in European Literature." Dylan tunneled his hands under her pajama top. He got his hands around her boobs, but she pulled herself away.

"Oh, Doctor, I'm so not impressed. And this degree in which you *Piled Higher and Deeper* qualified you for what?"

"To ascertain if a patron desires fries with the order." He reached for her again, but she slapped his hands.

"Yeah, I thought so. Keep your hands to yourself, big boy, before I get my handcuffs out. And I don't mean the breakaway bondage ones. I'll get my official ones I use for poachers around you."

Dylan tucked away his grin. She wore her Valkyrie game face, which clearly radiated, *Do not mess with me, you will not win.*

Maybe if Dylan behaved himself while she yakked away, she'd pull out the breakaways and let him use them on her. Being the sub in bondage games wasn't something he liked, especially after all the crap he went through in Hell Hospital.

"Listen to me. When you were eating, even awhile ago when we were starting to have sex, you didn't fully change into the jaguarondi. Do you have any idea what you were thinking at the time?"

"Sex?"

"Get your mind off your pickle, Pickle Head! Think."

"Oh, hell. Okay, okay. Let me think. When I was eating the steak, I wanted to get my face into it like a caveman, but I didn't want to embarrass myself in front of you so I forced myself to use a fork."

"Okay, that's a start. And when we started rolling around on the bed?"

"Hell. I was afraid if I made an ass out of myself by turning into a jaguarondi, I'd never get laid."

Haley patted the top of his head like he was a little kid who learned to tie his shoes.

He grabbed her hand and pushed it onto his dick. "It's called lap-dancing for a reason."

She had the gall to laugh. "If this works like I think, we'll get to that."

To his pleasure, she didn't remove her hand, even though she didn't massage his cock either. She just kept talking, "There is a part of the brain called the *amygdala*."

"Wasn't that the name of Luke Skywalker's mother in the old Star Wars movies?"

"That was Queen Amidala and shut up or I'll twist your balls until they turn blue."

"Yes, ma'am, Brunhilde."

"The *amygdala* is essential in decoding emotions, particularly those involving stimuli that threaten the host body. The hippocampus in the brain stores and retrieves explicit memories and reacts with the *amygdala* to provide strong emotions. If the memories are frightening, this can result in anxiety."

"I'd be impressed if I cared for a biology lesson. When do we get to the sex?"

"You are the perfect proof of men who can't use their brains and dicks at the same time. Not enough blood to work both organs. Now listen to my theory. The anxiety of trauma such as this gunshot wound," she patted the healing wound on his thigh, "or the realization that you were turning into a jaguarondi in the kitchen resulted in anxiety strong enough to send the *amygdala* into panic attack mode. This panic attack released the fight-or-flight adrenaline and somehow triggered the DNA to change you to the jaguarondi."

"Like I changed after you kicked me in the nuts?"

"Um, yes. Sorry about that."

"Kiss it and make it better?"

Brunhilde's eyes gleamed. "Now we're getting to my experiment. When you ate the steak, you wanted to not embarrass yourself by acting on the animal instincts. When I pointed out you were changing while we were on the bed, you controlled it. Now the pleasure of making love is similar to the same emotions that trigger pain. So," she slowly ran her hand up and down his dick, "if I do things like this, we'll reprogram the *amygdala* so it associates with pleasure. With enough work, you might even be able to learn how to control the change."

"I promise to practice all night if necessary." Dylan reached for the hem of her pajama top, but she stopped him yet again.

"No. You're going to have to be the sub in this. You're going to have to do what I say and let me do things to you so you can learn to keep the change from happening."

"Oh, hell." Dylan considered the scenario. He absolutely hated not being in control, but if the only way he was going to get anything was to be the sub, then, "Just don't handcuff me or tie me up. I might go into a panic attack after being in the Mexican cartel prison camp and Hell Hospital. Then you will be proved correct when I turn into a jaguarondi and start ripping things up."

"The object is to teach you to learn to not change into a jaguarondi."   Haley pulled the blanket and sheets from Dylan's body. "Hang onto the bedstead bars."

Obediently, he wrapped his hands around the bars behind his head. She pushed apart his legs until she had room to kneel between them. He watched her eye his body. To his frustration, she didn't touch him. He dug his heels into the bed and lifted his butt. He wanted her mouth on his dick. He saw the first drop of cum on his tip.

"Hildy, please. Go down on me."

"No, Pickle. You get no choice in what I'm going to do. No talking."

She sat back on her heels and continued to watch him. She took off her pajama top. Still sending her gaze roving over his body, she lifted her breasts with her hands and rubbed her nipples with her thumbs.

Dylan bit back his groan and instinctively arced his back. His hands and mouth tingled. No, he refused to allow the change to occur. He wanted to get laid. She wasn't going to participate if he turned into a jaguarondi. He forced the tingling to go away.

When he looked back at Haley, his Brunhilde was smiling at him. "You stopped it, didn't you?"

He nodded. She told him not to talk and, by damn, he wasn't going to say a word.

"Very good."

She leaned over his body. Her lovely hands toyed with his balls. As it brushed against his skin, her blond hair showed silver in the full moonlight. She blew lightly on his hot, hard dick.

Then she covered it with her sweet, wet mouth and began to suck.

Chapter 6

At the touch of Hildy's wet mouth, Dylan's balls nearly exploded.

She took her mouth from his dick. "Don't come yet," she ordered. She licked her lips as though savoring the taste.

"Are you fucking insane?" His dick knew what it was supposed to do. Cum started to pulse out.

Haley sat back and glared at him. "Make it stop. If you can't control your own cock, how the hell can you control the shift to jaguarondi? Don't let go of the bedstead and don't talk."

Dylan tensed, focusing all his attention on his dick before it made Mount Helen's most recent eruption look like a pot of vegetables boiling over.

His hands gripped the bedstead rails. The tingling in his fingers increased until he wanted to claw something. His teeth ached and his ears felt like they were being twisted off his head. Even his butt hurt like it was being torn in two.

He ignored all of it and concentrated on his dick. It jerked with a life of its own, desperate to come. His hands got slippery with sweat, but he held the bedstead rails. He nearly bit his tongue. With Haley glaring at him, he didn't groan or let out a single peep.

His dick finally subsided. It still stood hard and ornery, but it quit trying to spray the ceiling. The tension left him as though all the aching and burning never happened.

"Better," Haley crooned. "Much better. You see? You are a man, not an animal or just a cock."

Dylan glared at her. He wanted to get fucked, not be fucked around with.

"I'll be back in just a minute. Don't let go of the bedstead and don't talk."

Haley walked from the room, determined to get herself under control before she went back to him. Never had she been the Dom with a man as determined to maintain control as Dylan. Not only had he surprised her by keeping his cock from erupting, but he controlled and dismissed the shape-changing at the same time.

She only hoped when his instinctive desire to be the leader came to the fore, he satisfied his domination by pounding his cock deep inside her. She hoped she didn't have to face an enraged wildcat. She needed to get her supply of vet products and be ready if Dylan completely lost control.

But first...

She discarded her pajama bottoms and leaned against the hallway wall. She ran her fingers across her wet folds, imagining Dylan's fingers separating them while his tongue lapped her.

She rubbed herself harder and deeper, her womb clenched with tight pulses. She knew Dylan didn't know how hard it had been for her to stop sucking his cock. She wanted to drink his cum while it sprayed her mouth. She wanted to impale herself on that tall, thick cock while he sucked her nipples.

A brief orgasm shuddered through her

body and relieved some of her ache. Languidly, she pushed herself away from the wall and went to the kitchen to get the chocolate syrup and a couple of veterinarian tranquillizer slap injections.

Nice little gadgets those were. Just slap the animal and the tiny needle on the bulb sank into the animal's skin immediately releasing the trank.

On her way back to the bedroom, she made a brief foray into the bathroom. She promised not to tie or gag him, but she had a nice strip of velvet, a paintbrush for the chocolate, and some feathers she could use. She really needed to get a small nightstand with a drawer for her sex goodies. Not that she'd had much use for them since she was transferred to South Texas.

In her bedroom, Dylan still had his hands clamped around the headboard rails. His angry look subsided when he saw the goodies in her hands. Or maybe because she was naked, her thighs still gleaming from her own cream when she 'jacked herself. Whatever. He now looked like he was eager to try whatever she dished out. She set the trank capsules on the spindly table that held her lamp.

"Good boy, you didn't move," she crooned at him again, knowing damn well men hated the sound. She'd worked hard to perfect that grating tone, halfway between an indulged mommy-tone and a teacher comment to a not-too-bright-student.

She had the very hopeful feeling she was going to be screaming his name in delight in the not too distant future. She smothered her grin, knowing she needed to stay in charge.

"Turn your body so you're on your back and your butt is at the edge of the bed," she ordered.

At his obedient shifting, she knelt on the floor. Perfect. His balls, cock, and butt were even with her face. "You can put your feet on the bed, but keep your butt where it is. Pull your legs farther apart and hold your ankles with your hands."

Sweet women of all eternity, she'd forgotten how much it turned her on to have a self-assured man as her sex slave, one who trusted her enough to let her do whatever she wanted.

Slowly, she began to weave the feather around his balls loving the way they tightened and his cock jerked. When he didn't show any of the wildcat changing and his breathing had turned to pants, Haley decided to up the ante. She reached for the tiny paintbrush, then decided to hell with it. She wanted to touch his balls and cock.

She squirted chocolate syrup into one palm, then used just the tip of her middle finger to trace chocolate swirls and lines on the smooth insides of his thighs. Around each ball, she slowly drew concentric circles. With only a bit of chocolate left in her palm, she wrapped her hand around his cock. Under her sticky palm, the veins pulsed, thickening his cock as she held it.

She didn't bother to look at Dylan's face. She knew from his breathing and the sheen of body sweat glistening in the dim light he was almost at the edge. His body shuddered and she caught a quick glimpse of claws peeking from his toenails and fingernails. The claws disappeared quickly.

"Good control," Haley commented. The time had to come to reward both of them just a bit.

She lapped the chocolate off his thighs, then moved to his balls. His body twisted when she started to suck the first one, but she stopped and he stilled immediately. When she started again, he never moved. After licking the second one clean, she wondered if they both had the strength for her to lick his cock.

She started with a bit of licking, using just the tip of her tongue. His knuckles whitely gripped his ankles. Encouraged by his determination, she used her full tongue to lap first up the length, then around the girth.

Damn, damn, damn. She wanted this cock inside her muff, not her mouth. But she needed to make sure he still had control. She began to take him into her mouth, a few millimeters at a time. With one hand, she fondled his balls. The other hand she slid back and forth across his butt cheeks, occasionally touching his butt hole.

His cock jerked in her mouth. She suckled harder, pleased he didn't come immediately. She learned the shape of the smooth tip, then devoured him deeper to feel the texture of the ridged veins feeding its heavy girth.

Her nipples tightened unbearably. Her clit wept hot juices.

"Push yourself back onto the bed," she said hoarsely.

She sat back on her calves and touched her clit. She had to have him now. She climbed on the bed. He still kept his legs spread apart, his hands gripping his ankles. "Let go of your ankles and hold the headboard rails again."

She brushed a taut nipple against his mouth. Ah, a smart study. Dylan already knew not to do anything she didn't tell him to do.

She rubbed the other nipple across his mouth, daring him to taste it. Good. He kept his mouth shut although she saw the strain in his jaw and the taut tension in his body.

Haley straddled his body, then rubbed her aching, wet muff across his chest. Was he in full control?

She raised herself up to her knees, noting the trank caps were within easy reach to grab if she needed them. *Right, Lundberg, CYA in case the jaguarondi pops out.*

Time to test his control.

She moved up to his face and brushed her wet muff against his face. The claws popped out from his fingers again, but disappeared even more quickly.

She lowered herself to his mouth. "Eat me."

His tongue promptly plunged into her clit, lapping as though he were dying of thirst. His mouth sucked at her and pulled the tight knot of her clitoris into her mouth.

For a heartbeat, Haley felt stiff whiskers where her thighs pressed Dylan's cheeks and a scratchy tongue against her folds. They disappeared as fast as she realized what they were.

Rapidly, the essence of her being climbed higher. She rubbed her throbbing tits against Dylan's knuckles. If she truly tamed him for her sex slave, she'd keep this level of sensation with his sucking, lapping, and occasionally teeth scraping all night long. Her being stripped itself from her body. Her orgasm sent her into a frenzy, grinding herself against Dylan's mouth and tightening her thighs against his cheeks while shudders ripped through her.

"Dylan! Oh, women saints! Dylan!"

The last of the orgasm ignited through her and left her hanging limply onto the bedstead rails. His tongue and mouth moved more slowly now.

She felt cherished while he gently lapped and occasionally licked her clitoris to send aftershocks through her.

Stiffly, she unwound her hands from the rails, then moved herself from his mouth.

"Nice," she said, barely able to keep her eyes open. She patted his still erect cock. "Turn on your side so I can reach your cock."

Without saying a word, he twisted his body. Haley looked at the odd angle he lay at then laughed. "You may take your hands off the rails now and get comfortable."

For a moment his jaw worked, but he didn't say anything.

Haley took his dick into her mouth and began to suck. Dylan didn't know how much longer he was going to be able to stand this torture and stop his dick from exploding.

Her sweet muff, ripe with her juices that he still tasted, lay next to his face. The bountiful tits he wanted to suckle rubbed against his belly.

He wanted to grab her ass and eat her again. *Hey*, he realized, *he still had permission to eat her.*

He probed with his tongue, nudging her thighs slightly further apart. When he reached the ripe knot of her clitoris, she moaned against his dick. He suckled her knot enjoying the vibrations of her moans against his dick. Her body started shuddering. Her hand slapped with a sharp sting against his butt. She jerked her mouth from his almost exploding dick.

"Get rid of the goddamn tail, Gomez!"

He took his mouth from her muff and glanced over his shoulder. His furry tail lashed against her head and shoulders. *"Son of a bitch!"*

his mind exploded. He hadn't even felt the damn thing begin to extrude. At least he hadn't said anything out loud. Maybe she'd go on giving him head if he made the damn tail go away real fast. When it was gone, he cursed silently. He didn't have the energy to start this Dom/sub game again, at least not as sub.

His Brunhilde – and damn it all to hell and back, it wasn't *fair* that women got to be multi-orgasmic and most men were thrilled to get a single big one – lay on the wrinkled sheets glowing with sweat and post-clitoral satisfaction.

His dick still pounded with unfulfilled lust. The last time he had been this frustrated was when a girl cousin dared him to take one of his grandfather's *penis erectus* pills. Gawd-almighty, that had been the last time he let a female be a Dom until tonight. Just what had he been thinking? His dick throbbed and he smelled Haley's juices. Oh, yeah, he hadn't been thinking, just trying to control the damn wildcat urges to take care of his basic human needs.

"You just can't keep from pussy-whipping, can you?"

Dylan clamped his mouth shut against the curses curdling his brain.

"Dylan, as long as you continue to control the jaguarondi in you, I give you permission to pleasure me in any way you wish."

Chapter 7

As soon as the words left her mouth, Dylan had her on her hands and knees in front of him. He spread her legs apart. He eased the tip of his dick into her. He knew she was still wet for him, but he also knew some women needed a little time to adjust to his girth.

She let loose a long shuddering breath when his width fully stretched her. "About damn time. Harder, Dylan. Faster."

As much as he wanted to, he had permission to pleasure her however *he* wished. He slid nearly out, then slowly entered her again. Over and over, he continued the smooth solid strokes until she began to keen. When her orgasm began to shake both of them, Dylan pulled completely out.

"What the fuck?" She dropped to her belly and rolled over to glare at him.

Dylan pointed a finger to his chest, then to his mouth.

"Talk, you bastard."

He leaned over the end of the bed and found the long strip of velvet she'd discarded. "You said I had permission to pleasure you any way *I* wish." Rapidly, despite her kicking, he managed to use the strip of velvet to tie her ankles to two of the rails of the headboard.

"This is the way *I* wish to bring you pleasure." With her legs spread wide and her ass elevated, he kneeled between her legs and surveyed her wide-open clit. He held her hands with one hand, then drove himself into her. He sucked first one tit, then the other, all the while keeping up the relentless pounding his dick wanted so badly. His entire body shook at the pleasure of her sublime slickness and heated shivers against him.

The harder and faster he drove into her, the faster her breathing came. He felt the tingling in his fingers and toes, the sharpening points of his teeth next to his tongue, but forced the changing into abeyance. With a shrieking, unintelligible call, her body shook with her orgasm and he let himself go, joining her primeval scream with his own deep roar while his cum pumped out in sharp bursts.

Panting, he became aware of her body supporting his, her hands stroking his damp back. Her hands stopped, then her fingers began to lightly feather his. Her fingers stopped as though they found something.

"Dylan, untie me now." All the sex joy had disappeared in the First Sergeant order in his Amazon's voice. He always heard the Amazons knew exactly how and when to separate pleasure from business. "I want to see what's under your skin on your back."

"Goddamn it all to hell. Don't tell me I'm now sprouting some fucking wings." Dylan reached up his back, trying to feel what interested Hildy. He untied the velvet rope.

After she flexed her legs, she sat up. "Turn around."

Her fingers moved in small decisive strokes. She sat back on her calves. He turned to face her.

"The farmer who found the wounded

jaguarondi called me. How did you get shot anyway?"

"Trying to make connections with my human smuggler contacts to get them to stop until I got to the bottom of the Hell Hospital."

Hildy worried her lower lip. "When I took possession of the wounded jaguarondi, which the farmer tranked when he spotted it, I patched up the bullet hole," she patted the healing spot on his thigh, "and inoculated it for rabies, feline leukemia, and feline distemper."

"Gee, nice to know I'm protected."

"The vaccines probably aren't effective in your human body. If they were, all of us in animal protection would automatically be vaccinated against rabies the way the general population is vaccinated against the flu. It won't hurt you either," she assured him. "We stick ourselves all the time, dealing with unruly animals. Anyway, at the same time, I inserted a GPS unit to track the jaguarondi for our endangered species program."

"I have a GPS unit in me?"

"Actually, the one I put in is just below your shoulder blade. There's a second one between your shoulder blades."

"And there's only one place where it could have been inserted. The Hell Hospital," Dylan clamped his jaw shut. "You know what this means, don't you?"

"Just a wild guess, but I'd say someone's tracking you."

"Yes, that, too, but not for much longer."

Haley's eyes widened. "There's only one way to remove the tracking units."

"Yes. I know. Can you do it?"

"Can you keep yourself from turning into a

jaguarondi when I cut it out? I have some local anesthetic, but it's for animals. I don't know how effective it'll be on you."

"Just do it," Dylan said. He grabbed the briefs and scrambled into them and his jeans while Haley wrapped herself in a terry cloth robe. "You realize I'll have to run from here as soon as you get both of these out."

"Right. And I'm coming with you. Come out to the kitchen." They ran to the kitchen. "The light's better in here and I have a powerful flashlight also. I can get a scalpel from my vet kit."

"Why do you have so much veterinarian stuff? Are you a vet, too?"

"Qualified as a vet's assistant. Authorized to use some specific drugs." Dylan watched her lovely hands efficiently unpack instruments and packets of things. He recognized Instant Skin and one packet that looked like a general antibiotic. "Wildlife Control Management does a lot of treatment of injured animals. Most times the animal's injuries have to at least be stabilized before it's moved. And we always vaccinate animals we release back into the wild.

"Are you sure you want both units out? I don't think anyone will track the jaguarondi I tagged."

"If the Hell Hospital is responsible for my shape changing and put their own GPS tracking unit in me, I can bet they'll figure out about the jaguarondi's GPS. Take them both out."

She swabbed both areas with alcohol, then wiped them with another pad of something. "Where do you want to go? West Texas? The Davis Mountains?"

"Might as well. We'll need cash. They'll be

able to track us if we use money cards."

"I always keep cash on hand. Why let the bloodsuckers at the IRS know exactly how much money I have? And if we're going to West Texas, we can stop by one of the Indian casinos and run it up. Are you ready for me to cut?"

Dylan gritted his teeth. He focused on his internal clock. He was himself, the jaguarondi needed to remain deep within him. "Go ahead."

He hissed at the first sharp cut, then a sharp probe into his muscle. He forced his hands and feet to remain still. "How do you intend to run the cash up? Poker shark?"

"No," she said, calmly handing him a bloody GPS unit. "I have phenomenal luck at slots."

He felt her smoothing a stinging cream across the cut, then the soothing coolness of Instant Skin being applied. "Nobody has that kind of luck at slots."

"I do. Ready for the second?"

He nodded. "Go ahead."

"One of my sister's males got curious and ran a bunch of tests. I have a photographic memory and can calculate odds in a flash. I watch the slots for awhile and get the rhythm."

Again came the quick cut, then the digging probe. Again he made himself focus on remaining human despite the tearing pain in his hands and feet.

"The worse I ever do is double my money. And," she handed him the second gory unit, "if we go to the Indian casino I know, we not only can collect some extra cash at slots, but I can sell my car to one of the chiefs I know who lusts after it." She finished patching the second wound.

"Why does he lust after it and not after you?" Dylan flexed his shoulders, stood, and followed Hildy from the kitchen. He stopped by the bathroom and flushed the GPS chips down the can.

In the bedroom, Hildy had put on a pair of tiny panties and a lace bra. "He lusts after me, too. But you'll see. Let's get the hell out of here before your creeps come hunting us."

In the heat of the midday sun, Dylan marveled again at the depths to which Haley gave him unconditional support. Elliot Hawksky, not only one of the chiefs, but also the tribe's Head of Security, counted the last of the cash for Haley's pristine 1965 Shelby GT350 Mustang Hatchback into her outstretched palm.

"Haley," Hawksky's voice rumbled like distant thunder, as dark as the jet-black braid hanging down his back, "if you should choose to become one of my junior wives, I shall gift you back your car."

"Not even to be a senior wife, El. Come on, Dylan, let me show you how to play slots."

"Please do not break our bank, Haley," Hawksky told her. "Our visitor numbers are down with this virus frightening people. We must earn a living."

"You know no matter what I win, the other patrons will give you a profit. I'm ready to do some slots. Let's go, Dylan."

Hawksky touched Dylan's shoulder. "I wish to speak to you alone."

Dylan barely heard Hawksky's voice. He didn't know what the chief wanted, but he knew he needed to hear it, just like he needed to get into the Davis Mountains. "You go on, Haley. I'll catch up.

I want to cry over this Mustang just awhile longer."

After Haley disappeared into the casino, Dylan followed Hawksky to a hut set away from the modern buildings of the casino, the housing for the tribe, and the hotel for the guests. When Dylan ducked into the hut's door, he saw an old man sitting on a blanket on the hut's dirt floor. Facing the old man, Hawksky placed a palm to his head, then to his heart, and left them.

The old man waved a palm to indicate Dylan join him on the blanket. He offered Dylan the pipe he smoked. Always one to respect his elders, Dylan took a draw and returned it.

"I dreamed of you this morning as the dawn rose. I told Hawksky to bring me the wildcat shaper who comes with the woman with the moonlight silver hair. You are he."

After discovering he changed into a jaguarondi and struggling to control it, it didn't surprise him to have an old Indian he'd never met before calmly recognize him as a shape-shifter.

"I change into a jaguarondi, yes."

They waited in silence.

"Those of us who find our way to our animal shape are rare. You must celebrate your discovery of your inner self."

The smoke from their shared pipe curled around them. Dylan didn't want to celebrate turning into a jaguarondi, he wanted it to stop.

"You must embrace the change. You must become the jaguarondi. The jaguarondi must become you. If you do not, you will lose what you most need."

"What I need most is to control this changing. Can you teach me that?"

The old man shook his head. "You are the

one who knows what you need. You must embrace the jaguarondi to keep what you need."

The old man set the pipe on the ground in front of them, then close his eyes. As though he'd been summoned, Hawksky entered the hut again and motioned Dylan to leave. The old man's eyes remained closed, but Dylan copied Hawksky's respectful hand signals to the old man before he crawled out of the hut's small door.

Slowly, the two men walked back to the casino.

"Do you believe my father's grandfather?"

"Do you?" Dylan tasted the iron tang of fear at being stuck with this changing shit happening to him the rest of his life.

The chief laughed. Strong white teeth gleamed against his dark, bronze skin. "Hawksky is not just pleasant sounding syllables. It's what I am inside. You'll learn."

Hawksky's casual gaze sharpened suddenly. "What the hell is going on there?"

Dylan followed the direction of Hawksky's look and started running.

Both of them pounded across the empty tribal land determined to catch the men forcing Haley, his Hildy, across the parking lot. Hawksky barked orders into the communications unit on his shoulder.

His Brunhilde wasn't going without a fight. Like the Reservist Amazon Division First Sergeant she was, Hildy was fighting them. One man lay on the parking lot tarmac clutching his balls. Another still held her, but bled from scratches across his face.

A man in the uniform of Tribal Security lay in front of parked cars, bleeding from a head wound.

A popping sound came and windshields shattered from bullets fired by a man in the van to which four men were trying to drag Haley. Another Tribal Security officer spun with the impact from a bullet and dropped to the ground holding her shoulder. Tribal Security officers ducked behind cars and steadied rifles, obviously reluctant to return fire with Haley in the way.

With three men struggling to contain his fighting Valkyrie, the fourth man turned a gun to butt first and hit her across the head.

Dylan's mate drooped in the arms of three predators. Dylan pushed his way out of his remaining clothes and launched his jaguarondi body at the predators who dared attack his mate.

He added his own claw marks to the face his mate had marked and gained intense satisfaction at seeing the man clamp his hands to his bleeding eyes.

He bit a second man in the groin. His pointed teeth easily penetrated the man's uniform. Dylan hoped he'd bit the predator deep enough that the shrill soprano note the predator screamed was going to be that predator's natural voice for now on.

One of the three who had held his mate had a hawk tearing at his head and face.

His mate lay on the ground, holding her head and groaning.

Dylan attacked the predator who had struck her. When he was done, he shifted back into human form. He wiped the blood from the bastard's torn throat off his mouth.

The gunman who had shot from the van now slumped over the steering wheel with half his head gone from Tribal Security's bullets.

Several hours later, Dylan eased his body off Hildy's, grabbed a robe, and padded to the door of the high-roller's suite Hawksky had installed them in after the fight.

He wasn't surprised to see Hawksky standing there. "How are your officers?"

"One of them is in the hospital with a concussion from the bullet that grazed his scalp. The other has already been treated and released. Her husbands are trying to talk her into taking a desk job."

"If she's anything like Haley, they can forget that idea."

"She was my instructor in dirty fighting in the Amazons." Haley yawned and leaned against Dylan.

"You're supposed to be in bed. You have a concussion."

"I'm fine. What's going to happen to the predators who grabbed me?"

"We don't have to worry about them. Those who didn't die immediately must have had suicide capsules. They were dead before the medics had a chance to treat them for their wounds."

"Any charges being brought against Dylan?"

"What charges would those be? My officers and a bunch of tourists here to play craps, poker, and the slots saw nothing but a wild jaguarondi and a hawk attacking some turds with guns who were trying to kidnap a lady."

"Good," Haley nodded at Hawksky.

"Do either of you know who the turds were? The van has no prints and was stolen from

San Antonio two days ago."

"I think they're after me," Dylan said, "and were capturing Haley to get to me. You'll never be able to track them."

"Are you going to keep them off our land? Flying bullets upset the marks at the casino."

"I'll do my best."

"Good. You're free to go. Spend the night if you'd like."

"They may have reinforcements coming."

"They won't breach our barriers. We'll get you out in the morning. We have ways of getting people out without outsiders being the wiser. Haley, my Senior Wife has tendered an offer to you as Junior-to-Senior Wife."

"No, thanks. I'm going to hang with Dylan for awhile. He's got something to take care of in the Davis Mountains. I promised I'd help him."

"Suit yourself. Go back to bed and get some rest."

Hawksky shut the door to the suite. Dylan and Haley stumbled back to bed eager to once again explore each other's bodies.

When they exhausted themselves, Haley snuggled against Dylan's chest. She started to drift to sleep when she heard a rumbling. A slight vibration fluttered his chest under her cheek.

"Dylan, wake up. You, pickle head, you snore."

"Not snoring, wasn't asleep," Dylan said, cuddling her. "I'm happy. All cats purr when they're happy."

Black Panther

By
Myla Jackson

Chapter 1

Ramon Osceola blended with the shadows of the bald cypress towering over his head. The tree stood tall on the large hummock of land surrounded by swamp in the only place left he could call home. He stared out across the wide expanse of open water, the hair on the back of his neck standing at attention. The roar of an airboat propeller disturbed the usual stillness of the swamp, growing louder as the vehicle skimmed the surface of the algae-covered waters. The sound was headed his direction.

Access to his place was limited to land or air with no roads or bridges venturing this deep into the Big Cypress Swamp of Florida. Which suited him just fine. His special issues required space from other humans and the hammock of *land in the swamps* afforded a place where he could guard his solitude, as well as his life. Thank the gods the conservationists had saved the swamps from encroaching growth and development. They had even reestablished flow of waters to encourage the return of natural plants and animals to the area. Making his utter seclusion possible. He lived off the land and water, his sustenance that of his Seminole ancestors—fish from the water, plants and roots from the land.

He'd inherited the tiny island from his father and rebuilt it to be habitable after his discharge from the Army Special Forces. He'd distanced himself as much as any man could into total solitude. The occasional swamp tour guide ventured in looking for fresh routes to sell to eager tourists searching for the giant alligators and exceptional wildlife found nowhere else in the United States but that was pretty much it.

Inhaling the musty scent of decayed leaves and stagnant water, he much preferred the natural odors of death and rebirth of vegetation than the stench of sewage and trash of the city life. Especially the acrid smell of alcohol and disinfectant prevalent in hospitals and clinical laboratories like the one in which he'd been held captive for who knew how long. Even the thought of that place set his heart racing and he needed to take several deep breaths before regaining control.

But the airboat hadn't changed direction, and the noise grew closer. The operator ran it at full throttle--too fast for the twisting waterways leading to his remote house and too fast for swamp tourists. A *whop-whop-whop* sound joined the whine of the fan-powered boat.

Instinctively, Ramon tensed. The sound of helicopters — he'd heard them often enough when he deployed as a Special Forces soldier to the war in Iran. Before his capture. Before his alteration. Before his life had changed forever.

The helicopter appeared over the tops of the tallest bald cypress trees at the same time as the airboat rounded the corner of the jut of land blocking the view into his little hideaway. The back end of the craft slipped sideways before it straightened and shot forward.

From his vantage point beneath the cypress tree two hundred yards from his house, the animal in Ramon sensed danger and fought to unleash.

The aircraft was lean and black, an exact copy of hundreds of others in the military arsenal. The only difference being, this chopper didn't have the usual markings and it was operating in attack mode on the home front.

Clamping down hard on his back teeth, Ramon struggled to maintain his humanity in the face of a relentless metamorphosis.

He'd tried on numerous occasions to control the transformation only to fail, waking up naked in the oddest places. Thus his retreat to the Big Cypress Swamp. If he were to change out here, who would notice? He needed his humanity to face this kind of danger and he concentrated on the airboat and its occupant.

The driver's long blonde hair whipped around in the wind. A woman? Not the norm for the swamp, and she was hell bent on wrecking if she didn't slow down soon. For that matter, she headed straight for the house he'd built on the little island in the swamp.

As the airboat plowed through the lagoon's open water, its speed climbing to insane levels, the helicopter dropped low and a side door slid open, the snout of a machine gun pointing out.

Ramon pushed away from the tree trunk, and almost stepped out into the open to shout a warning to the driver, until he realized the sound wouldn't carry over the blast of the propeller jettisoning the watercraft closer. All he could do was watch as the gunner unloaded a rapid burst of bullets at the boat.

The woman at the helm cried out and jerked the steering grip away from the chopper, the rudders responding a little too well. The boat leaned on its side in the water and then straightened, moving in a zigzagging motion to avoid being peppered by the gunner overhead.

When the helicopter crowded closer, the woman wrenched her steering grip too hard. The front of the airboat lifted from the surface of the lagoon and the entire craft launched into the air, spiraling three-hundred-sixty degrees. The woman's body was thrown from her seat on the boat, landing hard on the algae-covered surface.

Heart hammering against his chest, Ramon watched helplessly as the empty craft hit the water upside down, the back cage and propeller separating from the boat, flying through the air in pieces. When the prop hit the water, it broke in two and finally sank beneath the murky depths.

Skin stretched and changed, hairs springing from follicles covering his body in a thick black pelt. Pain shot through every nerve ending as his bones shifted and contracted. Before long, he couldn't stand on two feet and dropped to all fours, fighting to retain his human thoughts and reasoning, a challenge he met through each transition. Anger pushed the transformation through his blood. Anger at the relentless and merciless pursuit of the woman who had fought to stay alive on the airboat, only to be thrown violently from her vehicle. The helicopter pilot didn't demand she stop over a loudspeaker, the crew didn't fire warning shots to get her attention. They wanted to kill her. Cop, judge and jury all wrapped in one package. What the hell was going on? Who was she? And why was the military helicopter chasing her? Was she a drug runner or a convicted felon? No matter what she'd done, she deserved a chance to defend herself.

As his transformation neared completion,

he shook free of his clothing. Then his haunches bunched, and he leaped through the underbrush, following the lay of the land until he was as close as he could get to rescue the woman without going into the water.

Overhead, the helicopter circled the airboat and finally flew off toward the house another hundred yards away.

A missile left the underbelly of the aircraft and flew straight into the house he'd spent the past two months remodeling. When the weapon touched the cedar exterior, it exploded in a blast large enough to rock the earth beneath Ramon's paws. The sound echoed against the tall stands of cypress.

Apparently the guys flying the chopper didn't think a rocket explosion was enough, they pumped several hundred rounds into the remains of Ramon's home. Had anyone been inside, they would have been dead by the time the helicopter took to the sky and made a wide, sweeping turn.

Instinct propelled him into action. Roman leaped into the lagoon and dog-paddled to the woman lying facedown in the water. He slid his head under her until she rested across his back, her face rising above the surface. Then he applied his paws to swimming with all his might to the shore farthest away from the destruction. He wanted to get her to the safety and anonymity of the shoreline before the crew of the helicopter returned to finish her off. And if he didn't resuscitate her soon, she'd suffer irreparable brain damage. As he struggled to balance her body on his back and paddle to shore, the rage that somehow seemed to control him burned inside.

The house in the swamps had been his

sanctuary, his escape from the harsh world. And now that was gone too. After losing his humanity, he'd come to the only home he knew to lick his wounds and hide in the swamps away from prying eyes and heartless scientists who would want to poke and prod the freak.

Sinking his teeth into her shirt, he lifted her and dragged her in the shadows of the banks until she was completely out of the water and invisible to the helicopter circling over the demolished airboat.

The helicopter wasn't the only danger to contend with. Ramon's gaze darted around, searching for the alligators known to frequent the lagoon. He had to get her up and moving to keep her from becoming an afternoon snack.

Out of the water, he walked up her back pressing his front paws into her, pushing the liquid from her lungs, the blades of the helicopter whipping the vegetation into his face.

He ignored the sound of the killing machine and concentrated on shifting into his natural form. Closing his eyes, he willed his body to change back into a man, human frustration warring with animal instinct to run deeper into the woods. To save this woman, he had to be a man to help her. Still pushing against her back, he stared down at his paws as they stretched and extended. Excruciating pain ripped through his muscles and joints as his body lengthened and expanded, the fur retracting into his skin until long slim fingers lay against the woman's shoulders.

When the transformation was complete, he straddled her buttocks and leaned into his effort to expel all the swamp water she'd inhaled. As he pushed against her back, he studied what he could see of her body and the side of her face turned toward him.

She was petite, possibly only five-feet tall with nicely rounded hips and a narrow waist. The bit of her face he could see was pale, the skin smooth and creamy where not covered in mud and algae.

His hands slid up the side of her ribcage, urging the water up from her lungs. As his fingers curled around her, he could feel the swell of her breasts beneath her damp clothing. Ramon groaned, his cock resting in the indentation of her ass. The transformation back to his human form always left him horny as hell. At that exact moment, he didn't care what woman, as long as he had a slick pussy to slide his engorged cock into. He alternated between disgust at where his thoughts were headed and desire for the woman lying beneath him — a woman whose eyes had yet to open.

Would her eyes be the color of cornflowers in the spring to match the long blonde hair he'd seen blowing in the wind before she'd been tossed from the boat? Her hair now lay in dark wet strands plastered to the back of her head, and she was as still as death. He pushed harder, and she finally responded, water gushing out of her lungs.

As he worked over her, he prayed to the gods that rescuing her wasn't another mistake on his part. Why had she been racing through the swamps as if being chased by the devil himself? And why had she found her way into his lagoon? Was she from the government? Or worse. Blood ran cold in his veins and his hands hesitated in their work as dark thoughts raced through his mind. Was she one of the sadistic bastards from

Hell Hospital? If she proved to be a threat, he'd have no other choice but to kill her.

*****

Dr. Hannah Richards surfaced from the black lagoon of her nightmare when the pressure on her back forced water from her lungs. She gagged and choked, struggling to move only to find herself pinned to the ground, her face lying against the cool, slimy shoreline.

Whatever pressed against her back let up and she sucked in a deep breath, liquid gagging her lungs again. She coughed to force up the remaining water while clawing against the tangle of vines and decayed leaves. Desperate to climb to her feet, she tossed away a stringy mass of the muck and tried again to push up. The briny taste of swamp water registered on her tongue and her stomach heaved, projecting the vile contents into the dank vegetation.

Weight lifted from her lower back and she was free to climb to her knees where she puked and hacked all the water from her system. Exhausted, she rolled over to her back and opened her eyes. Sunlight trickled through the branches overhead warming her face until a shadow leaned over her, blocking the gentle rays.

As her gaze cleared and adjusted to the lack of sunlight, she stared up into the near-black eyes of the man standing over her. His long, straight black hair lay plastered to his scalp and shoulders, damp from his dip in the lagoon. Besides the hair and eyes, his square jaw, dark skin and high cheekbones gave him away as Ramon Osceola, the man she'd risked her life to find. "Thank God, it's you," she said, her voice gravelly from her bout with swamp water and coughing.

Black brows furrowed on his smooth dark forehead. His hair had grown even longer since the last time she'd seen him in his cage at Hell Hospital.

"God has nothing to do with me." He stood to his full height of six-feet-two, towering over her, naked and as beautiful as she remembered, his dark skin not a result of tanning, but a tribute to his Native American heritage.

Her gaze traveled upward, from the well-defined calves to thick, muscular thighs.

Hannah stopped when her perusal reached the swath of curly black hair surrounding his erect cock. A gasp escaped her lips. No matter how many times she'd witnessed his transformation from human to black panther and back, she couldn't get over the tantalizing residual effects. Every male subject in the hospital experimentation showed the same result. When they shape-shifted back to their human form, invariably they were left with a painful erection.

Ramon cleared his throat, the small amount of movement making his cock jerk as if beckoning her to touch. How many times had she been tempted in the past? Hiding behind her mask and smock, she'd been anonymous to the Special Forces captives. Now her face and every expression became exposed to his advanced interrogating skills and techniques. She could hide nothing from this man.

Her face flaming, Hannah forced her gaze past his magnificent cock and upward over rock-solid abs to the rippling muscles stretched taut across his chest and finally to the strong chin and high cheekbones of a Seminole Indian.

"Ramon Osceola?" she asked, although she

knew every incredibly sexy inch of this man. Hadn't she studied him for the four months she'd conducted experiments on him and other members of the Special Forces units they'd stolen from? A fact for which she would never forgive herself, for the immoral experimentation and irreprehensible consequences she'd have to live with for the rest of her life.

Yet hidden behind her doctor's mask, she'd studied him the most, drawn to his dark skin and brown-black eyes. By day, she'd donned her professional demeanor and masked anonymity to perform the highly successful experiments demanded by her captors. But at night she couldn't block her dreams of lying naked with this man, imagining those hands and that incredible cock doing all the things she wanted him to do but didn't dare suggest.

He stared down at her, eyes narrowing into slits. "Do I know you?"

"Yes." Crawling to her knees, she pushed herself to her feet, swaying slightly. Once there, she met his gaze head on. "And no."

He crossed his arms over his bare chest, seemingly unconcerned with his nakedness as if daring her to say something. "Who the hell are you and why did that helicopter attack you and my home?"

For the first time, she glanced around, noting the small rise of land on which they stood. She panned the lagoon to the larger hammock where only a few short minutes before a rough-hewn cottage had been. Except for a few framing timbers still left standing amidst the smoke and debris, the house was a complete loss. Her chest tightened. Because of her, they'd destroyed

Ramon's home. If she'd left him alone, would they have let him survive? Had she sentenced him to death by seeking him out? Yet another layer of guilt she'd have to live with. "I'm glad you weren't inside when it happened," she said softly.

"Your concern touches me." His lip curled on the edge. "I'm waiting for answers."

Looking at him she was hesitant to spill her story and her plea for help.

Living from moment to moment since her escape from Hell Hospital, Hannah had known her share of terror. Having played life safe up until the day she and her daughter had been kidnapped, she'd been a model citizen. Never hurt another soul, never committed a crime. For all she'd done over the past year, they could lock her up in prison and throw away the key. Short of murder, she'd committed enough crimes to invalidate her Hippocratic Oath several times over.

And she'd do them all again for Lilly. She'd do anything for Lilly. After a difficult pregnancy, during which her husband left her, her baby girl had been born two months premature. She and the doctors had fought to keep her alive, succeeding beyond her most fervent hopes. The struggles they'd endured together just to keep the girl alive bonded them for life.

She took a deep breath and launched into her story, hoping he'd listen and understand why she'd done what she did. "I was one of the doctors working at GeneTech in Dallas, researching gene splicing in crossing different species of animals."

His forehead dipped into a scowl. "Animals or humans?"

"Animals only," she said, her words firm. She hadn't willingly signed on for human testing.

"Until Vaughan Mitchell's men stole my daughter, Lilly, from the home we shared in the suburbs.. They'd left a message on my phone link that if I wanted to see my daughter alive, I had to go along with everything Mitchell demanded. Which included working in Hell Hospital for the past year."

His lips thinned into a straight line, the muscles in his jaw tightening. "You expect me to believe this?"

"Yes."

"That makes you one of the enemy." A growl rumbled in his throat and his gaze darted to the sky. "How do I know you're not a set up for them to recapture me?"

Her chin dropped to her chest. "If I were you, I wouldn't believe anything anyone said, but please hear me out." Then she looked up and pinned his deep brown gaze with her stare, willing him to understand and forgive. "What I did, I did to save my daughter. They held her captive and threatened to kill her if I didn't. The experiments had been conducted on chimpanzees at first. Then they brought in humans to test the effects of the genetic reengineering program. As long as I did what they said, they let me have my daughter with me." With a deep breath, she turned and walked to the doorway. "Lilly and I talked about escaping, but they kept us under lock and key when we were together, and I didn't dare leave when we were separated. I didn't know if I'd ever see her again.

"When one of the men escaped before they could "release" him and still remain anonymous, Vaughan took Lilly away, blaming me for assisting with the getaway. I had nothing to do with the escape, and I pleaded with Vaughan to return my daughter. When he refused, I planned my own escape, determined to find and free Lilly." She turned to face him, tears pooling in her eyes. "You see, I have to find her before they kill her. Vaughan insisted he'd taken her off the hospital compound. I have an idea where, but they're sure to be waiting for me. I knew I couldn't do it on my own. That's why I had to find you. Don't you see? You're the only one I could trust to help me."

"Damn it! You're the fuckin' enemy." He strode toward her, his hands clenching into fists. "I should kill you now."

She stood firm, refusing to allow his anger and the fire in his eyes to intimidate. Hair sprouted on his cheeks and arms, evidence his control slipped. "Yes you should. But you won't." Her voice was calm, steady, soothing.

"What makes you so sure?" The rumble in his voice was more pronounced.

"You're an honorable man." She hoped she'd read him right—praying he wouldn't slay her. "If you kill me, my Lilly will surely die."

"Why me?" He waved his hand at the murky water. "Why track me down all the way out here in the swamps?"

"You're one of the only people I knew with the training to pull off a raid on the compound where they're keeping her. Only a man trained by Special Forces has a chance to get through their defenses. I need you." She needed him to help find her daughter. What she wouldn't tell him was that she also needed him in a way a woman needs a man, had longed for him throughout his stay in Hell Hospital. Having him pace in front of her completely naked, his gleaming brown muscles larger than life and within inches of her fingers itching to feel them. No, he would never believe her.

Would he understand why she had to do what she did and help her to rescue her daughter? "When I ran from Hell Hospital, I stole one of the high-tech tracking devices. I wasn't sure which of the subjects I'd find when I managed to track him down, but I hoped it would be you." No, she'd prayed it would be Ramon.

"Let me get this straight. You worked at Hell Hospital tampering with monkeys. What else did you do? Were you involved with the human program?" His face was still as if etched in stone, awaiting her response.

A chill slithered its way down Hannah's spine. Now that she'd found Ramon Osceola, she hesitated to tell him the full extent of her role in the experiments. Disclosure of her part in this scheme could possibly infuriate him. If he became angry enough, he could shift into the form of a black panther. Would he consider her a threat and kill her as was instinctive to a cornered panther?

She gulped back her fear and squared her shoulders. Her daughter's life depended on her and this man. He was her last hope. "Just remember, everything I did was under duress. They were threatening my daughter's life. I was always behind a mask and smock, so you probably don't remember my face, but you'll remember my name. I'm Dr. Hannah Richards. I'm the geneticist from Hell Hospital who made you what you are today."

Chapter 2

That tingling, burning sensation exploded through his veins as the transformation struck him like a blow. His incisors pushed against the inside of his mouth and elongated into feline fangs. He inhaled several times, willing the change to abate. It slowed, but didn't retract. "What did you say?" Words came out in a husky growl, understandable, yet no less animalistic. He hated that. In all his military training, he'd always been in control. Until Hell Hospital and this woman screwed with his DNA. His hands bunched into fists, his cat-like fingernails digging into his human flesh, reminding him of his abnormality.

"Look, I know this is a shock, but I had to find you." She reached out and laid a hand on his arm.

Jerking back, his first instinct was to hiss at her and slap her hand away with a powerful swipe of his paw. She was the enemy. Because of her, he was a freak, part man and part animal. And she'd tracked him down in the swamps. "How did you find me? What tracking device?" His gaze panned the sky and he listened for the return of the helicopter. Would they come back to claim their prize? Would they drag him back to Hell Hospital where they'd perform more experiments?

They'd have a helluva fight on their hands this time because he'd die rather than go back. He already had enough problems dealing with his sudden transformations. What more could they possibly do to him and the others he knew were there as well?

His enemy stood in front of him, a petite woman, five feet tall and probably weighing no more than one hundred pounds dripping wet as she was. She wasn't in the bloom of youth and the lines around her eyes put her closer to his thirty-eight years. But her beauty was ageless, her appearance fragile.

How could he attack a woman no bigger than a child? And he wanted very badly to wreak his revenge on the person responsible for the current hell he'd been living since his return to the States.

Dark smudges beneath her eyes indicated sleepless nights. She coughed and her entire frame shook with its force. "I'll help you if you'll help me free my daughter," she said, straightening to her full height. In the proud tilt of her chin, he sensed strength. In the hollows of her cheeks, he saw fear and desperation. Had remorse set in? He snorted. A little late for regrets.

The cat in him could have cared less about her difficulties. The human in him responded, a matching ache building in the region of his heart.

"How can you help me?" His teeth shrank back into his gums, the black panther fur retreated back into his skin, and his voice returned to normal. He was back in control of this situation. He couldn't hear the sound of a helicopter hovering over the horizon, even with his heightened senses. As long as it wasn't coming back, he knew without a doubt that he could handle one small woman. He could snap her neck and kill her with very little effort at all. He'd done it enough in covert operations where silence was the key to surprise, allowing his troops to overcome an enemy twice their strength. The thought of killing her rubbed against his mind like a cat pressing into his leg.

Screams of others trapped in their cells in Hell Hospital echoed through his mind and his lips pulled back from his teeth. How many others were there? He'd known of at least three. Were there more? How could this woman look at herself in the mirror after what she'd done? And why was he hesitating to kill her? She deserved to die.

She inhaled a shaky breath and blew it out before speaking. "You have a GPS tracking device embedded in your skin. I'll dig it out."

"That's all? I could do that myself." He moved closer, his bare feet soundless against the damp leaves and decaying vegetation covering the tiny island. "The only way you can help me is to undo what you've done. Can you do that? Can you take away the beast inside me and make me the man I was?"

Her shoulders sagged and she stared at the ground. "No. I'm sorry. Your condition cannot be undone."

"Sorry? You've made my life a living hell and all you can say is 'I'm sorry'?" If you can't undo your chemistry experiment, how did you plan to help me?" His voice ended on a roar, his teeth elongating, hairs pushing through his skin. The fur on his arm caught his attention, reminding him he was losing his temper and that always made him lose his humanity. After several deep breaths, he was back in control, the thread holding him in check frayed but holding.

Her eyes widened and she took a step

backward.

He could smell her fear and it made his body quicken, his cock grow harder. She was pretty in a petite, fragile way. Not the kind of woman he was normally attracted to, but she was female and he was...horny.

The fear disappeared and her face hardened into a tight mask. She stood her ground, refusing to back down.

"Not good enough." Ramon continued forward until he stood within an inch of her, his thick cock nudging her belly. Then he dropped his head to sniff her neck and rub his face across the side of her cheek. "I can think of another way you can help me."

"Whatever it takes," she said, her gaze staring straight forward as if she could see through his chest into another world. "I'll do anything you want if you'll help me find and rescue my daughter."

Her determination and willingness to sacrifice everything touched a chord inside him. He squelched that sudden urge to feel sorry for this woman. Pity wasn't an emotion he could afford with the person responsible for ruining his life. But he couldn't help it.

What he'd lost at Hell Hospital was only of him. If this woman spoke the truth, she'd lost more than her morality. She'd lost her child. As a mother, she was bound by the unwritten duty to protect and care for her offspring, her cubs.

Where was the anger he'd felt a moment before? Since he'd returned to the States and the subsequent discovery of his...abnormality, he'd had to give up his career in the military, the life he'd built for himself as a soldier. The life he loved.

He'd hidden in the swamps afraid to venture out for too long for fear he'd change form and find himself naked in an awkward place, turned over to a scientist to be poked and prodded like they'd done in Hell Hospital. For two months, he'd lived on the edge of a society he used to be a part of. Now he belonged nowhere. The only home he knew was destroyed. Anger pushed up into his chest, again. And the person responsible for his anger had dared to ask for his help?

Revenge could be sweet. And revenge would be his.

Grabbing her arms, he pulled her to him, rubbing her body against his nakedness. "You'll do anything?"

The sweet scent of skin and the heady fragrance of her fear drifted up to tantalize his nostrils. He ground his cock against her belly, wondering what it would feel like to fuck her until she screamed. Would he morph into an animal as he slammed his dick into her pussy?

He could imagine her horror if he became a panther while buried deep inside her. Any woman would be frightened and disgusted if it happened. One of the reasons he'd chosen to remain celibate. If he turned while fornicating, the authorities would hunt him down and kill him.

Nails dug into his palms again. She'd done this to him. Made him a freak. He could never trust himself with a woman again. Transformations happened sometimes with no warning. How could he have a meaningful relationship—no, how could he fuck someone—if he was afraid of what he might become in the process? He lived in fear that the panther in him would strike out and kill.

Dr. Hannah Richards drew a sharp breath between her teeth and stared up into his eyes. "I'd sleep with the devil himself if it means getting my daughter back safe."

"Good, because I'm the devil." He bent and claimed her mouth, his kiss angry, punishing. His hands slid down her back and up under her wet blouse.

Her skin was cool and damp, but it made the fire in his veins burn hotter. His grip was punishing and he'd snap her neck in two if he thought it would make him feel better, but nothing short of making him whole again would make him happy. After he'd been discovered on the outskirts of Johannesburg, South Africa, he'd thought he was rescued, freed from the hell he'd been forced to live. At that time, he didn't understand the full extent of the experimentation done on him in Hell Hospital. Nor had he known what other kinds of hell awaited him back at home. He could never go back to being the man he was.

The starch faded out of her body as he dug his tongue into her mouth, sucking at her lips, delving deep as if he'd crawl down her throat. Releasing her back, his hands circled to her front where he grabbed the lapels of her thin cotton blouse and ripped the buttons loose from top to bottom, laying her open for his perusal.

She gasped, her eyes wide, scared. Then she pushed her shoulders back, her full, rounded breasts jutting out beneath the scrap of apricot lace. "I know the animal in you has a greater sex drive and you might have a more difficult time controlling it. If you need the release, I'm willing to let you fuck me in order to secure your promise to help me free my daughter."

The thought of sinking into her luscious channel lit his insides like igniting aviation fuel, burning hot and fast through his system. Was she really willing to sell her soul to the devil just to save a child? He laid the side of his cheek against her bra-clad breast and slid his face across until his mouth poised over the lace hiding her nipple. He reached behind her, ripped the shirt from her shoulders and unclasped the bra from behind. With deliberately slow movements, he slid the straps over her shoulder until she stood before him naked from the waist up.

Rosy brown nipples puckered into tight beads, from the tips of her rounded flesh. Her breathing came in short, shallow gasps, but her hands didn't rise to cover her nakedness. She stood like a virgin at the sacrificial altar — an offering to the beast.

That she was so willing to give her body over to his sick pleasure only angered Ramon more. He stared down into her wide eyes as he cupped each pendulous orb in his hands and squeezed her, knowing his grip was bruising her, wanting to cause her some of the pain he'd felt every time his body changed from human to animal.

A gasp escaped her and she bit down on her lip to keep from crying out.

He bent and ran his tongue up from beneath her left breast to her nipple, tasting her skin. She was like honeysuckle and catnip. Sweet and overwhelmingly tempting. His mouth closed over her other breast and he sucked it between his teeth, biting down until she clasped his head.

"You have every right to hurt me and I won't stop you, but please be quick. I want to save my daughter before it's too late."

Ramon's head jerked up and he reeled backward. A bucket of ice-cold water couldn't have doused his desires anymore effectively than her words. With Ramon uncaged and holding her close, Hannah was frightened of his fierce power more than she'd been during her entire stay at Hell Hospital, but she couldn't deny the sensations building low in her belly, the purely physical response to this dark-skinned soldier standing naked in front of her.

His skin glistened a deep reddish brown, still damp from his dip in the lagoon to save her life. Muscles stretched over impossibly broad shoulders, narrowing to a firm abdomen and sexy ass. No droop in those cheeks. How long had it been since she'd had her birth control inoculation? A glance at the tattoo on her arm confirmed it. Too long. If he wanted to fuck her, she shouldn't be concerned. At thirty-eight, she was long past the government-declared "prime" for childbearing. She shouldn't have to worry about pregnancy. Hannah's fingers twitched, the sudden urge to test the firmness of his cock almost overwhelming her good sense.

Ramon had every right to hate her and she wouldn't blame him if he lost his temper and killed her. But her daughter needed her and she had to free her from Vaughan's treacherous hands. If giving her body to this man would secure his promise to help her, she'd do it. She'd already sold her soul to the devil back at Hell Hospital. Her body was just a vessel, a tool she could use to save Lilly. That she quivered in anticipation wasn't something she wanted to admit to herself, much less to Ramon.

Her hands shook as they rose to the button of her trousers. She flicked it open, slid the zipper down and pushed the damp fabric over her hips. "Please," she said, easing the trousers down her thighs. "Take what you want. I deserve it. What I did was wrong." She stepped out of her trousers and stood in nothing but her apricot-colored lace panties, her hands fluttering at her sides, the temptation to cover her breasts from his intense gaze instinctive. Then she slipped her fingers beneath the elastic band of her panties and jerked them down her legs. When she stepped out of them, she was naked, vulnerable and breathless.

She'd put herself on equal footing with Ramon. Both stood in the shadows, without clothing, wary and unsure of what the other would do next. Whatever he demanded, she'd comply.

But he stood unflinching, his eyes narrowing to slits.

How much more did she have to beg? Her teeth ground together. Begging grated on her even though the pride and independence that once thrived in her had been completely shattered in her desperate attempts to save her daughter. Pride fell by the wayside months ago. If begging was what he wanted, she would drop to her knees and beg.

Still Ramon stood like a statue, unmoving, unbending except for the slight twitch in his cock. Although he'd backed away, his erection hadn't slackened in the least.

Aware the helicopter could be back at anytime, Hannah didn't have the luxury to wait for Ramon to take her. She had to grasp matters in her own hands. With a deep breath, she did just that.

Her fingers reached out and circled his cock.

Ramon's hands clamped on her shoulders, the rough texture of his skin sent mixed signals throughout her body. Fear warred with desire, desire winning the rush to her brain and the lower regions governed by her physical need. Hannah held on, her grip tightening around him, her hands sliding up to the tip, circling the velvety ridge until he gasped.

Fingers dug into her arms, but he didn't shove her away. "What do you really want?" he demanded through clenched teeth.

Her gaze met his. "I want you to make love to me." She told herself she only said the words in order to buy his assistance, but the more her hand moved across the sheathed steel of his cock, the more she couldn't deny her attraction. She'd seen him naked in the hospital, pacing the length of his cell, his body strong and proud. Of all the specimens, she'd been drawn most to this one. Perhaps it was his Native American heritage or the proud tilt of his chin, the dark intensity of his brown-black eyes.

Standing naked in front of him without the benefit of the cell bars, her smock and surgical mask for anonymity, her emotions lay raw and exposed to his whim. He'd never seen her behind the mask, but she'd seen all of him and wanted him then. Now their roles were reversed and the danger only increased his desirability. Moisture beaded on her upper lip. A drop of sweat slithered down between her breasts, causing her nipples to tighten and pucker.

His gaze followed the path of the bead of sweat between her breasts and lower.

Her hands moved downward to where his penis emerged from the nest of dark hair. One hand skimmed over his balls and cupped them, rolling the hard-packed orbs between her fingers while the other hand traced his length out to the end of his penis, finding the tip and circling the moistened hole a creamy drop of cum adding lubricant to her ministrations.

"I can't be bribed." His hands tightened on her arms, making as if to push her away. "Especially by you."

"No?" Her own grip tightened. Though her own desires were climbing rapidly, she forced herself not to dart a glance to the sky. The threat of the helicopter returning was real. They might decide to come back and drop ground troops to search for her remains to ensure her silence. To guarantee her survival and his, she had to hurry this effort along. "I'll do anything." Pressing her breasts to his chest, she rubbed the nipples against his, still massaging his balls.

Though he remained still, he wasn't immune to her. His cock twitched in her palm and his body was as stiff as his heavy penis, his breath shallow and restricted. His chest heaved as he drew in a deep breath, his head falling back. Strong hands planted on her shoulders and pressed her down. "Then suck my dick," he commanded.

For a moment she stared into his eyes, wondering if she was being a fool. As a man, he could hurt her, as an animal, he could easily kill her. Deep inside, she knew he wouldn't harm her intentionally, and she wanted him.

She dropped to her knees, her fall checked by the padding of vegetation and soft, moist soil. All the hours spent in Hell Hospital observing this man had led her to many hot fantasies and cold showers. Fraternization with the patients was prohibited. But that didn't stop her own fantasies about this one. How would it feel to hold his hard length in her hand, to pull him into her mouth and suck him until he reached orgasm, his cum running down her chin?

On her knees in front of him, her heart pounded against her ribs as she smoothed her hands up his muscular thighs, enjoying the feel of his steely strength encased in dark skin. Her own hands looked pale next to his skin and she liked the contrast. With a glance up into his unwavering face, she took his cock in her hands. Without breaking his gaze, she ran her tongue from the base of his penis upward to the tip. Would he like it? Would he want more? Would he find her desirable? Thoughts tumbled through her head even as waves of desire raced south, making her moist in that one special place.

Ramon groaned, "All of it." Then he dug his hands into her hair and shoved his cock into her mouth until it bumped against the back of her throat.

Instead of annoying her, she found his force even more stimulating. The caveman approach only fueled the fire burning between her legs. With his cock in her mouth, she circled one hand behind his ass, grasping his cheek to push him away then pull him all the way into her mouth again. Her teeth nipped at the ridge of his dick, her tongue flicking the tip in tiny strokes.

Her pussy ached to be touched and she ran her free hand down over her belly. She dipped into her juicy depths, swirling around and tempting with her smooth hand. Her moan wrapped around his cock and she pushed his hip away, slamming him back into her mouth.

With both hands clutching her hair, he pumped in and out of her mouth until his body stiffened and he jerked back on her until her scalp burned and tears came to her eyes. Satisfaction curled in her belly as Ramon lost himself in her.

Cum spurted over her chin and down her neck and the fingers holding her hair, curled, the tips sharpening into claws. She knew what was happening to him, but she was too caught up in fantasies she had harbored for months. Her roots ached as she strained against his hold on her hair. She wanted him in her mouth, wanted to taste his musk. When he refused to let go, she whimpered, her hands rising to cup his balls.

Glancing up into his face, she saw evidence of what she'd done and her heart compressed in her chest. His irises had formed a long slit and his lips peeled back exposing long feline fangs. "What do you want from me?" His voice was a harsh growl, lashing out as he released her hair. "Tell me!"

Guilt warred with her longing to be with this man and she hung her head and sobbed, "I want you to fuck me. Then I want you to help me save my daughter."

"Damn you!" He stepped away and pushed a hand through his thick straight hair. "I shouldn't have done that. You push me, woman."

She knew she should be totally focused on getting her daughter back. Yet, with Ramon standing over her, naked and gleaming in the shadows, her needs overwhelmed her. "I'm not sorry."

"Well I am. I'm an animal, for godsakes!" His fist pounded into his palm. "You should be afraid."

Pushing her shoulders back, she sat on her haunches. "I'm not afraid of what you are."

"Why me? Why follow me out here?" He waved his hand at the swamp surround them.

"Yours was the only tracking device I could steal before I escaped, and I'm glad it was yours." He was the one man of all the others she'd altered that she'd felt drawn to in a way even her ex-husband hadn't been able to touch when they were married. It was Ramon Osceola who'd filled her sleeping and waking dreams, making her hot and needy, her body aching for fulfillment. A desire she didn't think herself capable of until she'd seen him naked and pacing in a cage.

He held out his hand. "Get up." His words were spoken gently, but they were a command, nonetheless.

When she placed her hand in his, he jerked her to her feet and into his arms, her bare breasts against his equally bare chest.

Red-hot electric currents seared through her veins and she fought to breathe.

"You don't even know me." He rubbed the side of his cheek against her ear and licked a path across her cheek until his lips hovered over hers. "What makes you so sure you want me to fuck you?"

Hannah grappled with coherent thought, her breathing now at marathon pace. "I know you as well as I know myself." At least that wasn't a lie. Since her daughter had been taken, Hannah hadn't known what she was capable of doing. In all her education, she never thought she'd use her knowledge to alter a person's DNA. For the sake of her daughter, she knew of no limits to the sacrifices she'd make.

Making love to Ramon would be no sacrifice. "I watched you while you were in Hell Hospital. The way you paced your cage, kept in shape and fought back in every way you possibly could. I knew you'd survive. Your determination helped show me that I too could survive and eventually escape. Which I did."

"And you came after me." He pressed his rock-hard cock against her belly.

Fire raged below. He had to take her before she spontaneously combusted.

He set her away. "This isn't going to work."

A scream burbled up her throat and Hannah swallowed it back. "Why?" As soon as the word left her mouth, she knew her answer. The whopping sound of helicopter blades slashing the air filled made her stomach flip over and her pulse pound against her ears.

Ramon stared down at her with his deep brown eyes. "They're back."

Chapter 3

"Damn!" Hannah ducked farther into the shadows and grabbed for her clothing. "Come on, we have to get out of here."

"No shit, I'm not going back to Hell Hospital," he said. "And neither are you."

"Oh, they won't take me back." As she shoved one leg after the other into her trousers, she muttered, "They'll kill me first."

The words spoken so softly froze his blood in his veins. "Why?"

"That's what they were trying to do when I landed in the water." She zipped and buttoned before she looked into his eyes. Her breasts were still bare, the sun filtering through the trees broke up the shadows across her creamy white skin and rosy areoles.

The animal in him responded to the musky scent of her creamy mound. Despite the danger, he wanted to grab her to him and drive deep into her pussy. He forced his mind to remain human and wrapped around their current dilemma. "I would think they'd want to keep you alive to do more experiments. You already know the program and have the requisite skills." He ground out the word "requisite".

Her lips twisted. "I know too much and they'd rather have me dead than my revealing all their dirty little secrets or bring the authorities down on Hell Hospital."

Ramon grabbed her arms and halted her struggle to slide her hands into her shirt. "You know where it is?"

"Yes. I know where Hell Hospital is and I know just about everything they're doing there. I can barely sleep nights knowing what I know." She shook his hands loose and pulled her shirt down over her shoulders, tucking the bra into her pants pocket. "And they don't want me back—they want me dead. And they didn't want me to reach you because I'd alert you to their plan."

"What plan?" he asked.

"I'm not sure what they wanted to do with you but when they released you, I figured it was all part of the same plan. They converted a group of Special Forces guys into shape-shifting cats."

The echoes of screams and other voices filled his head, stabbing pain into his temples. As his incisor teeth lengthened, he pressed fingers to his temples and fought the change. He remembered things, horrible things that would make a man scream in agony and then blubber like a babe. It tore your soul away and Ramon was certain it never returned. "You mean there are others like me?"

She nodded.

"How many?"

"I know of at least three others."

The approaching thunder of the helicopter blades forced Ramon into action. "Come on, I know of another place we can stay."

She stared up into his eyes, her baby-blues filled with tears. "So you'll help me find my daughter?"

"What makes you think your daughter is still alive?" He knew it was harsh. But if she knew enough to think they wanted her dead, they wouldn't have any trouble disposing of a kid.

Hannah flinched.

Although he didn't hold out hope for the girl and he had good reason to hate this woman, he shouldn't have squashed her hopes. Revenge wasn't a valid reason to take a dig at her obvious love for her little girl.

"They won't kill her until they know for sure I'm dead." It sounded as if she was trying to convince herself. "She's their leverage to keep me from going straight to the authorities. They'll use her to their advantage. Besides, they have another geneticist on staff."

Ramon's fists clenched at the thought of potentially more victims of the DNA tampering. "We have to stop them."

"You can't if you don't know exactly where the compound is. Or at least you'll take a long time finding it." She tied her button-less, damp blouse around her middle, the effort pulling it taut over her breasts. Without a bra, her rosy nipples made dark round shadows beneath the fabric.

His cock hadn't calmed from her blowjob and his previous transformation. If they didn't get a move on, he'd be tempted to take her then and there, damn the helicopter!

At just that moment, the aircraft came into view over the lagoon. Hannah shrank against a tree, hugging the shadows, her eyes wide and wary. The helicopter hovered over the shattered airboat and a man wearing scuba gear and flippers rappelled from the skid, sliding down the rope, the hand holding the rope behind his back to slow his descent. When he was within four feet of the water, he let the rope feed out through the D-Ring and he dropped into the water, submerging beneath the wrecked craft.

"We need to move while their attention is on the airboat," Hannah said. "And before they use the tracking device to find you."

"Then come on." He grabbed her hand and led her through the dense foliage. "Stay close to the trees and watch for alligators."

She sucked in a breath and blew it out slowly. "Alligators will look easy after what I've been through. Let's go."

Ramon helped her over the little hummock of land, leaping from shadow to shadow until they'd left the helicopter and diver behind. For nearly an hour, they alternated between walking and wading from island to island until they came across a hut thatched in palmetto fronds. In the water close by was a skiff with a trolling motor attached.

"Yours?" Hannah asked.

"One of my escape hatches. In the past six months, I've learned not to rely on anyone else. And I refuse to be a prisoner ever again. If it means having redundancy in my escape plans, so be it."

A smile curved her lips and she ducked her head to enter the primitive hut.

Because of his sudden transformations, Ramon had made a habit of stocking various locations with clothing in case he found himself close by after a transformation. His condition was too hard to explain to the tourists and Game and Fish Wardens wandering through the maze of tributaries.

His eyes adjusted immediately to the dark and he noted the undisturbed neatness of the tiny hut, glad others hadn't wandered in and taken his belongings.   Without a lock on the door, he couldn't guarantee the security. Besides, a lock on a thatch hut would appear as a challenge to whoever ran across the small dwelling, while traversing the twisted channels. Who would stop someone from breaking and entering in the depths of the swamp? For that matter, who would hear Hannah's screams if he decided to take her and damn the consequences?

As if sensing his thoughts, she glanced up, her eyes wide, pupils dilated, making her blue eyes appear black in the limited lighting cast by the setting sun through the open doorway.

"We'll rest for several hours and give the helicopter and search parties time to clear the area."

"We can't leave now?" She wrung her hands together, her gaze darting to the single cot standing against the wall of the building.

"If we take the skiff out in the swamp before it's completely dark, we stand the chance of being spotted. If we go too soon, they might detect our departure. I'd rather wait until they bug out before we make our move."

"We need to get that tracking device out of your back. Do you have a knife, antiseptic, anything?" she asked, searching the dark interior for surgical instruments she knew she wouldn't find.

"I have a knife." He crossed the room to a wooden box nailed to the wall. Inside was a pocketknife and first aid kit complete with alcohol pads and bandages.

"I'll bet you were a good boy scout," she said, a smile tilting the corners of her lips.

He snorted and handed her the items.

"Where did they bury the device?"

"Centered between your shoulder blades. It'll only take a minute to get it out. It might hurt a bit since we don't have any pain medication."

"Can't worry about that now. We can't stand around waiting for your friends to blow this place while we're in it."

"They're not my friends." She ripped the foil wrapping off the alcohol pads, opened the knife and swabbed the blade. "Not the most sterile means, but it'll have to do. She held the knife out in front of her and raised her brows. "Ready?"

Ramon had a moment's hesitation. Turning his back on a woman holding a knife wasn't his idea of smart.

As the moment dragged on, Hannah rolled her eyes to the ceiling. "If I planned to kill you, I would have found a way to do it already. Come into the light and turn around." Her tone left no room for argument.

Without thinking too hard on the subject, he strode to the open door and turned his back. "Just do it." As the knife pierced the skin on his back, he clenched his teeth and thanked the pain for distracting him from her body. Nothing like a knife in the back to take the starch out of his penis. He stared down at the limp appendage. *Not so impressive now, are you*? He almost laughed at the course of his thoughts if she hadn't chosen that moment to dig into his flesh. A roar rose in his throat and his claws extended from his fingers.

"There! I got it." She held the bloody knife in front of his face to show him the miniscule computer chip. "Hell Hospital tagged all of the subjects so they could keep track of your movements." She handed him the knife, chip and all. "Hold that while I clean you up."

Gentle fingers cleaned the blood from his back, applied antiseptic ointment and patched him with a small adhesive bandage. "All better and there won't be much of a scar."

"If you'll excuse me, I'd like to get this tracking device as far away from here as possible." Even before he could root around for clothing, he stepped out the door and strode several hundred yards away from the hut before he stopped. He had to get it farther away than that or the helicopter would find them. Frustration bubbled up in his chest, triggering the animal transition within. He placed the device gently between his teeth and concentrated on remembering throughout the change overtaking his body. He was much faster in feline form than in human form.

Several minutes later, he raced through the swamps farther and farther away from the hut and Dr. Richards. Deep inside, he knew he had a mission and it had to do with the bite of something in his mouth. In order to protect his den, he had to take this thing deep into the swamp.

When he'd gone as far as he dared, he located an alligator sunning near the shore. He knew they were dangerous, but deep inside that other part of him he knew this would be the place to drop his prize. Sinking his claws into the bark of a cypress tree, he climbed. On a limb out over the water, he remained balanced on his paws until the alligator maneuvered beneath him. Then he opened his mouth and screamed. Below, the alligator's tail swished and the giant reptile looked up, his mouth opening wide in the direction of the scream, ready for attack.

Before the massive jaws could close, he

dropped the tiny prize into the alligator's gaping maw. Without delay, he eased backward down the tree and raced through the swamp back to his den and his mate awaiting him.

Retracing his path, he could feel his muscles stretch and the bones pull and lengthen. By the time he reached the hut, the transformation was complete. He stood on two legs, not four, and he recalled almost all of what had occurred. Elation filled his chest. This was a first. By concentrating on his goal, he'd been able to control the animal inside and to remember the details of his transition and subsequent execution of the mission. With the tracking device far away in the belly of an alligator, they'd be safer and he could figure out what this woman really wanted from him. Then there was the matter of the incredible hard-on he had following his change back into a man. He shrugged. It couldn't be helped. But it sure as hell hurt, demanding some relief.

She stood in the doorway, a frown denting her lovely brow. Though the sun had fallen below tree-level, he could read her features. When she saw him, her frown cleared and she raced out, throwing her arms around his neck, her belly bumping into his distended cock.

He winced and set her away, rubbing at his engorged penis to ease the pain.

"I'm sorry," she said, glancing down to where his hand stroked his flesh. Her face flushed red. "I was afraid you wouldn't come back."

Refusing to turn away, he continued the steady rhythm, his hand barely easing the tension. He wanted more…distraction. "The device," his voice rumbled in more of a growl than normal. Clearing his throat, he started over. "The device is several miles away.   Hopefully, the helicopter won't locate the hut until we're long gone."

"Yes, of course." She looked out to the swamp and back to the hut, avoiding looking at his face or his hands.

The idea that she was unsettled by what he was doing amused him. He stepped into the hut, hiding his smile.

"Perhaps you should get some rest before we leave. I'll watch for intruders outside." Hannah hovered on the threshold, her lip caught between her teeth.

Ramon's hand shot out and he snagged her elbow. "No. With your shiny blonde hair, they could spot you in a moment. Best to stay inside and rest. If they don't see movement, they might not investigate.

Her gaze darted back to his naked body and the single bed in the corner. "You can have the hut, I'll rest outside."

The edges of Ramon's lips twitched. Clearly the bed and the close quarters with him had her worried. "What's bothering you? It's not as if you haven't seen me naked."

"I know. It's just—" Her hand waved as if she were trying to pull a word from the air. "I don't know…intimate."

Despite Hannah's role in his transformation, Ramon couldn't help chuckling at the doctor's inability to articulate her misgivings. Twin flags of color stained her cheeks and her lips pressed into a straight line. Ramon relented. "If I promise to put on clothes, will you stay inside?" He expected a look of relief. Instead, her gaze ripped across the breadth of his chest and traveled downward.

Blood surged through his penis, swelling it to full in a matter of that one glance. Heat flooded his own cheeks and he felt compelled to dive for the trunk at the foot of the bed. Why should he be embarrassed in front of the doctor? Hadn't he been naked in front of her for over four months? He willed the heat to fade from his face before he could turn.

"I don't know that it will help," she whispered behind him.

"What do you mean?" He straightened, his hand wrapped around a pair of worn jeans. Did she think of him as a freak? The animal she'd created? Anger spread through his body and he could feel the stiff black hairs pushing through his skin. "Don't you trust me to keep my hands to myself? Afraid I'll change into a panther if we get intimate?" Damned if he wasn't afraid exactly that would happen. He glanced down at his arms growing darker, the hair lengthening and thickening with each passing second. She should see this, face what she'd done. Ramon turned.

Her steady gaze met his. "No, I'm not afraid."

"Well, you should be. I haven't made love to a woman since you and your buddies did this to me." He turned his back to her. "I have no idea what will happen."

A hand touched the pelt on his back, smoothing down over his shoulder blades and down to his waist. "I'm not afraid of you or what you might become," she said, her voice at once soothing and exciting, like thick cream running down his throat.

He stiffened, his anger invariably fueled his change, pushing the chemical reaction that morphed his bones and muscle tissue into that of a black panther. Over the past two weeks he'd learned to control the change, but he never knew until he stopped whether or not he'd be successful.

His incisors spushed against the inside of his lips and his fingernails lengthened into sharp claws. "Why do you want this?" He didn't even recognize his voice. It came out like the scream of a wild beast instead of the angry tones of a frustrated man. He wanted nothing more than to take this woman and fuck her like there were no tomorrow. But he couldn't. He couldn't trust himself as a cat, a wild beast whose instinct was to kill its prey.

Her hand slipped around his waist and she pressed her face to his back, fur and all. "I'm not afraid of you. I've seen what you become. I know." Her hands turned him to face her and she pulled him close. "I'm afraid of myself. If I let you make love to me, will I be able to leave? I have a daughter who needs me even more than I think you do. I can't leave her. If I fall for you, I don't know if I can walk away." She pressed her forehead to his chest. "I know you must hate me for what I did to you, and you might find this hard to believe, but I've been attracted to you since you were in Hell Hospital. I can't help myself."

Her words hit him square in the chest and he could feel his claws retracting, the anger waning in the light of her revelation. He didn't want to believe her, couldn't. She was *them*. One of the sick bastards that had changed him into a monster. "Why should I believe you?"

"You shouldn't. I'm one of the enemy," she said, her words echoing his thoughts. The slender arms around his waist tightened and tears moistened his chest. "But believe this. I love my daughter and would do anything for her."

"Does that include sleeping with an animal?" He shoved her far enough away he could look into blue eyes swimming with tears.

"I won't lie. I told you I'd sleep with the devil himself to keep my daughter safe. But with you, I don't want you to make love to me in order to save my daughter. I need you," she said, her voice fading into a sob. "I need you to hold me and remind me that I am alive and away from that horrible place. I want you to be inside me to fill me until I don't remember the hell it was, the voices screaming in my memories, the look on my Lilly's face when they took her away. I need you to make me forget." She clawed his arms trying to pull him close.

But he held her away.

"I'll hold you and I'll make love to you, but it will be because I want to, not because I owe you anything. And I'm not promising I'll help you in any way."

"I understand. If you choose to help me, great," she said. "If you don't, I'll go on without you. Just hold me now until I have to leave."

Against his better judgment, he pulled her into his arms and crushed his mouth to hers. She smelled earthy like the Florida everglades he loved. A pleasant side effect to the swim she'd taken when her boat had been attacked, but he wasn't thinking clearly. He just wanted to touch, taste and feel again. Since he'd been held in captivity, he hadn't been with a woman. Hannah was convenient and Ramon was horny. Perfect combination. That she had hair the color of spun gold and eyes the blue of a summer sky didn't mean anything.

"You're taking your life into your own hands," he growled against her lips.

"I'm willing to risk it." Her hands crept up his chest and circled behind his head. "I want you no matter what you are."

A rumble started deep in his throat and he slid his cheek against hers, trailing kisses and nips down her throat.

"Ouch!" Her hand swatted at his cheek. "Not so hard. Besides, your teeth are showing."

Ramon sucked in a deep breath and willed the change to abate. He wanted to make love to her as a human, not an animal. He could do it, with enough restraint. The teeth pushing against his lips retracted with each breath he took until he knew he was back in control. Best to take things slowly.

Her fingers slipped to the front of her blouse and she untied the knot holding it together.

Ramon opened the edges of fabric, pressing his lips against her collarbone, the swell of her breast and the dip between. When the blouse was completely open, he pushed it from her shoulders. Her pale skin almost glowed in the shadowy room. Her full, bare breasts jutted out, tipped with tight round buds, begging to be taken.

As he gazed his fill, Hannah went to work on her trousers and panties, slipping them from her hips until she stood naked in the dusk.

Ramon fought back the animal surge flowing through his body. He wanted this female, wanted to claim her for his own, mark her with his scent, and fuck her until she cried out his name. Hairs sprang up along his arms and neck, his fingers curled, the nails lengthening into claws.

"Okay, you're starting to scare me," she said, her voice shaky. Her arms crossed over her breasts, barely covering the milky mounds.

Tipping back his head, Ramon concentrated on returning to his human state. He'd done it before and he sure as hell needed to now if he wanted to make love to Hannah. And he did. Oh yes, he did.

His cock was hard and aching to fill her. After several long moments, he could feel the change receding.

"That's better." Slender fingers slid around his waist and pulled him against that sweet slim body. He inhaled the scent of her, the musky sexy scent of a woman in the early throws of passion. Her hands dropped lower to cup his ass.

With his cock pressed into the silky skin of her belly, need ached in him like a strong physical pain.

But she was petite and fragile, compared to his six-foot-two frame, and he didn't want to scare her again. Despite what she'd done to his genetics, she was a woman, the weaker sex, to be cherished, her body worshipped.

He dropped his head to one of her breasts and sucked it into his mouth, his tongue circling the hard round bead, his teeth clamping down, tugging gently.

Hannah arched into him, her head falling back exposing the long line of her throat to him, pressing her breast deeper into his mouth. "I want you, Ramon," she moaned and swayed against him. "Now."

"Patience," he whispered against her other breast, treating it with the same attention as the first. He could feel the heat building within her, smell the warm scent of her excitement.

His own body quickened, his cock filled,

straining to be inside her. But he wanted her need to equal his before he took her—wanted her to beg him to take her inside him, to spread her thighs wide and show him how ready she was for him.

"You don't know how often I dreamed of this," she said, her leg sliding up the back of his.

Moving his hands lower, he traced the line of her waist downward to her hip and across to the silky blond hairs covering her *mons*. He parted her folds and rubbed a finger over the swollen nub. She gasped, her fingers digging into his shoulders. "Oh, yes. Oh, yes." The leg circling his calf convulsed, clutching him nearer as she tried to angle herself closer to him.

"Not yet."

"Why?" she breathed. "I want you now."

"You're not ready."

"Not ready?" she wailed. "I've been longing for this for months. I'm so hot I could spontaneously combust. And you think I'm not ready?"

He smiled down into her face as his fingers dipped lower. First one, then two fingers entered her channel, sliding into the creamy depths clenching around his digits. She was hot and wet for him, but he wanted more. "I want to taste you here."

Her body trembled, her eyes widening. "There?" Her hand slid down his arm to where his fingers lay buried inside her and hers joined his. "Then do it."

Ramon bit hard on his tongue, hoping the pain would keep him focused and stable in the throes of his rising passion. Often he changed without warning and he didn't want to blow it now. He wanted this woman and he wanted to prove to himself that he could have a woman again without succumbing to the animal within.

With a low growl in his throat, he shoved her against the wall and dropped to one knee.

She steadied her hands on his shoulders and looked down. "What are you doing?"

His answer was a long gentle flick of his tongue.

She moaned and her hips undulated to the rhythm of his strokes.

He trailed her juices up to her sensitive nub and flicked and teased it until she screamed, her body stiffening, her orgasm pulsing all the way through her.

Without relenting, he continued his assault until she sagged against the wall. "Umm, Ramon?" Hannah's hands dug into his hair and pulled him away. "Are you changing again? Your tongue is a lot rougher. Go easy."

He breathed deeply and held still for several seconds until he had it in control again. "Sorry."

She shrugged and smiled down at him. "Not to worry. I kinda liked it. Just not so intense."

"I don't want to hurt you. I have other plans before we're done here."

"Ummm. Show me." She guided his head back to her pussy.

With her juices on his lips, Ramon didn't know how much longer he could last. If he wasn't careful, he'd come like a teenager all over himself or worse — he could change into a panther and hurt her.

With one final lick, he eased her leg from his shoulder and stood, sliding his chest up her torso enjoying the sensation of his body rubbing against hers. Then he lifted each of her legs and settled them around his waist. "Ready?"

"You should know." She eased down over him, her slick channel sheathing him in heat and moisture.

Ramon closed his eyes as sensations rippled across his nerve endings, the need building in his balls making them tight to the point of exquisite pain. Then he was pumping into her, thrusting deep until his balls slapped against her. She met him thrust for thrust, balancing her hands on his shoulders.

When his orgasm hit, he raised his face to the ceiling and screamed his release, all the primal feelings of man and cat rolled into the sound.

"Ouch. Careful with the claws, big guy," she said into his neck. "You're scratching my ass."

Immediately he dropped his hands and noted the hairs springing from his skin. Damn. The orgasm waned as he realized he'd lost control of his change. A knot formed in his belly and he couldn't look at Hannah. "Get off."

"Why?" Her legs still wrapped around his waist tightened, refusing to release the hold her cunt had on his cock. "I like it just where I am."

"Get off," he growled. His lips curled back baring his feline teeth.

A stubborn look crossed her face and her arms circled his neck, her lips hovering close to his. "No. I told you I want you any way you come."

And he came.

Not once, but twice before they had to leave.

Chapter 4

He was still angry. She could see it in his eyes. Several hours later when they were settled in a 787 airplane heading west, he sat with a pout as good as any eight-year-old's. He'd been half changed, buried inside her and she hadn't let him go. He'd felt so damned good that she'd refused to let him off the hook.

And she didn't care. The man had to know he was sexy and she wasn't afraid of a little cat hair or pointy fingernails. She'd wanted him as badly as he'd wanted her. And she'd known the dangers of fucking a genetically altered man. If anything, his alteration only improved his attraction in her mind. And she could swear his cock was bigger than when he'd been a mere human.

Her panties grew damp at the visual conjured of him standing in the hut, erect and proud. Hannah wiggled in her passenger seat, hot and wanton. If the flight attendants could read minds — oh, boy!

Ramon's nostrils twitched as he sat next to her, his eyes closed as if in sleep. But he hadn't let sleep claim him. While trapped on board an airplane, he'd been extremely alert to any changes in his body chemistry. If the change came on while he was in the air, they'd be hard pressed to explain it, and Hannah wasn't so sure the animal in him would respond well to the close environment.

As nervous as he was, she was even more

so. She'd sat clutching his hand, trying to appear relaxed while hoping he wouldn't change into a panther. Not until the wheels touched ground in Dallas did she breathe a sigh, hurrying him off the plane and out of the airport as quickly as possible. They still had quite a distance to cover to get to the compound in Waco. The two days that had passed since her escape seemed like a lifetime. She hoped to hell they still thought she was alive. As long as they did, her daughter had a chance.

"Worrying won't change anything," Ramon said from the passenger seat of the transport they'd rented at the airport.

"Maybe not, but I can't help it." She shot a glance his way, admiring his high cheekbones and the straight sleek black hair secured in a leather strap at the nape of his neck. During his time in captivity, his hair had grown longer and despite his release, he hadn't bothered to have it cut. It was as much a part of him now as the Seminole blood flowing through his veins. As a member of the Special Forces, he'd had his own choice of hairstyles. They were encouraged to grow their hair if they wished to erase all connection with the military. Blending in was their directive. Once back on American soil, the military granted him an extended leave of absence after his ordeal in captivity. He'd not had call to cut the long, thick black hair.

Hannah was glad. She liked it when it brushed over her skin, the coarse texture stimulating her nerve endings. Her hand twitched on the armrest, her fingers aching to run through the length. For more reasons than his military abilities, she was glad he was with her. He grounded her in confidence, made her feel like they could conquer the world together, or, at the very least, rescue Lilly.

The drive to Waco took a little under an hour, the traffic heavy and slow at times. Based on information Hannah had overheard over the past few months, the Branch D compound was located on the historical landmark where a religious cult had fought to survive against fanatical American forces in the early nineteen nineties only to burn to the ground-women and children dying in the flames. The history of the site and political significance had appealed to the leaders of the Genetic Research Institute when choosing to build an alternate complex.

As they drove into the city of Waco, darkness settled over the dry, Texas landscape so foreign from the swamps of Florida. Their timing was perfect. With little vegetation in this part of the state, darkness would be their only cover to allow them to sneak past the security sensors and into the compound.

Hannah's stomach knotted in anticipation. She prayed she was right about where they'd taken Lilly. It only made sense. The other geneticist had visited the alternate site on multiple occasions, commenting on the sparse medical facilities available there and the prison-like accommodations.

"Do you think we have all the tools we'll need?" As if checking off a list, she went through the items she thought they'd require to break through the fences. Then came the high-end security system and concertina wire around the compound. Ramon was a professional, he'd know all there was to know about infiltration and attacks. More so than a geneticist. She only understood how to muck up a human's DNA structure. She bit the inside of her jaw. Her nerves made her want to run off at the mouth.

"We have what we need," he responded, his tone clipped, discouraging further talk.

But Hannah couldn't sit back in the heavy silence they'd shared since leaving Dallas and she needed to clear the air between them. Reaching out, she touched her hand to his arm. "I want you to know I'm sorry for my part in your genetic reconstruction. If it had only been me, I wouldn't have done it."

The only indication he'd heard her was the tightening of his hands on the steering yoke. His attention remained focused on the GPS direction finder on the transport dashboard.

So he wasn't ready to forgive her. What did she expect? Would she have forgiven a person so readily if the circumstances had been reversed? Probably not. Her hand dropped to her lap and she stared forward, letting the silence stretch between them like a tightrope on which neither would venture out.

When they were within a mile of their destination, Ramon drove the transport off the road and parked it behind a stand of mesquite and scrub oak trees. Climbing out, he broke off several branches and stacked them against the vehicle on the side visible from the road, effectively camouflaging it from curious eyes. "We walk from here."

Her heart thundered in her chest, Hannah fished the backpack loaded with the tools they'd need from the back seat.

Ramon took the pack and slung it over his shoulders. "Perhaps you should stay here," he said.

Hannah shot a glance at his rigid face. What a difference from the man who'd made love to her in the Big Cypress Swamp. Gone was the passionate lover and in his place was the taciturn soldier, the Seminole warrior bent on going to war without the women. To hell with that! "You don't know what my daughter looks like. I'm going."

"It'll be dangerous."

"I don't care. That's my daughter out there. She might not go with you unless I'm with her."

"So be it. But don't get in the way. I want to get in, get your daughter and get out. Then you can tell me where Hell Hospital is located and we can call it even."

The wind sucked out of her sails, Hannah walked beside Ramon, the lead lump in her belly weighing her down with each footstep. The tall dark warrior meant to be done with her after he'd fulfilled his promise to rescue Lilly. The thought of never seeing him again left her chest hollow and achy. Hadn't she gone into this deal with her eyes open? Hadn't she known this man would travel alone and avoid lasting relationships and commitment?

His profile spelled it out. He'd never married, only dated once or twice before moving on, and he never took a woman home to meet the family. Not that he had much family left. His love life read like the history of a sailor with a girl in every port, but none for long. Then why did she feel empty, as if she'd lost her best friend? She couldn't lose something she never had. Besides the great sex they'd shared in the swamps, what did she have?

Nothing.

They moved along in silence. The anticipation of seeing her daughter again, lifted Hannah's spirits, tempered by the realization that they might be in the wrong place. Doubt set in, taking hold and scaring the shit out of her.

For all she knew, Vaughan could have hidden her daughter in Hell Hospital and told her he'd taken her to an alternate site, just to mislead her. When she'd escaped, she knew she was taking a chance. She hoped she'd taken the right chance. If her daughter was inside the walls of the Branch D compound, with Ramon as her guide, they'd bring her out. Of that, she had no doubt.

Stars lit their way across the flat landscape with the occasional live oak tree casting moon shadows across the grasses. After what felt like an eternity, buildings appeared on the horizon, rising up from the lonesome prairie, the boxy lines stark against the endless night sky.

With her heart pounding against her ribs, Hannah fought to remain calm. She couldn't afford to lose it now. Her daughter's life depended on her and Ramon getting inside the compound.

As they approached the outer chain-link fence, Ramon's steps slowed and he ducked low to the ground, his head turning left and right, observing everything.

"Are we going through the fence? Should we get out the tools?" she whispered, her nerves making her mouth shift into high speed.

Ramon held a finger to his lips and eased along the fence line toward the road leading through a gate. A lone guard stood in a lit gate shack, armed with an automatic weapon like those used at Hell Hospital.

Despite the warm night air, a chill shivered

down Hannah's spine. "How are we going to get in?"

The low rumble of a cargo transport came from the distance. Ramon's head cocked in its direction. "Come on." He backtracked until they were out of sight of the guard shack and headed away from the compound.

"Where are you going? We can't turn back now! My daughter could be in there! Are you quitting on me?" Her voice rose in a hysterical whisper. Although she'd said she'd get her out by herself, Hannah had no idea how. Ramon was the key to freeing Lilly. He couldn't walk away now. "Fine, I'll go back on my own. I won't let them kill my daughter, even if I get killed trying to free her. And I have no idea how I'll do it, but I'm not a quitter." She stomped back across the grass toward the compound, tears blurring her vision.

A hand clamped down on her shoulder and jerked her around and into Ramon's arms. "Don't you ever shut up?"

Before she could respond, his lips clamped down on hers.

All thoughts of conquering the compound single-handed flew from Hannah's mind in that one blinding, kiss. When his mouth left hers, she gasped for breath and sagged against him.

"At least now I know how to shut you up," he said against her hair. Then he shoved her to the ground as lights from a cargo transport lit the road a few hundred yards to their south. It was headed toward the compound, slowing as if looking for the gate.

Hannah shifted closer to Ramon as the sting of prickly pear cactus needles pierced her right arm. "You could have found a better place to hit the dirt than a cactus," she grumbled, her words trailing off as the vehicle grew closer. It would pass within ten feet of where they sprawled in the dirt.

Hannah held her breath, afraid of what would happen if the driver spotted them.

After the transport passed, Hannah let out a sigh, which was cut short when Ramon grabbed her hand and yanked her off the ground. "What the hell are you doing?" she hissed, trying not to yell loud enough the driver could hear her.

The muscles in her arm screamed as she raced to keep pace with Ramon. He was chasing the back of the transport. When he reached it, he jerked the handle of the rear door and a miracle occurred. It opened.

Without warning, he hurled her into the back and leaped in after her, closing the door behind them.

She laid flat on her stomach, her lungs hauling in huge gulps of air. A genlight glowed green, illuminating Ramon's face and the grin tilting his lips.

"What the hell did we just do?" she gasped.

"Hitched a ride inside the compound. So shut up and hide behind those." He motioned toward some boxes stacked against the inner walls.

The transport slowed and a shout sounded outside.

Hannah scrambled to her feet and threw herself behind the stacks. Ramon slid behind her just as the door burst open. Peeking around the corner of the boxes, Hannah could see the gate guard's weapon aimed inside.

From her perch behind the box, nestled in the warmth of Ramon's arms, Hannah could just barely see the guard standing at the rear of the transport.

"Look, I've been driving close to nine hours to get this stuff here. Mr. Mitchell wanted these supplies delivered ASAP. Check the invoice. It's all in order," the driver said.

"I don't care how long you been drivin', this load ain't goin' nowhere until I have a look."

"All I know is Mitchell wanted it fast. If you delay the goods, it's your funeral."

"What's in the boxes?" The guard stepped up into the back of the cargo hold, the bed of the transport shifting with his weight.

Hannah pressed her fingers against her lips to stifle her gasp. A few more inches inside and he'd see them hiding in the shadows like the fugitives they were. Ramon's arms tightened around her and he pressed a kiss to her ear.

The frantic beating of her heart calmed a fraction. If the guard saw them, Ramon would deal with him. No problem, right? Ramon was Special Forces. He could handle anything. Hannah sure hoped he could. They couldn't afford to alert the entire camp before they had Lilly safely away.

"Hell if I know what these guys are sending." The driver stood on the ground outside the door. "I don't ask. I'm not paid to know what's in the boxes. I'm paid to deliver and keep my mouth shut."

"Pretty trusting, aren't you?" said the voice in front of the boxes.

"I like living with all my body parts arranged just the way they—"

Rumbling filled the air as a helicopter swooped low overhead.

"Wonder what the fuck all the excitement's

about." The guard leaped from the back of the cargo hold and turned toward the sound of the chopper. "Helicopters have been comin' and goin' all day."

"Beats the shit out of me. Now, if you're done holding me up, I'd like to ditch this stuff and get the hell out of here."

"I guess you're okay. Go on." The door shut, extinguishing the light from the guard shack and the stars.

In the dark interior of the cargo transport, Hannah inhaled a long shaky breath and snuggled into Ramon's arms.

*****

Not for the first time that evening Ramon regretted bringing Hannah along. She didn't have the military training to perform this mission. And the more she was with him, the more he felt responsible for her well being. He needed a team of highly trained Special Forces men to get in and free the girl, not just one man and a geneticist. What had he been thinking?

That was the problem. He hadn't been thinking with his brain. Yup. That was his problem. He hadn't been thinking with the proper organ. Since he'd joined the service, he'd made an unwritten rule that he'd never get involved to the point he'd lose focus. And he'd done just that. Lost focus.

The scent of woman filled him and made him want to take her in the back of the transport. If he were any less of a man, he would. But they had a job to do first. Like it or not, he was stuck with Hannah as his assistant.

He shifted her out of his lap and felt his way out from behind the boxes to crouch between the stacks. "When the transport stops, wait for my signal to move, and don't make a sound. Got it?"

"Got it," she said from the darkness.

The vehicle rumbled through the compound and came to a stop a few minutes later.

"Hey, Osceola," Hannah whispered.

He could smell her fear and wished he could reassure her, but he didn't have so much as a plan to get them through the next few minutes. "Yeah."

"Thanks for helping me."

She risked making noise just to thank him for helping her. Ramon would have shaken her, if he could get to her and back to his position before the door opened. But he remained in position and shook his head in the dark. "I just want to know what part of Africa Hell Hospital's in." That place needed shutting down before anyone else was hurt.

"It's not in South Africa, Ramon. Hell Hospital is here on the southwestern border of Texas in the Davis Mountains," she said.

"What?" Ramon tilted back on his heels as if he'd been slammed in the gut. "It's in the States?"

"Yeah."

"How the fuck—"

Before he could say another word, the door flew open and a forklift slid up to the back of the transport.

Ramon had been captured on a mission in South Africa and when he'd been released, he'd been in South Africa. He'd assumed Hell Hospital was somewhere in Africa, not the United States. How the hell did something so horrific operate without detection in his home country? How could the government allow it to happen?

Unless the government was involved.

Chapter 5

Hannah hadn't meant to tell him about Hell Hospital until they'd freed Lilly. But if she didn't make it out alive, she wanted Ramon to know where it was so he could stop what they were doing before other innocent lives were ruined.

She knew the staff at the hospital took great pains to keep the location secret, especially to the experiment subjects, but she wasn't prepared for the shock in his voice. And now with the door wide open and a forklift's prongs reaching inside their hideout, she didn't have time to explain or reassure him in any way. They had to get out now, or risk discovery.

"In here," Ramon whispered. He slit the plastic wrapped around a group of boxes and tossed one out on the bed of the truck. Then he grabbed her hand and pushed her between the boxes, shoving the backpack in after her. He followed her into the tiny hole he'd made where they crouched between stacks of cardboard boxes. They were hidden on the very pallet the forklift prongs slid under.

The pallet beneath her feet shook and rose from the ground and the beeping sound of heavy machinery made when in reverse echoed off the metal walls of the cargo transport. They were moving out of the vehicle and from what little Hannah could see between tiny spaces between the boxes, transferring them onto the loading dock of the largest building in the compound.

If Lilly was here, the biggest building seemed the most logical place to hold her. And if Hannah knew Vaughan Mitchell, he'd have set guards all around her in the event anyone was fortunate enough to make it inside the compound.

The close space and dread robbed Hannah of her ability to breathe properly. Her head felt light and her knees buckled. If not for the hand resting on the small of her back, she'd have passed out already. But that hand grew heavier and claws poked into her before long.

"Damn," Ramon said behind her. "I'm sorry, but sometimes, I can't stop it." The words started out sounding normal, but by the end of his sentence, they were more of a rumble than coherent sounds.

Her heartbeat skittered to a stop for two full seconds.

The pallet jolted against the concrete floor and she gasped, her heart slamming against her chest. The warmth behind her disappeared and she knew Ramon had slipped out of the hole and onto the loading dock.

Before she could ease completely out from between the boxes, she heard the scream of a large cat and the startled yell of the forklift operator. Another yell sounded from the direction of the truck. Hannah cleared the boxes in time to see a sleek black panther clamp powerful jaws into the neck of the truck driver, piercing his vocal chords and killing the man instantly.

"Who the hell are you?" a voice asked behind Hannah.

Fear sent tingles across her skin, raising the flesh in goose bumps. But she couldn't turn and face this new threat. Her gaze was riveted on the huge cat, staring straight at her with blood dripping from wickedly sharp teeth.

When the panther's muscles bunched and he moved toward her, Hannah's knees shook and she almost fell to the ground. She backed against the boxes and tried to scream, but nothing would come out. The creature leapt toward her, missing her by mere inches.

The man behind her yelled, "What the hel—" his voice cut off and reduced to a gurgle as the cat snapped his neck with one potent bite. The panther dropped the man and stared at Hannah for a moment, then he ran for the door leading deeper into the building. His sleek movements were soundless in the dead silence of the loading dock.

Hannah fought the bile burning a path up her throat and gathered the backpack and Ramon's clothing and shoes from the ground, before racing after the vicious animal he'd become. As she sidestepped the dead men whose blood spilled onto the concrete from the gaping wound in his throat, she wondered if she'd made the right decision to enlist his help. It wouldn't be long before someone discovered the dead men and the rest of the compound would be alerted. With only minutes to spare, they had to hurry and find Lilly. Then get the hell out.

*****

With the metallic taste of blood in his mouth, his stomach rumbled, but he didn't have time to feed his ravenous appetite. A sense of urgency pushed him through the overhead door standing open and ready for the forklift to carry the load of boxes into the storage room. In the far corner of the cavernous space, another door was secured with an optical scanning device. Ramon struggled to understand its significance, knowing he couldn't get past it without an appropriate scan.

As Hannah hurried up behind him, the handle twisted and Ramon growled a warning, shoving her to the side with his nose, using a little more force than was necessary. She hit the wall and gasped, her eyes going wide. He didn't have time to worry about whether or not he'd hurt her.

When the door opened, a man stepped through.

Ramon lunged at his face, sinking his teeth into the unsuspecting victim's windpipe. The man died instantly, his body falling across the threshold. The door swung closed, but the dead man's body blocked it from closing all the way.

Leaping across the inert man, Ramon led the way down the hall, sniffing every door for the scent of a child or someone resembling the woman hurrying to keep up. He could sense her horror, smell her fear and something deep inside him hurt. Even in his present form, he knew she was the one that made him this way, but he also knew she was forced to. But her horror at how he'd killed those men had shaken him down to his paws. Although he knew he could think more rationally as a human, he didn't want to change back into a man at that moment. The pain was easier to take as an animal, his emotions more readily masked in the black-as-night face of a panther. If he could, he'd stay a panther forever rather than witness that look in Hannah's face again. She'd been terrified of him and repulsed by what he'd done. How could she ever look at him like a man again without fearing the beast within?

A shout heard around a corner and the

vibration of booted feet pounding against the tiled floors, reverberated through his paws.

Hannah opened a supply closet door. "Get in," she said, holding the door wide for him to comply.

He hesitated, resisting the thought of being restrained in a small closet.

"They'll kill you and then how would Lilly and I get out of here?"

Another shout echoed in the hallways, energizing him into action. He leaped into the closet as men in solder's uniforms rounded the corner. They carried the same automatic weapons as the gate guard and they headed for the loading dock.

"They must have discovered the bodies," Hannah said, sneaking a peek out into the hall. She gasped and jerked her head back when another person hurried by in a white lab coat. "I know that man."

The transition back to human would happen no matter how much Ramon fought against it, but the change overcame him so fast he couldn't focus enough to try to halt it. His bones and muscles stretched and lengthened, the pain of the quick alteration blinding him for the few short minutes it took to complete the transformation. When his vision cleared, his heart sank to his knees.

Hannah stood silhouetted in the limited light coming in from the vent in the door. The clothing and backpack was held close to her chest like a shield, her eyes wide and wary.

When he straightened into a standing position, he held out his hand.

She jerked away, and then her face softened,

a frown denting her brow. "I'm sorry, it's just a lot to handle."

He reached out and tugged on the clothing she held against her body. "Do you mind?"

"Oh, I'm sorry. Here let me help you." She dropped the backpack on the floor, flung the jeans over one shoulder and held open his shirt.

"I'm perfectly capable of dressing myself," his voice sounded gruff, the residual of a growl making it harsh. He reached out to snag the shirt from her hands.

She held it away from his grasp. "I know that, but this way will be more fun."

What game was she playing? "We don't have time for fun."

With a brow arched, she shook the shirt. "Then quit arguing."

He shrugged, refusing to read into her gesture. Instead he turned sideways and slid his arm into the shirt. When he had the other arm in the sleeve, she moved around to his front and pulled the shirt over his shoulders and together.

When she leaned close to secure the buttons, the lingering effect of his transformation nudged against her belly.

Her brows flared and she gasped.

Ramon tilted his head back and tried to breathe normally to will the reaction to abate. He wanted her so badly his cock throbbed with need.

It didn't help that her scent wafted toward him, her arousal apparent in the musky aroma filling the confined space. How could this happen when she'd been terrified by him only moment before?

With a deep breath, he snatched the jeans from her shoulders and turned to dress facing the door. Better to resist temptation. When fully dressed, he reached for the door handle. No time like the present to find her daughter and get the hell out of there.Hannah leaned over Ramon's shoulder, absorbing the heat from his body as he eased the door open and sniffed the hallway.

"Stay behind me." He settled the backpack over his shoulder and slipped around the door and down the hallway, slowing at each door until he stopped in front of one.

Hannah's heart hammered in her chest. "What is it?"

"I think your daughter is behind this door."

"How can you be sure?"

He tapped a finger to his nose. "She smells like you."

"Lilly?" Hannah pressed her ear to the door and called out a little louder. "Lilly?"

"Mom?" a female voice said from the other side of the door. "Oh thank God."

Hannah almost cried when she saw the door was equipped with an eye scanner-locking device. "How can we get in?" She glanced both ways down the hall.

Ramon calmly shrugged the pack from his shoulders, dug inside and pulled out a wad of lumpy clay. He packed it into the doorjamb next to the handle.

"What's that?" she asked.

"A little old-fashioned explosives."

"Won't it be really loud?"

He shrugged and pressed a metal device into the putty. "Probably."

She twisted her hands together and darted another look up and down the hallway. "Well, then do it." She leaned against the doorframe.

"Get behind something, Lilly."

Ramon grabbed Hannah's hand and pulled her away from the door and down the hall twenty feet, then pressed a remote control device.

A small bang shattered the silence and a puff of smoke filled the air around the doorway. Other than that, it didn't appear to have budged the door. Hannah's stomach dropped to her knees, her disappointment a sour taste in her mouth. "What now? How can we get her out without someone who can activate the scanning equipment?" As the words left her mouth, alarms rang out. "Great, now they know where to look."

Chapter 6

If the entire compound wasn't due to converge on them any moment, Ramon would have laughed. "Have faith, doc." He loped to the door. Just as he reached it, the door swung open and a young lady the image of Dr. Hannah Richards, twenty-years younger stepped through.

Hannah rushed forward and wrapped her arms around the blonde woman. "Lilly!"

"Mom!"

Ramon reeled backward, his mind having a tough time wrapping around what he saw. "What the fuck?"

"We can do the introductions later, let's get the hell out of here." Hannah let go of the young woman and grabbed her hand, hauling her back the way they came.

Ramon shook his head to clear the wool gathering there. "If you want out, going back to the loading dock might not be a good idea."

Dr. Richards turned to face him. "You're right. Got a better idea?"

"We find another exit before they find us."

"Any idea where we could start looking?" Hannah asked Lilly.

"This way." Lilly led the way around a series of corners and down several hallways until she stopped in front of a door with a brass nameplate. Engraved in brass was the name Vaughan Mitchell.

"Got any more explosives?" Lilly asked.

"Yeah." Ramon stepped to the door, digging out another clump of the plastic explosives. As he smashed the pliable product around the door handle, he shot a glance at Hannah. "I was picturing a little girl in pigtails."

Hannah's face flushed and she stared at down at him. "Would you have refused to come if I'd told you she was full grown?" Hannah hooked an arm around her daughter's waist. "Lilly's eighteen. But she's still my daughter, and I'd still do anything to save her from these people."

"I get the feeling there's something going on here, but could you two hurry it up?" Lilly glanced over her shoulder. "I hear people shouting down the hallway."

Ramon glared once more at Hannah and then pressed a detonation device into the explosives. "Get back." He herded the women down the hallway and pressed the remote detonator. The bang shook the floor and the puff of smoke filled the hallway.

When it cleared, the door stood slightly ajar.

"Is there an exit from inside his office?" Hannah asked.

"Even better." Lilly hurried around Ramon and into the office.

Hannah followed with Ramon close behind her. He had a few questions to clear up with the doctor. But first they had to get out of the building.

"Vaughan's the top-dog around here and kinda thinks he's above all the precautions," Lilly was saying.

"So? Where's the door?"

"He doesn't have a door, but he has a helluva big window." Lilly pressed a button on the wall and a shield slid sideways, revealing a floor-to-ceiling plate glass window with a view of the fields beyond the compound.

Ramon lifted a heavy office chair and flung it at the window. The window cracked, sending a long fracture across the center, but it held. He lifted the chair and slammed it against the window again. This time a tiny hole appeared and several shards of glass fell to the carpeted floor.

Hannah lifted a smaller chair and crashed it against the window in the same spot. Between the two of them, they enlarged the hole until it was sufficient for them to fit through.

Dropping the chair to the floor, he stripped his shirt from his back, laying it over the jagged edges. Then he motioned to Lilly. "You first."

Lilly hugged her mother and ducked through the hole, dropping to a crouch outside on the ground.

When it was time for Hannah to go through, a noise caught Ramon's attention, and he glanced toward the doorway.

"Stop right there!" A man stood at the threshold, pointing a pistol at Hannah. "Take one more step and I'll shoot Dr. Richards."

"Vaughan Mitchell, don't you ever get tired of threatening people to make them do what you want?" Hannah stepped in front of Ramon but far enough away that he couldn't knock her aside without lunging toward her. "Don't worry about me, Ramon. Get Lilly out of here."

"What the hell do you think you're doing?" Blood jettisoned through his body and the hackles rose on the back of his neck. The change was on him and he could do nothing to stop it. If only he could hold on to his humanity until he figured a logical way out of this mess. But the transformation surged forward. "I'm not leaving without you."

"Don't worry. You won't have to leave without her because you're not leaving." Vaughan said. "You don't have a chance of getting off the compound, even if you make it out of this office alive. Security is on alert and they've been ordered to shoot to kill. That goes for anything that moves." The man's eyebrows rose and he stared straight at Ramon. "Including large animals. Good to see you again, Sergeant Osceola."

Rage mingled with the pain of his transition and he fought to keep from crying out. He knew this man's scent and he knew what he'd ordered done to others in Hell Hospital. Beyond that, his mental functions were sliding into a more primitive instinct for survival and protection of his territory. His mate was being threatened and he had to do something about the predator.

He dropped to all fours, an angry cry rising from his throat in a roaring scream. With slow, deliberate steps, he stalked toward his prey, sliding his body against his mate as he moved by.

"No!" she shouted.

But Ramon wasn't listening. The scent of fear emanated from the man with the hard metal weapon. Good, let him worry. Let him fear the power of a pissed-off panther.

"Stop there or I'll shoot."

His words were garbled, almost foreign to Ramon's hearing, but he understood the intent and his footsteps halted, his back legs bunching up behind him, getting ready.

The man's hand shook, and the weapon wobbled. He spoke again.

This time, Ramon wasn't listening. All his concentration was centered on the scent of blood running through warm flesh. He knew he couldn't attack straight on. Cunning would be key to taking down this creature.

Ramon leaped to the left as a shot rang out, echoing against the walls of the room. His feet barely touched ground and he pivoted and lunged at the man's throat, his jaws clamping into the jugular. With a twist of his head, he ripped open the throat and blood spurted out. The weapon fell from his victim's hands and he crumpled to the floor, his body jerking several times before he stilled.

"Ramon!"

Someone was calling to him.

His teeth remained buried in the throat, and he refused to let go. He wanted to rip out the heart and guts of this predator in warning to others who dared threaten his clan. Hands grasped the ruff on the back of his neck and tugged.

When he looked up, he recognized the eyes of the human staring down at him. Tears streamed from them and she shouted in a language he struggled to understand. She let go of his neck, grabbed the backpack and clothing from the floor, and then moved toward a hole in the window, waving at him to follow.

Ramon spared one last glance down at the dead creature lying on the floor before he released his victim and followed the woman. When she motioned him through the hole, he stood firm.

After she stepped through and down onto the ground below, he leaped through the opening and out into the night air.

Sirens pierced the air, ringing in his ears,

urging him to run as fast as he could to get away.

Two women stood in the grass, urging him to follow them. His mind told him they were his family, and he needed to protect them and get them away from this terrible place. Trotting ahead, he spied men carrying long weapons.

Keeping to the shadows, he worked his way toward them. When he was within striking distance, he lunged at the one nearest him, knocking him to the ground and snapping his neck in one fatal bite. The other man aimed his weapon and fired off shots, the rounds missing their mark.

Ramon leaped into his face, his teeth ripping into his eyes and dragging skin and tissue down over his nose. The man screamed, dropped his weapon and clutched at his face. A quick glance behind him indicated the women were still following and he moved on.

When they came to the fence, Ramon set to work digging a hole beneath the wire. Within seconds, he had a hole large enough for all of them to fit beneath. Hannah and her daughter scrambled on their hands and knees, shimmying beneath the wire to the other side. He followed and they ran as far and as fast as they could away from the compound.

The whomping sound of helicopters filled the air and lights beamed out over the landscape. They had to find cover quickly or risk being captured. Ramon led the way, searching for something to crawl under. Behind him, the younger woman stumbled to her knees and fell, crying out. His Hannah dropped back to assist her. Her gasp and shout alerted him to stop his search and return to help.

The scent of another of his kind filled his

nostrils and his feet slowed. The woman on the ground writhed, twisted and changed before him.

His humanity struggled to surface from the animal clouding his brain. He needed to understand the significance of what was happening to the woman. The animal in him recognized her as one of his kind.

When the transformation was complete, a sleek jaguar shook out her coat and stood on all fours.

Hannah dropped to her knees, hands over her mouth, her eyes streaming with tears.

Ramon understood grief and rubbed against her, trying to soothe her, to take away her sadness. The jaguar eased up next to her and stared into her eyes as if to reassure her. She nudged Hannah's cheek and licked at a tear sliding off her chin.

With one hand, Hannah hugged the jaguar to her and circled the other arm around him, pulling him close, her tears still falling. For several long minutes, they crouched in a huddle, absorbing their combined strength.

The longer they stayed in one place, the nearer the high-powered beams from the helicopters swept, moving closer to their position with every passing minute.

Ramon urged Hannah to her feet. She gathered their belongings, tucking clothing and shoes into the backpack. With the jaguar on one side of the woman and him on the other, they ran and ran until Hannah could run no more. When they stumbled into a dried-out gully, Ramon left them to search the creek bottom for shelter from the searchlight. A few hundred yards down the gully, the banks were overhung with tree roots and large boulders sufficient to hide a human and two large cats.

Racing back to the Hannah and the jaguar, he urged them to follow him. They ducked beneath the overhand just in time as the helicopter's floodlight swept the length of the gully.

Tucked beneath the overhang, Ramon could feel his body shifting and changing until he lay as a human once again, the rocks and roots digging into his naked skin.

Behind him, the jaguar shifted and changed into a beautiful young woman. Hannah gathered her daughter against her and rocked her, sobbing into her silky blonde hair. "Oh baby, I'm so sorry. I was too late."

Chapter 7

After a tense half hour, the helicopters moved on. Ramon, Hannah, and Lilly climbed out from beneath the overhang and continued following the path of the gully until it crossed a road. Moving under the cover of night, they found their way back to the transport hidden in the bushes and drove back to the city of Waco and then headed south toward Austin, each quiet, lost in their own thoughts.

Hannah moved in a daze, knowing what had to be done, but refusing to talk about what had happened back at the compound. She should say something, but she didn't know where to begin.

"Mom, don't shut me out," Lilly said from the backseat of the transport. "I need you now more than ever."

"I'm not, honey. I'm just not ready to talk about it."

"Well, you'll have to someday," her daughter said, settling into the back seat.

"I can't. Not now." Hannah buried her face in her hands, the tears returning. "This is all my fault."

"No, Hannah. The Genetic Research Institute was responsible for all this." Ramon reached out and grasped her hand in his. "You were a pawn in their plan. They used you."

"Look, Mom. I'm alive," Lilly insisted.

When Hannah turned to look at her lovely

daughter, the tears fell faster. *They'd fucked with her DNA!*

Lilly shrugged. "I'm a little different, but I'm alive. And that's what counts right?"

Hannah stared out at the dry Texas landscape, her deeds weighing heavily on her soul. "I should have refused to perform the experiments. I played God and this is my punishment."

Ramon slowed the vehicle and pulled off the side of the road. Grasping her chin in his hand, he turned Hannah to face him. "If you hadn't done what they demanded, would your daughter would be alive today?"

She shook her head. He used the same arguments she'd used when she'd gone to ask for his help—the same rationale she'd used when she'd altered human genes to become animals. Another glance back at her daughter made her feel like someone was stabbing her heart, it hurt so badly.

"Is the problem that you can't accept me for what I am?" Lilly leaned over the back of the seat, her hand resting on Hannah's shoulder. "Is that it? Do you hate what I've become?"

"No, baby." She grasped her daughter's hand. "I could never hate you. I love you more than life."

"She shanghaied me into helping in this rescue, at great risk to herself." Ramon smiled at Lilly. "I'd say that's proof enough."

"Then don't be sad," Lilly said, smoothing the hair back from Hannah's forehead. "I can't stand to see you like this."

"I'm just sorry it had to happen to you. I wanted so much for you. A life, a family, love someday."

Lilly squeezed her hand. "Who's to say I can't have all that still?"

Ramon's gaze met Hannah's. "She's right. Who's to say she can't have all that?"

What was he trying to say? Was she trying to read more into Ramon's words than what she heard on the surface? Did he want her in his life? Had he learned to trust her? Hannah's head spun with hope and the possibilities. Then she fell back to the earth. *Get a grip, girl. He's just trying to help you fix things with your daughter.* "You're right, honey," Hannah said, though her gaze never left Ramon. "With the right man, you can have all that."

"I know, Mom. You were the one I was trying to convince. Frankly, I think it's kinda cool to be part human and part animal. I've always wanted a fur coat but never wanted to kill an animal to get it."

Laughter bubbled up inside Hannah and she shot a twisted smile at her daughter. "I can count on you to look at the bright side."

"Yeah, I learned it from my mother." Lilly glanced ahead. "Now, what are we going to do to shut down Genetic Research Institute?"

"You two aren't doing anything," Ramon said, his mouth firming into a line. "I'm dropping you off in Austin and going on without you."

The hope she'd felt a few moments earlier crashed around Hannah's ears. He'd had no intention of continuing on with her.

"Like hell you are!" Lilly leaned over the back of the seat. "We're going."

Lilly's declaration shocked Hannah out of her quickly growing depression. She'd just gotten her daughter back. She didn't want to lose her all over again. "Maybe Ramon's right. We aren't trained to launch an attack on Hell Hospital."

"I don't care," Lilly said, crossing her arms over her chest. "I want to be a part of taking them down. I want to be there when Hell Hospital burns to the ground."

The more Hannah thought about it, the more she agreed with Lilly. Her daughter was old enough and had endured enough to make her own decisions. When she opened her mouth to protest Ramon's edict, she halted when he raised his hand.

"It's not up for discussion." True to his word, Ramon refused to discuss his decision all the way to Austin where he left them standing in the parking lot of a transport rental company.

After all they had been through together, and the incredible sex they'd had, Hannah couldn't believe he'd just drop them off and leave. For all she knew, she'd never see him again and that made her saddest of all. A knot formed in her throat, choking off any final goodbyes as she stared after his vehicle speeding out of sight. Even though she had her daughter back, her life still felt empty without Ramon.

"So, what's it to be?" Lilly asked. "Are we going after him?"

*****

The drive to Southwestern Texas was long and lonely, especially since he'd left Hannah in Austin. He missed her more than he cared to admit. But she'd gotten what she'd been after. Lilly. Not a small child, but still her daughter and someone she loved very much. How would it feel to be loved like that?

He didn't know and probably never would. Now that he was part man and part beast, he may never know that kind of love. What woman would accept him if she knew?

Hannah would accept him. Although she'd been heartbroken by her daughter's transformation, she still accepted and loved her. Nothing could ever change their connection.

Then why was he, Ramon Osceola, confirmed bachelor and loner, dreaming of happily-ever-after? Even if he hadn't been a mutant, he wouldn't have wanted a woman permanently ensconced in his life. Hadn't he worked hard at discouraging commitment?

Absolutely!

Until Hannah. Her fierce love and sexy curves wouldn't quit clogging his brain. He couldn't think without a memory of Hannah taking root in every thought. Her honey-blonde hair, pale, silky skin and her ability to love so deeply had slipped beneath his defenses. Now all he wanted was to go back and claim her as his own.

Deep inside the foothills of the Davis Mountains, Ramon knew he couldn't go back until he'd done what he came to do. Hell Hospital had to come down. After he accomplished that, he might just go back to Austin and look her up. If she was still there.

Fuck!

He slammed his palm on the steering yoke, sending the transport skidding sideways. He hadn't made any arrangements to meet with her. He had no idea where to find her.

Fuck!

With his heart firmly lodged in the pit of his belly, eating a hole through his gut, he pulled into the Last Watering Hole, the combination bar and filling station Hannah had mentioned as the place to stop before he ventured into the Davis Mountains to Hell Hospital.

He'd rather go on, but his mouth was dry and he needed to load up on food and water in case he ended up hiking the rest of the way to his destination.

When he stepped into the shadowy bar, a familiar scent crowded his senses overwhelming him with memories of the cells back in Hell Hospital. Not the smell of Dr. Hannah Richards, but the smell of another. A tall blond-haired man Ramon had never seen before, stood next to the bar, his hand holding a drink frozen midway to his mouth. The glass slipped from his fingers and crashed to the floor, shattering into wicked shards, the liquid spewing across the concrete floor.

"Hey, buddy, that'll cost you," the bartender shouted.

The man didn't answer, instead he stared at Ramon, his head tipping upward slightly and his nostrils flaring as he sniffed the air. "I know you, don't I?"

Ramon nodded without thinking and sniffed. "Yeah."

A man walked in behind him and the same sense of recognition struck Ramon. He spun to face the new arrival, his heart pounding against his ribcage. *What the fuck?*

The new arrival, a shorter man with dark brown hair and olive-toned skin, stopped in his tracks and stared from Ramon to the man at the bar and back to Ramon. "What's going on?" he asked, his brows dipping toward his nose.

"I don't know, but maybe we better take it outside," the man at the bar suggested.

A creepy feeling slithered across Ramon's

skin, the tingle of transformation threatening to launch inside him. He fought back the change and led the way back out into the oven-like heat of late afternoon in South Texas.

As he stepped out into the sunshine, a transport skidded to a halt in front of them.

Lilly leaped from the passenger seat, a grin spreading across her face. "You can't stop us from helping, you know. As soon as you left us, Mom and I rented another transport and here we are!"

He'd never been happier to see someone as when Hannah climbed out of the vehicle, her gaze locking with his, no smile on her lips, her eyes wide and concerned.

With the two men emerging from the building behind him and the two women standing in front of him, Ramon was struck with the feeling something big was happening.

But first things first, he wanted Hannah in his arms.

As if sensing his need, she moved forward, falling into his arms, kissing his face as if they hadn't seen each other in a long, long time, not just half a day.

"I didn't think you'd be happy to see me," she said, laughing and crying at the same time.

"I forgot to get your communication link for when this was all over," he said. "I'm glad you came. I never realized how much I could miss you."

"Me too." She rested her forehead against his chest and took a deep breath. "We wouldn't let you go back in there without help. We care about you." She inhaled a deep breath and let it out. "I care about you. I couldn't bear the thought of you going in alone."

"We didn't have to worry about it," Lilly said.

Suddenly remembering the young woman beside them, Ramon stared across at Lilly. "What do you mean?"

Lilly sniffed the air and nodded to the men standing behind him.

Hannah shot a glance at her daughter and then peered around Ramon, her breath catching in a gasp. "Lilly's right. I believe the cavalry have arrived."

White Tiger

By
Delilah Devlin

Chapter 1

"Either he's the dumbest terrorist I've ever seen, or he wants to get caught."

Casey McTaggert blinked at the burly Military Intelligence officer beside her and pushed her glasses back up her nose. She wasn't accustomed to sitting thigh-to-thigh with a man — and definitely not one of such awesome proportions. She wasn't sure whether she liked it or not, but the skittering nervousness gripping her each time she addressed him was...interesting.

"Khalid's not a terrorist, and he isn't stupid," she shouted over the roar of the turbine engine and the *whomp-whomp* of the helicopter's blades.

Captain Sorensen snorted and turned his attention back to his small handheld satellite link-up. "I'll take your word on the first," he said, in his thick Texas accent, "but the bastard's headin' straight toward the southern wall. You'd think he'd zag at least once."

Scooting as close as her harness allowed, Casey peered down at the small screen showing the infrared feed. Khalid Razeh's pale-colored SUV traveled in the dark down a rugged, gravel road at a fast clip.

"Does he think he can outrun the Border Patrol's Incident Response Team?"

She shrugged, unwilling to share at the moment what she thought about the Afghani national's most recent activities.

The square-jawed soldier didn't appear to want her opinion anyway and continued to scowl at the screen. "It's like he's telegraphin' his destination—hasn't veered off his course once. If he knows we've spotted him, I have to wonder whether he's just tryin' to draw us out." He pounded his fist against his thigh. "Shit!"

Sorensen unsnapped his tactical radio mike from the shoulder strap of his web gear. "Oscar-three-one, this is tango-four-niner, over."

"This is oscar-three-one."

"Scramble the anti-artillery. We may be headin' into an ambush."

Casey tugged at his sleeve. "Captain, I really don't think that's something we have to worry about. I believe he intends to turn himself over to us."

"He's a wiley fucker—pardon my French, ma'am. I'm not takin' any chances with my team. And get that damn helmet back on!"

The helmet lay at her feet, just beyond her reach over her fat briefcase. She strained against her harness until her fingertips touched the fabric covering the hard shell and dragged the helmet up.

When he gave her another pointed look with his ice-chip blue eyes, she sighed and plopped the heavy helmet on her head, tucking her hair behind her ears to snap the chin strap closed.

Somehow, she didn't think the desert camouflage quite matched her neat, navy-blue suit.

The helicopter swung like a pendulum, buffeted by the heavy winds preceding a line of thunderstorms heading toward the Texas's Big Bend country.

Casey clasped her briefcase tight against her chest and swallowed against the urge to empty her stomach on her escort's suede army boots. "Khalid isn't stupid," she repeated under her breath.

"Well, ma'am, you should know."

And she should. She'd been following this particular combatant's career for the past eight years, exclusively.

"That's why you're here. God, help us." He muttered the last under his breath and shook his head at the vagaries of his commanders who had placed a desk jockey in his care.

Casey wrinkled her nose in irritation, but kept silent, just thankful to be "here" and a part of this momentous event.

"Here" was the newest model Dark Hawk helicopter, speeding toward the southern border wall. Wind shear continued to batter the helicopter as it swung right and dropped, taking her stomach with it. Casey was several hundred feet above her comfort zone. She hated flying. But she'd jumped at the chance her superiors gave her to finally get a close-up look at the man who'd fascinated her for all her professional career.

The past several weeks had been filled with excitement. When the photo taken by the spy-cam at a Parisian coffee shop frequented by Arab extremists had surfaced, giving a grainy but definable image of his face, she'd been shocked at how young he appeared.

Reviewing the snippets of data she'd gathered over the years, she'd calculated he had to have been an adolescent when he'd participated in the Kandahar Offensive. A child reared on a war front. But somehow he'd managed to educate himself. The communiqués he'd issued in Arabic indicated he wasn't a radical Muslim Shi'ah bent on martyrdom — he was a Muslim who supported

secular policies to strengthen coalitions in his part
of the world.

A focal point now for dialogue rather than
violence, his actions most recently indicated he was
weary of war. God knew, two decades of
unrelenting violence had taken its toll on the entire
world.

His tactics often put him in direct
confrontation with the United Amer-Euro nations,
but having immersed herself in the culture and
history of the Middle East, she'd secretly come to
admire him—a modern David with unshakeable
principles fighting an equally zealous Goliath.

Or so the official dossier she'd compiled
said. One of the reasons she'd come this far from
her Washington bureau desk concerned a second,
even more tantalizing revelation about Khalid's
shadowy past.

She pulled out the photograph one more
time. Now in his late 30's, the strength of will that
had enabled him to escape the expeditionary forces
in the mountains of the Hindu Kush through a
maze of networking tunnels for weeks on end
wasn't evident in the lean, almost ascetic face. He
looked like an artist rather than a warrior.

Long, straight black hair brushed the tops of
his shoulders. The features of his slender face were
oversized—large brown eyes, lush lips, a nose with
only a slight hook, and a strong, square chin with a
cleft. He was beautiful. His features could easily
have graced any Byzantine icon -- so
indistinguishable from any particular Middle
Eastern ethnicity did he appear.

Why was he here? What monkey wrench
was he preparing to pitch into the works? What
greater plot had he hatched? With the upcoming

peace talks, his presence so close to the U.S. border boded ill for the outcome. Had she misjudged his evolving role at the center of the peace movement?

If their sources were right, the man they watched approach the southern fence was indeed Khalid. Little was known about him, except that he'd been on Interpol's Most Wanted List for ten years — a known operative from the Black Jihad Coalition, labeled a terrorist by most of the western alliance nations.

But as an analyst working deep inside the U.S. intelligence community, Casey was savvy enough to understand he was just like most of the operatives her agency employed. No less deadly. No less secretive or obscure. No more a terrorist.

Khalid was a master tactician, a soldier in a global war able to infiltrate and blend in with any environment. The question was why he'd blown his carefully guarded cover a week ago and allowed himself to be photographed, and then followed, by a surveillance team.

From the profile she'd compiled and maintained over the years, she knew he never made careless mistakes like that, so his action had to be deliberate.

Which was what made his second suspected identity that much more plausible. If he was indeed "The Tiger", it was her job to ID him and bring him in from the cold.

The SUV had come to a halt near a lonely stretch of wall. The surveillance cameras trained on the vehicle as Khalid stepped out on to the dusty trail.

He strode to a point just below the wall, looking as though he gauged the height. Which was nuts. If he tried to climb it he'd be barbequed by the electric wire stretched across the uppermost level of the walkway at the top of the thick wall.

Then he walked back a hundred paces and stood, moonlight silvering his midnight hair.

If she had blinked, she would have missed the transformation as his body seemed to shiver and melt, and suddenly, a white tiger stood in his place.

"Mother fuck—"

Casey's fingers dug into the captain's arm as she realized what had happened—what Khalid really was and the true significance of his code name.

The tiger charged at the twenty-foot fence—its lithe, but powerful frame gathering speed until it leapt, clearing the height of the fence, not touching down on the top of the five-foot-wide walkway. He'd cleared the fence entirely!

"We have a breach! Shoot to kill!" Sorensen shouted into his mike.

"No!" Casey bit out. The need to capture and glean intelligence from Khalid's mind had been her primary directive. Now a new imperative presented itself.

However, Sorensen ignored her, continuing to shout orders to the airborne team in their stealthy helicopters, dropping like vultures to the desert floor, soldiers spilling from their bellies as the din of gunfire and commands erupted in a cacophony of organized confusion.

At the center of the melee, the white tiger leapt to a rocky outcrop to shield its body from the gunfire.

A line of fast-moving Hummers with men standing in machine gun turrets burst over a rise. Just as the helicopter she traveled in touched the ground, an explosion ripped apart the aircraft to their right, sending a fireball into the air.

Sorensen reached across her to unlatch her harness. "Get to cover!" he shouted as he freed himself.

Casey fell out the door of the helicopter, still clutching her briefcase close. Her heart pounded in her chest. Her movements seemed to slow as though she'd entered a bad dream where her body and feet were mired in quicksand.

An arm circled her waist—Sorensen's, she saw—and he was shouting still. But she couldn't hear him above the salvo of explosions ripping apart the ground around them.

"Get to the rocks," he roared into a lull between blasts, and shoved her forward.

With her precious briefcase still clutched to her chest, Casey landed on her knees, shredding her nylons. She picked herself up, half running, half crawling up the outcrop—away from the vehicles that were one by one exploding around them.

When she found a large boulder, she slid behind it and covered her ears, and then realized Sorensen hadn't followed her. She peered over the rock and saw him lying several yards away, his hand outstretched on the dirt, his helmet nowhere to be seen.

She started for him, determined to bring him to safety—no matter he topped her weight by at least a hundred pounds, but something hard snaked around her waist.

With the incoming artillery from beyond the southern border slowing, she turned a wary glance behind her, only to see the object of her professional obsession holding her.

"Come with me," Khalid said, strong British inflections apparent in his clipped tone.

The hard set of his jaw told her there was no use arguing, but she cast a wild glance toward the captain lying so still at the foot of the outcrop.

Khalid shook his head once and lifted a rifle, Army issue in appearance, from along his naked thigh—his message unmistakable.

Hoping she hadn't misjudged the man who held her life in his hands, she let him lead her down the other side of an escarpment to an abandoned Hummer, its driver and crew nowhere in sight.

"Get in!" he said, his voice brusque, as another large explosion had her ducking her head.

With her heart hammering at her chest, she dumped her briefcase in the backseat and scrambled into the driver's side, following the point of his weapon. She started up the vehicle as he climbed into the seat beside her.

"Drive!"

She wiped her sweaty hands on her skirt and set the vehicle in motion, backing away from the chaos beyond the hill. "We can't escape the artillery!" she shouted. "It's aimed at you, not those guys!"

His stare was level, no trace of acknowledgement for what she said in his expression. She tried again. "You have a GPS chip—they're honed on you. But you already know that—it's why you were traveling so fast."

His stoic expression gave no hint of his thoughts. "You will remove it. Now!"

Aghast, she glanced in the rearview mirror only to see another round churn the dirt in the road behind them. "We can't stop! We're still in range of their fire from the other side of the border."

"You have something to cut with?"

"On my key chain—a mini-Swiss pocketknife."

"Where?" he asked, eyeing her suit.

"I-In my briefcase."

"Drive very fast!" He reached behind her, his arm close to her shoulder.

It finally penetrated her thoughts that he was entirely naked. Of course, she thought, how was a tiger supposed to bring a change of clothing?

The briefcase banged against the back of her seat as he pulled it over his knees. The latches sprang open with their familiar click and before she could remember to voice a protest, he was staring at the photo on top of her stack of files.

Casting him a wary glance, she pointed the vehicle down a trail and kept silent, letting him figure out for himself what she was doing with a dossier of Khalid sightings and analysis in her case.

He paused only a moment and snorted and then unsnapped a pocket. Pulling out her wallet, he eyed her Universal ID card and tucked it back into the pocket. Next, he reached inside for her keys. "Pull over. You will cut out the tracking device."

She blinked. "You trust me not to slit your throat?"

He held up the tiny two-inch blade and lifted one dark eyebrow.

With a sheepish shrug, she said, "So, it might take some serious sawing to do any damage." She pulled to a halt and held her hand out for the knife. When he set it in the center of her palm, she twirled her finger. "You'll have to turn around. The chip is behind you...embedded in the back of your neck."

"How do you know this?" he asked, his dark eyes narrowed in suspicion.

"You think you're unique? Shifters like you have been turning up around the world."

"You know so much. Do you know why I am this way?"

"No, I don't. I also don't know who's responsible. But until you showed your fur back there, we thought only our guys were affected."

"I am singled out."

"Yes, but why?"

His jaw tightened. "You know so much—you tell me."

Casey eyed him, every lean, muscled inch of his broad chest and shoulders, as she thought about her answer. "Because they know who you really are. They figured out you're one of ours."

Chapter 2

"I'm right, aren't I?" Casey unsnapped her helmet and let it drop to the floor behind her. "You're 'The Tiger'!"

His expression shuttered closed. "The tracking device." He turned abruptly, and drew his hair away from his neck.

He may not want to talk about it, but she was too excited to let the subject drop. She knew she was right! "I knew it even before you showed off back there. But how'd *they* figure it out?" she asked as she ran a finger over the back of his neck, feeling for the slight bulge that would indicate the device.

He snorted. "I was coming to ask you that question."

Gritting her teeth, she pressed the tiny blade to his skin, pushing it just deep enough to lift a little flap. The tracking device slid out, and she held it on her fingertip to bring it around for him to see.

For a moment, he glared at the small square chip, and then he reached behind him and pressed his fingers to the small wound that had released a trickle of blood down his nicely shaped back. "Throw it out the window and drive."

She did just that, not making conversation again until several miles lay between them and the tracker. "We have to get you some clothes and find a phone."

"Just keep driving — and turn off the

headlights."

She didn't argue. The sky was mostly cloudy, but a little moonlight peeked through to provide enough light to guide her down the gravel path. "You've barely an accent. Middle Eastern, anyway. Must have spent a lot of time in the UK. How'd you manage that?"

"You ask too many questions."

"I'm guessing that since you've been pretty busy from your teens on, you spent time there as a child?"

"Do you nag your subjects to death?"

"I don't know—you're the only 'subject' I've studied for the past few years." She shrugged at his narrowing glance. "I can't help it. This is so much more exciting than intercepting transmissions or eavesdropping on snippets of cell phone calls."

"You have a very boring job."

Casey blinked. Was that a sense of humor? In the distance, she saw a lone light.

"Pull in there."

She slowed, but approached cautiously. "It doesn't look like anyone's home."

"Precisely the point."

"You don't have to worry about a repeat of what happened back there. With that chip gone, we can go anywhere. You know, the military was there to act as escort. I only have to explain who—"

"You will not get a chance to explain. You will die."

Casey gulped, realizing her bubbling excitement over finally being proved right had let her forget she was a captive. "You're going to kill me?" she asked, more curious than afraid.

He rolled his eyes. "I cannot be brought in.

Whoever is responsible for my current state has more planned for me."

"I don't understand."

"I carry an image in my mind—of a place. I have never been there, but I am compelled to follow a path."

"The shifters we recovered don't have that same...compulsion."

"I do not believe it is connected with the change to my DNA. It is something else."

Curiosity was Casey's middle name. It was what made her excel in her profession—how she'd earned the plum assignment of following Khalid's career exclusively.

Sitting before her was the greatest, most intriguing puzzle she'd ever encountered, and she wasn't influenced one little bit by the fact he wasn't hard to look at. She just wished he'd lose the briefcase draped over his lap so she could satisfy another "need to know" fact. "I have a credit card in my wallet—we could stop at the nearest Wally World for some clothes."

"Why do you not have a cell phone?"

"Captain Sorensen took it from me." At the lift of one eyebrow, she added, "He was my escort. He was very thorough—didn't want me to compromise the secrecy of the mission." A twinge of regret had her fingers tightening on the steering wheel. Sorensen might have been a bit overbearing, but she hadn't wished him harm. She hoped he hadn't been killed in the attack.

"As much as you talk, I can understand his concern."

"Oh, I'm great at keeping secrets! Really! It's just meeting you..."

He tapped the top of the briefcase. "This

means nothing now. After I have proper clothing, I am leaving you behind."

"But you can't! You need me. I know things about your…condition."

"Do you know who held me? Who experimented on me? Do you know how they found me in the first place?"

"Well, not that. But I do know that a few others seem to be converging on this area of Texas. A few we haven't been able to get to. It's what clinched it really."

He shook his head, wincing as though it hurt. "I don't understand."

"Before I saw you shift—I knew." She shrugged. "In our daily briefings, we've been following ex-POWs, or trying to. They're gathering in this region. The agency doesn't know why either."

"Do you know where they go?"

"I know where to start looking." He couldn't get rid of her now—he needed her! She lifted her chin. "I'll show you."

"You will take me there. But first, we must find another vehicle."

His gaze swept over her, leaving goose bumps prickling across her skin. "Gotcha, we have to ditch this Hummer. We are kinda conspicuous."

"When you get me to where the others are, you must leave me."

Casey was ready to promise him anything not to be left behind now. She nodded.

She spotted the outline of a pickup truck, parked beneath a corrugated tin carport. "Can you hotwire a car?" Khalid watched the woman's mobile mouth curve into a mischievous smile. She had no idea how close he was to pouncing. Her scent beneath the sweat and dirt teased his nostrils like the flick of a cat's tail. She teased at his senses, tugging at his cock which jerked against the smooth leather case he'd perched on his lap.

Never had he been so distracted from his purpose. Just another thing he hated about the changes in him. He seemed to have lost control over his ability to shut out physical needs. His mind was no longer the captain of his body.

It was just an added irritant that he really did need her to accompany him. The woman obviously spent too much time in a sheltered cubicle — far from the harsh glare of reality. Her unshakeable enthusiasm and curiosity contradicted the image of the stale, world-weary analyst he would have conjured. She was almost…innocent…in her wonder.

His instinct for self-preservation reared up, reminding him not to relax his guard in her disarming presence. She was a woman — an attractive one despite the wire-rimmed glasses sliding down her nose and the messy knot of blonde hair pulled tight at the back of her head. The prim suit hugged slender curves, almost boyish in their lack of definition. Her legs, however, were extraordinary.

Neat, slender ankles, long straight calves, and smooth round knees.

His cock approved, straining against the case.

"Do you know how?" she asked, her eyes shining in the moonlight with a hopeful glitter.

Most assuredly, he knew how. But he did not think he was responding to the correct question. He shook himself and looked around. The truck. "Yes. I can…hotwire it. Cut the engine."

With the M-19 he'd "acquired" back at the wall strung over his shoulder, he bounded from the vehicle, supremely aware of the wag of his rigid cock. He didn't bother to turn away from her. Better she should know her affect on him now. Perhaps it would curb her…enthusiasm.

Her gasp was gratifying, but he ignored her and strode barefoot to the dented truck.

Minutes later, he sat behind the wheel, glad to have something else to occupy his attention— besides her ripening arousal.

He could smell it.

She shifted on the truck seat and cleared her throat. "Daylight's gonna be upon us soon."

He wanted her relaxed. Pliant. Women loved to talk, he recalled. "You don't sound like you're from Washington."

"I'm not. I'm from Oklahoma."

"Your accent isn't very southern."

"Well, when you're blonde and blue-eyed, and you have a thick twang to your voice, no one takes you serious."

"I take you seriously." He turned to give her a look filled with sensual promise. "I thought you should know," he said softly, curious now to see her response.

She blinked rapidly, her expression dumbfounded. "You mean…as a spy-catcher?"

He frowned. "As a woman I intend to fuck."

Her jaw dropped open.

"Why do you think I brought you and not one of the soldiers back there?"

"Because I was the only woman and you could more easily subdue me?"

"You weren't the only woman. But you

were aroused."

"What?"

"Before the attack, the scent was fading, but I caught it still. I was drawn by it. Were you flirting with the soldier who shoved you out the helicopter?"

"I certainly wasn't flirting. And I certainly wasn't aroused!"

He liked her embarrassed outrage, and it amused him how easily she could be riled. "You're aroused now." He dragged a deep breath into his nostrils. "You can't lie to me about that. There is one good thing about the changes in my body. I have an excellent sense of smell. I can smell arousal and fear. I was curious at first about your absence of fear. Now, I realize it's because you haven't any better sense."

"That's...that's insulting!" she sputtered. "I'm not really afraid because these things are all new to me. I'm still...processing."

"You sound like a computer."

"I work closely with one."

"You make it sound like a friend."

"It's an AI—we have the most fascinating conversations."

"I bet you do."

A long pause stretched between them, then...

"Besides, we don't have time to fuck."

A smile stretched his mouth. She was thinking about lying with him. "Sure we do. We have to find a place to hide before daylight rises and wait until the stores open. I might get arrested in this condition."

Her gaze dipped to his cock, and her cheeks flamed. "Right. An arrest for indecent exposure would cap a really hellish night."

He rolled down his window, letting the cool night air fill the cab, enjoying the brush of it over his skin. But it did nothing to cool his ardor.

Then he saw the gravel track to the right that led to a copse of trees in the distance. He followed the track away from the road, far from any sign of human habitation, and parked the truck. Determined now, he let himself out of the cab. He smelled water nearby and followed his nose.

A door slammed behind him, and Casey followed more slowly into the shadows cast by moonlight and leaves. "Are you taking a leak or something?"

"No. We'll stay here until the stores open in the next town." He pushed back more branches, forging a trail.

"So, tell me," she said, sounding a little breathless. "Just how do you think you're going to go into town naked and buy clothes?"

"I'll stay here. You'll go."

Her footsteps ground to a halt. "Why would you trust me not to call the agency?"

Khalid's gaze captured hers. "By the time you leave for the store, you'll do anything I ask."

She gave a short gust of laughter. "And you're going to persuade me how?"

"I'm going to show you what kind of man I really am — you will believe in me." He continued toward the sound of running water.

"I'm not some Pollyanna," she said, stomping in dried leaves. "I don't believe the world's a happy place, and I know what kinds of atrocities 'good' men can commit against each other. Why do you think I'll believe you — and *help* you, for God's sake?"

He halted again and turned back to face her. "Because you already believe in me — and you're dying to know what happens next. Take off your clothes."

Her eyes widened like saucers in the moonlight. "I will not!"

"Suit yourself." He turned and parted the brush, slipping through it and into a clearing at the edge of a narrow stream.

He wasn't disappointed long. Casey crashed through the vines and branches behind him, emerging with her hair straggling around her shoulders.

Not waiting for her reaction, he set his weapon against a tree and stepped into the stream, wading toward the center. The water came to only mid-thigh, so he knelt and let the fresh coolness sweep between his thighs and around his raging cock.

"You could have mentioned the creek," she grumbled.

"I did not wish to agitate you further. I prefer to begin sex with a clean body."

"I wish you'd stop saying that. You're just doing that to discomfit me."

Khalid couldn't help the grin stretching his lips. "You think I'm wearing this erection because I want to annoy you?"

"It doesn't take much to get a guy going." Under her breath, she added, "I know that much."

"You think I get this way around any woman?"

"Any woman who smells of arousal apparently — or so you said." She sounded grumpy, edgy — she smelled deliciously horny.

"Casey McTaggert, take off your clothes and join with me."

Her hands fisted at her sides. "I'm on a mission. I can't compromise myself."

"We are on the same side," he said softly.

"Are we? I'm not so sure any more."

"You like being right. Why do you doubt yourself now?"

"Because…" Her eyes glittered in the darkness. "I'm not used to wanting anything this much."

"Ahhh…" He nodded. "You are missing holes—huge caverns—in your notes. Will you not fill them? Won't you let me…fill them?"

"I don't like being a source of amusement," she said, her voice tight now.

"You think I ridicule you?"

"Look at me," she said, spreading wide her arms. "I'm not exactly…fuckworthy."

She believed it—he could see it in her pink cheeks. "Why not let me be the judge?"

She drew a ragged breath and stepped closer to the edge of the creek. "This is like recreational sex, right? Just to get the tension out?"

"Are you very tense?"

"Uh huh."

"Then, yes. We will have recreational sex. But you still have to remove your clothes."

She swallowed and cast a wild glance around them. "Is the water clean? Cows aren't pissing in it upstream?"

"Where is your optimism? Of course it's clean. I smelled it, too."

"You don't know how unsexy that nose of yours is becoming."

"But you will take off your clothes."

"Yes." She sighed as though this was a great effort. "How about turning around until I'm in the water."

"It's dark here."

"Along with that awesome hooked nose of yours, I know you also have enhanced night vision."

"I'm going to taste every inch of you, Casey. Do you think I'll keep my eyes closed the entire time?"

She sucked her lower lip between her teeth. "Guess not."

His heart pounded faster when she shrugged off the jacket and turned to hang it on a branch.

"I feel like there ought to be some cheesy music playing."

"I like the sound of the water. It's soothing."

"If you say so." She ducked her head and unbuttoned the row of tiny buttons down the front of her blouse, then gave him a quick, nervous glance before opening it and letting it too slip from her shoulders. The pale cups of her bra glowed in the moonlight.

Khalid's balls tightened, drawing closer to his groin. He dropped his hand below the surface of the water and caressed his cock, warming it with his hand.

The skirt quickly followed, as did the frayed hose and her plain pumps. When she stood looking awkward in just her underwear, he turned his back.

The sound of silky garments sliding over smooth skin sent shivers along his neck. His skin prickled with awareness.

The first sloshing sounds had his back

stiffening, fighting the urge to turn toward her and gather her close. He needed so badly to sink inside her body—find ease for the ache in his groin, growing more painful by the moment.

But he let her make her own way toward him, timidly, hesitantly.

What he didn't expect was that she would circle him to stand in front of him as he knelt.

Her hands settled on his shoulders. "I'm not sure what happens next…what you want."

His gaze roamed her small, round breasts and the narrow curve of her waist. Afraid to touch her, he gripped his thighs under the water and leaned forward to take her nipple between his teeth.

Her nails bit into his shoulders as his teeth nipped the hardening bud.

"Aw, God," she moaned and leaned closer, pressing her breast deeper into his mouth.

He opened wide, sucking her breast into his mouth, working the nipple with the flat of his tongue. The velvet softness of her areola invited the stroke of his tongue, so he circled it, pausing to gently chew her hardened nipple.

Still, he didn't reach out to hold her. He feared he'd leave bruises if he did now.

"Khalid, please, please," she moaned. She widened her legs and her rich, ripe scent filled his nostrils.

He let go of her breast and moved across to the other, nudging it with his nose while he breathed in her delicate scent. When his teeth closed around this nipple, she shivered and her hands clasped the back of his head.

Khalid liked the way her fingers sank into his hair to curve around his scalp. She combed through his hair, dragging hard when he suckled deeply. He released her breast, but continued to lap her skin with his tongue, laving the soft underside of her breasts, then working his way down her quivering belly. Groaning, he traced the contour of her belly button, pressing his tongue hard against the soft button and enjoying the throaty moan it produced.

Then he leaned down to lick his way toward her sex. Crisp, clean hair — curling, but soft — tickled his nose and her legs widened again, inviting him lower still. When he tongued her cream-coated folds, his sex jerked between his legs.

"Oh, God," she groaned, her fingers tightening around his head.

Khalid sucked on her outer lips, savoring her salty-musk flavor. His whole body tightened against overpowering need to plunge inside her…fuck deep into her moist, hot core.

"Inside me," she whispered. She pulsed her hips, her movements a little jerky. "Lick inside me, please, Khalid."

With his own body shivering now with restrained lust, he let go of his thighs and lifted his hands to carefully part her folds. His thumbs opened her like the petals of a fragrant rose. When next his tongue slid between, he hardened it to spear inside her portal.

A deep shudder racked her slender frame, and she cried out, her whole body growing rigid as she strained against him. "Please, please…more."

Allah! He'd not known a woman's softness or her many flavors in so long. He'd withheld himself, kept true to his faith. But his hunger, his *beast's* hunger, overrode his strict personal code. He meant to devour her.

Chapter 3

Khalid inserted shaking fingers inside her channel and glided them in and out of her moist heat, mimicking the movements he would make when his cock entered her sweet body.

He leaned toward her, inhaling her fragrance, closing his eyes for a moment to savor and commit it to memory. Then he opened his mouth and suckled the small hard bud that peeked out from the top of her folds, swirling his tongue on it until her begging ceased. Soon, she shivered like a leaf clinging to a branch in the wind.

Her response was gratifying and made him feel powerful, masterful in a way he hadn't in a very long time. When her moans became a soft, never-ending wail, he lunged up from the water and grasped her hips, pulling her up flush against his body. Her arms eagerly wrapped around his shoulders, and he cupped her buttocks, lifting her higher until the head of his cock slipped between her legs. Her eyes clenched tight and her breath hitched as she waited for him to make his next move.

Staring, studying the way her mouth pouted and her features strained, he slowly rotated her hips until he found her opening with his sex.

At the last moment, she opened her eyes and stared back at him. Holding her gaze, he said, "I can't be gentle." The roughened quality of his voice didn't surprise him. Every part of him was reined tightly on the verge of violence.

Her hands tugged his hair hard, and she leaned close to brush her lips along his cheek. "Just fuck me, Khalid. Fuck me hard."

His fingers widened to grip her ass hard, causing her to cry out. Then he drove her down his cock—all the way down—not giving her time to catch her breath, not letting her body adjust to the size of his cock.

Casey screamed, her cry strangling at the end while he lifted her off. When he jerked her down his length again, his buttocks flexed and drove his cock upward. He forced himself deeper inside her then let her slip off, only to drive hard inside her, again and again, while she writhed, her thighs clasping tight around his waist.

Casey's hot, tight channel drenched him in liquid fire, rippling around him, squeezing, welcoming his harsh invasion. With her hands clutching his shoulders, she labored to lift and grind down in opposition to his movements, increasing the friction between their bodies— building a slippery heat between his cock and her channel. Her lips drew back in feral grimace as she matched his ferocious strokes.

Up and down, they strained against each other, grinding their bodies close, groans escalating as the carnal violence they did to each other reached its climax.

At the last moment, Khalid held back, gritting his teeth against the need to release the beast growling and clawing to be free. Instead, he grunted and tucked his face into the crook of her shoulder and let his seed pump inside her, aided by the rhythmic pulses caressing the length of his cock.

Her channel milked him, squeezing tight

around him as her rocking movements slowed, soothing him as he hugged her close.

Her fingers dug into his hair, and her cheek glided like a kitten's against his. Her breaths gasped softly -- ragged little sobs that had him feeling as powerful and victorious as a conquering hero.

"I think I really need that bath now," she said, rubbing her nose in his hair.

He smiled against her shoulder. "You smell divine. Lickable."

She pulled away and wrinkled her nose, her gaze sparkling with humor. "That's just gross."

Feeling lazy and happy, he lifted one brow to mock her. "Will you argue with me, now?"

Slowly, her expression grew solemn, and she sighed. "I have to—or I might just take this a little too seriously."When Khalid's expression grew stony once again, Casey schooled her mouth into a tight smile. "And we both know this was all about blowing off some steam." She wiggled her butt, trying to clue him in to the fact he should let her down now.

But Khalid seemed content to stand in the water with his dick still crammed all the way up inside her. And the Lord knew, she found that sensation entirely too cozy.

She didn't want to break the connection either, but she really, really didn't think she could pretend she wasn't singing a chorus of "Wows!" inside her for a moment longer. And that was so *un*cool.

Khalid will think I never get any. Although considering where he'd been most of his adult life, he should have been every bit as nervous and unsure as she had been—as she *was!*

However, his hands had mapped her body as though he knew very well the destination. He'd shown no hesitation — just a relentless, flattering need.

"I'm sorry I was so quick," he said, his voice soft.

"Quick?" she repeated dumbly. "Yeah, I guess."

But he hadn't been — he hadn't hurried through a thing. If he'd taken his time, she wondered whether she would have survived.

For once his gaze didn't look right through her. It wasn't amusement or ingrained caution she saw reflected in his dark eyes. His eyes were soft, his mouth no longer a firm, thin line.

As they stared at each other, Casey realized her body was priming itself again for another round of unbelievably primal sex.

"You didn't take off everything."

She gave him a quizzical glance.

He tapped the side of her glasses.

She'd made love to him, and never thought to remove her glasses. *I'm surprised the lenses didn't fog up!* "I didn't want to miss anything."

His gaze fell to her breasts. "I can understand the sentiment."

"Maybe..." She bit her lip when his gaze came back up, sharp and searching. *No guts no glory.* "Maybe, we should do it again."

"Just to be sure we didn't...miss anything?" His cock stirred inside her.

"Uh huh," she said, trying not to give him an answering squeeze. She didn't want to seem *too* eager — *too desperate!*

Apparently Khalid wasn't as keen on the idea of seconds. He lifted her up, letting his cock slip free and set her gently on her feet.

Stifling her disappointment, Casey stood still as he scooped up handfuls of water and sluiced them over her body, gliding his palms along every inch of her until she was clean. Her scraped knees he paid special attention to, taking care not to abrade them and blowing against the raw flesh to ease her hurt.

When she was washed to his satisfaction, he led her to the shallow edge of the creek bank.

She gave him a questioning glance when he halted there.

"Lie down."

"Here?"

His eyelids dipped and his nostrils flared. But what caught her attention most was the slow rise of his cock. "Tigers like the water."

Her whole body quivered at the deep, growling inflection in his voice, so at his urging she lay down. With the stream giving her bottom and legs buoyancy, she let her arms rest above her head on the bank.

Khalid stepped back into the water and knelt, bending to submerge his head below the surface. When he rose up, he flung back his hair, silver water arcing in the moonlight.

He looked like a dark god come to earth. Every curve of muscle defined by glittering droplets in moonlight. His dark-hooded eyes lent him a sinister appeal, as did his cock rising high against his belly.

Casey dug her heels into the gritty sand at the bottom of the creek and lifted her bottom above the water, spreading wide her legs in a crude but unambiguous invitation.

Khalid's chest expanded, and he pushed

back his long hair with one hand as he strode through the water to stand over her. He lifted a foot and nudged her knees wider apart and stared at the part of her that gleamed with her own juices.

Casey didn't know what guided her actions, but she reached between her legs and trailed a finger along her cleft, sinking one digit inside herself. She swirled her finger in her cream, circling while she watched his gaze follow her slow movements.

His hands fisted at his sides and his thighs tensed.

When she pulled out her finger and trailed it up the inside of his calf, the muscles jumped beneath her light touch. She slipped her legs between his and knelt at his feet.

She hadn't patience for prolonged foreplay. Instead she reached between his legs to cup his balls and pressed her mouth to the base of his cock. His breath hissed between his teeth, and his fingers speared into her hair to cup her head as she glided her lips and tongue up the outside of his shaft. She tugged and caressed his scrotum, and firmed her lips along his length, using her mouth and tongue to kiss and taste every inch of him.

When his fingers tightened, she relented and grasped the root of his cock between both her hands and swallowed the silky-soft cap at the tip. Khalid groaned and flexed his hips to glide along her tongue. Letting instinct guide her actions, she relaxed her jaws and sank deeper, urging him to fuck deeply into her mouth.

She moaned and twisted her head, swallowing to take him deeper and caress him with the muscles at the very back of her throat while she stroked his shaft with her clenched fists.

Over and over, she pumped him with her hands as she sucked him, countering his strokes, gliding faster and faster, waiting for the quivering of his thighs to tell her when he neared his orgasm.

At the last moment, she ringed the base of his cock and squeezed, halting his eruption. She reared back, coming off his cock. "Inside me," she said, and gave his plump crown a lick like it was a sweet candy. "I want you to come inside me, Khalid."

Khalid stood over her, his body tense and shuddering, his fists clenched at his sides. His chest rippled as another shudder racked him. "You've tempted the beast."

Casey had never been so turned on, knowing she was responsible for bringing this man to the edge of his control. Her own body shivered, releasing a gush of liquid desire. "I want all of you. Wild. Hard."

"Turn around," he ground out.

She released him and faced away, shaking when his thighs and belly snuggled against her bottom. His cock slid between her legs, and he glided his length along her cleft, delivering teasing strokes that had her wriggling to help him find her entrance.

But his fingers dug into her buttocks to hold her still. "You have given yourself into my care. Let me see to your pleasure."

"Please," she moaned. "It won't take much, I swear. Just come inside me."

His body left hers, and Casey sank on her elbows, frustrated, aching, her pussy clenching around air.

Then his mouth opened around her engorged outer lips and suckled.

Casey raised her bottom, encouraging him to delve deeper, but he continued to suck and tug her outer lips until her hips pulsed, following the rhythm of his lips.

When a finger followed the crease between her buttocks, Casey gasped. "Fuck! Oh, please." One digit fingered her tiny opening, circling the tightly pursed lips, smoothing around the circle until she realized her whole body clenched tight.

She forced herself to relax, sighing as the tip of his finger pressed inside.

Her belly and bottom quivered, but she widened her stance in the water, giving him greater access to any part of her he wished to explore. She gave over her trust, knowing he'd lead her on an exquisitely torturous journey.

Just when her ass began to burn, his tongue lapped between her labia, moving down to find the hard button of nerves that swelled with her arousal.

His lips pursed around it and he sucked it, while his fingertip fucked in and out of her ass.

A sob tore from her throat, but she kept her body poised on hands and knees for his pleasure. When he sank the entire length of his finger into her ass, she cried out.

The tight ring clenched hard around his finger, and Casey held herself rigid, wanting to pulse against the mouth suctioning her clit, yet afraid to drag on the finger stretching her.

His lips released her clit. "What do you want, Casey?"

"You…inside me."

"My cock?"

"Yes, your cock…inside me," she said in a rush, then biting her lip against a groan.

His finger swirled.

"Oh, God! I can't take it!"

"Not yet. Can I keep my finger here?"

"It hurts."

"Later, then." He pulled out of her and snuggled his thighs and hips closer. "Is this what you want?"

Her forehead sank to the surface of the water. "Yeeesss." His laughter, low and wicked, spun around her, leaving her feeling nervous and…expectant.

He shifted behind her, and then he felt for her pussy, spreading her lips with his fingers, his cock nudging between her clasping folds.

Then his hands came down on either side of hers—his belly, hot and solid, blanketing her back. He surrounded her with warmth and his musky-male scent. "Shall I be gentle, Casey?" he whispered into her ear as he teased her pussy with shallow probes of his blunt head.

"*Pleeeease,*" she keened, clenching tight her jaws, trying not to let him see how much she needed this, how far beyond control he'd pushed her.

His hips flexed, and his cock slid inside. Not far enough.

She squeezed her inner muscles around him and pushed back, trying to drive him deeper.

His laughter gusted against her ear. "I was rushed the last time. Can I not savor?"

"Oh, God, Khalid. Anything—" she gasped. "Do anything you want. Just move!"

"Anything?" One hand lifted from the ground and palmed her spiking breast. He squeezed the nipple between his thumb and forefinger. "Will you be so compliant later when I take you again?"

"Again?" How could he take time to tease? Didn't he know she was a second from exploding? She drew a jagged breath. "I'll do anything. Give you everything. Suck you dry, if you like—just please move."

His nose nuzzled her ear. "So coarse. Do I make you this way? Or are you like this with other men?"

"Huh?"

"You came willingly to me. I wonder if you are so eager, so accommodating, with others. I find I'm a little jealous."

"Jealous? Because of me?" A strained gust of laughter erupted from her throat. "Khalid, I have no sex life to speak of. Did you see the tattoo on my arm? I haven't had an injection of birth control in a couple of years."

He stopped nuzzling her ear. "You aren't afraid of becoming pregnant?"

Her breath hitched. "You aren't protected?"

"I'm Muslim, *habibah*."

"So?" she said, her voice rising along with her alarm. "You've lived in the West. You know our conventions."

His body tensed. "I am a Muslim," he repeated, firmness in his tone as he squeezed her nipple harder. "Some things I will not compromise for convenience sake."

"But you've done this before. Fucked."

He sighed, and his cock grew still inside her. "Yes. I've done this—but in my youth."

"Isn't it against your beliefs?"

"I find I am…overcome with my need. This," he said, spearing once, deeper than before, "I cannot control."

While her mind shouted a warning, her body melted, mollified by his confession. *Shit!* But really, what were the chances of her becoming pregnant? It was just one night. "You seem to be controlling *this* just fine," she muttered, hot and very bothered.

His body relaxed against hers again, and he pressed a kiss to her shoulder. "I mustn't disappoint. Think of my honor. I have a reputation to enhance."

"More notes for me to take?" she said, bracing her hands firmly in the sand, readying for him to unleash a storm all over her.

"If you wish to write about it. Perhaps you need more inspiration?"

"Definitely." Her breath hissed between her teeth when he circled his hips. "Deeper, please."

"I'm getting there. Have patience."

"You're killing me."

"Shall I stop?"

Casey groaned in frustration. "I'm through talking to you. You don't understand a thing I'm saying."

"Really?" He nipped her neck. "Shall I translate?"

"I speak perfect Arabic, thank you very much."

"But you are lacking in your understanding of a man's physical forms of communication."

"What the hell am I missing?"

"I am talking because I need to get my mind off how delicious you feel squeezing around me. You're so wet and hot my body is primed beyond restraint to take you."

"What the hell have I been begging for?"

He nipped her ear. "Shhh. Your begging

only makes it harder for me to keep you safe."

"Unnnh," she groaned, aching to respond to his admission, but mindful of his need to explain.

"When I am aroused," he whispered, "...whether in anger or lust, I cannot control the shifting. I would not want to become an animal when I am inside you. I might do you great harm."

She opened her mouth to reassure him she was ready to take the risk.

"No! I know what you are thinking, but a tiger is very large, very heavy. And I cannot swear I would be able to control the urge to hold you with a tiger's grip while I take you."

Sounded kinda sexy to her, and a lot kinky. "A tiger's grip?"

"A tiger holds his mate still with his teeth."

"Oh!"

"Do you understand now, why I need to do this at my own pace?"

She got the point all right. "Do I have to pretend patience?"

"Of course not. Your lack of patience amuses me."

"That's what I'm here for — to provide the comedic relief."

"I swear I am not laughing at you."

"Really? I can feel you grinning against my neck."

"This is a grimace. Can I proceed now?"

"With what? The conversation?"

"No, with the taking."

Chapter 4

That silenced her complaints.

Khalid squeezed her soft breast one more time, and then dropped his hand to the ground. Gently, he gripped her shoulder with his teeth.

A reminder for her to behave.

Casey shivered beneath him and her channel tightened. Slow and easy. That's how he intended to build her release. He'd show her he could control his inner beast. Prove to himself he had the upper hand in this challenge. And what a challenge she was. The frosty little analyst in her conservative suit had become a water nymph. A temptress with golden hair and skin that glistened in the moonlight.

He released her shoulder and started to move, pushing into her body, her inner tissue and muscle wrapping around him like a moist, hot fist. He stroked in and out, his breaths deepening gradually, the depth he plumbed increasing by centimeters. He'd take it slowly, incrementally, committing these moments to his memory. If Allah were kind, this would be his last thought as he slipped away from life.

For he had no doubt he headed toward his death.

Casey whimpered and fell forward on her elbows, her face above the water, her hips remaining high. In this position she could not press back, couldn't encourage him into a blinding flurry of passion. She had to take him—however he chose.

He chose faster, deeper, his chest tightening, his breaths heavier. His balls drew tautly against his groin as he neared the precipice.

He widened his knees between hers and leaned back, grasping her buttocks to force them against his belly, sharpening his own strokes as the clawing need built tension in his thighs and belly.

Deeper, harder—he closed his eyes and concentrated on the escalating pace of his motions, striving to deliver thrusts that would ignite her ardor. The slap of flesh—her bottom to his lower belly and thighs—had him tightening his grip, forcing her faster to meet the hammering of his cock.

Casey whimpered and groaned. Her breaths gusted loudly with each jarring thrust, until she gave a strangled scream and arched her back, her head flinging back as he powered into her.

Unrelenting, he held off his release, determined to make this moment last a lifetime. But the black wave roared up, cresting over him and his balls emptied, cum spurting in endless, throbbing bursts to bathe the womb of the woman who held on, barely keeping her head above the water.

Khalid pulled her into his arms, maintaining the glorious connection until his body was spent. His breath rasped harshly and he turned her head with his fingers to kiss her mouth, sliding kisses over her swollen lips, her nose and her chin.

When at last his body and mind calmed, he leaned his forehead against hers.

"Wow," she whispered, her eyes still closed behind her glasses.

A smile stretched his lips at her reverent

tone. "Did I disappoint?"

Her eyes opened and tears quickly welled in them. "Are you kidding? I think I died for a second there."

He hugged her close, sighing when her arms slid atop his to return the caress. "I will have to strive for longer next time."

"Make sure I never wake up."

*****

"I can't sleep here like this," Casey whispered, although she had slept for some time if the graying light was any indication. She hoped like hell she hadn't snored.

"Is the ground too hard?" he murmured sleepily beside her.

She liked his deep, sleepy voice a little too much. Made her think about what it would be like as a regular occurrence in her life. "No, not hard. Bugs," she said, forcing the words through a constricting throat.

"Bugs?"

She felt him smile against her shoulder. "Something crawled across my ankle," she lied. "We should sleep in the truck."

He pulled away and helped her rise from the ground beside the creek bank. "You go," he said, standing close enough to heat her skin, but not touching.

"What about you? You need sleep, too."

"I want to run."

Her eyes widened as she realized what he meant. "Oh. Should I roll up my windows, then?"

"Do you think glass would stop me?" His smile was self-derisive. "I will harm no one. I just need to run."

"All right," she said, as she rubbed her arms

against a sudden chill. "Wake me when you come back?"

He waited while she dressed in her rumpled clothing, and then picked up his M-19 and led her through the brush, taking care to hold back vines and branches so they wouldn't scratch her.

At the truck, he waited for her to climb in. "I won't be long past the dawn."

She watched him walk away, reminded by the set of his shoulders at the pride and strength held within his beautiful body — and the loneliness he wore like a shabby coat just beneath the surface.

"I really need to get him some clothes."

The cab of the truck proved too stifling, so she lay in the bed of the truck, her suit jacket rolled into a ball for a pillow, trying to catch a few minutes of sleep. But her thoughts were troubled. She'd let him get too close — too fast. His prediction appeared to be coming true. She was poised to aid him in escaping.

A branch snapped nearby, the crisp sound making her jump.

Sure a small animal rustled in the underbrush, she settled down again and tried to logically address the issues that niggled at her conscience. She was an analyst from the very agency that was set on taking him in. She ought to get into the truck and drive like hell away. It was her duty to escape him and report his location.

However, he was the most intriguing puzzle she'd ever encountered. Part soldier, part criminal. Maybe part double-agent.

And then there was that little thing about him being a tiger, too...

She shivered, remembering how forcefully he'd taken her, how strong his arms had felt as he held her, how fiercely he'd thrust inside her, allowing her no place inside herself to hide her response. She'd never experienced anything like Khalid Razeh. The thought that she might never again saddened her.

Another snap sounded nearby, and she tensed.

Suddenly, a large creature landed in the truck bed beside her and she shrieked—until she noted the white fur with black stripes.

Khalid, the tiger, was enormous. By the creaking of the truck beneath his weight, she guessed he easily topped six hundred pounds. She gauged his length at nearly ten feet, maybe more, which would have made the fit snug inside the truck bed if the tailgate hadn't been down.

Remembering his assurances, she remained still as he stared down at her. A low growling rumbled from his mouth, causing her jerk, but he didn't pounce. Instead, he tilted his head and stared. His blue eyes didn't blink as she stared back. She remained rigid, not breathing, as he bent his giant head and sniffed along her body, pausing over her sex, then snuffling softly upward until she felt his breaths gust from his moist nose against her throat.

With his large head blotting out the brightening sky, she knew if she didn't draw a deeper breath she'd faint. She gasped, but her sudden movement didn't cause a reaction. His prickly fur brushed her cheek and he withdrew, letting her draw a deeper, steadying breath.

The large cat settled on its haunches beside her and rolled to his side, lifting a heavy paw over her belly.

She didn't mind the weight. Too curious to

hold onto her alarm, she studied him and realized he was fully sentient.

He allowed her to take his measure. His head was wide, his snout long—the long teeth peeking between his lips, frightening. She slowly lifted a hand to smooth over his fur and found it slightly coarse. She rubbed slowly, noting he held himself still and guessed he didn't want her frightened. The paw resting on her belly fascinated her. She hadn't realized how broad it would be. She turned it, marveling at the fur surrounding the pads. This adaptation was what had allowed it to slip so silently through the woods. His claws were thankfully retracted.

When her gaze rose to his once more, he opened his mouth around a wide yawn, and she felt her heartbeat skitter once again. A mouthful of white, curved fangs—any one of them alarming on their own—gleamed like mini-scimitars.

His head settled to the truck bed, and they lay side by side as the sun blinked on the horizon at their feet.

"We should sleep," she said, hoping he understood.

He yawned again and stretched, his rear paws sliding beyond the end of the truck.

With his paw warming her stomach, she snuggled her cheek against her jacket. She blinked once, then her eyes widened again as the tiger lying beside her shimmered, his shape morphing before her eyes, an image of his human body limned in light, superimposing over the tiger's.

Before her gasp ended, Khalid lay beside her, his breath panting, his hand curving around her waist to pull her flush against his body.

With his head buried in her hair, his whole

body shuddered, then lay still. "I think that should warrant another 'Wow'," he said, his voice unsteady.

She smoothed a hand over his shoulder. "Does that hurt—when you make a shift?"

Khalid rolled to his back. "Not really. I feel a jerk, and all my muscles constrict. But it's not really painful."

"Are you sentient after you shift?"

His head turned toward her, and his dark brows drew together in an irritated frown. "Must you always analyze?"

"I'm sorry. I'm just so curious. I know it's a fault." She withdrew her hand and tucked it beneath her cheek. "I'll shut up."

A muscle at the side of his jaw flexed. "Are you tired?"

"I barely slept, but no. I'm too keyed up to sleep."

"Good." He rolled over her, pressing her to her back.

When he nudged her legs apart with his knees, she opened to him thrilled he still wanted her.

Settling his hips between her thighs, he pushed up, resting on his elbows as his hands cupped her face. "This bed isn't very soft."

"I don't care. I swear it." With the long, thick ridge of his cock grinding against her sex, she really, really didn't.

Khalid sat up, his knees sliding to either side of her thighs and he slipped his hands beneath the hem of her skirt to push it slowly upward.

Casey helped—lifting her bottom to let the skirt bunch around her waist.

Then he stared, unmoving for a long

moment, at the tiny triangle of fabric concealing her sex.

Casey watched Khalid, as fascinated by the size of his erection as she was the expression he wore. Fiercely frowning eyebrows framed his dark, unblinking eyes. His cheeks and jaw were taut. His lips parted and his tongue swept out to wet them. Then he shifted his gaze to her. A wicked grin curved only the corners of his mouth.

Stinging, electrical excitement swelled her labia and tightened her nipples to scrape against her blouse. When his hand cupped her breasts through the fabric, the charge arced like lightening from breast to womb. As she sighed, her back arched, pressing her breast harder against his palm.

He opened the top three buttons of her blouse, then pushed her bra up, forcing her breasts to squeeze under the bottom elastic. Her nipples swelled, poking straight up. When he leaned down to suckle them, one by one, Casey mewled.

He straightened and gave her a look so filled with sensual promise that her clitoris began to swell.

Her only thought was to help him build this delicious moment. She lifted her hands to cup her bare breasts and thumbed her aching nipples, knowing he'd watch. His cock jerked, and his hand sank between her closed legs as he watched her pleasure her breasts. He traced her cleft through the fabric, growling in the back of his throat when moisture seeped through her panties. When she pinched her nipples hard, causing herself to gasp, he tore the skinny elastic bands on both sides of her panties and swept the silky underwear away. This time when his fingers traced the length of her pussy, they sank into creamy heat.

One at a time, he lifted his knees to allow her to spread her legs. She did so without hesitation, bending her knees to tilt up her hips and provide him the view she knew he craved.

His chest rose with his indrawn breath, which was very gratifying to Casey. She liked knowing she took his breath away. He held the strings to make her body and soul dance. He leaned over her and kissed the nipples peeking between her fingers, and then he lay fully on top of her.

Resting on his elbows, he kissed her mouth, stroking his tongue inside to mate with hers. He kept his eyes open as he kissed her. Although this close his features blurred, she watched him right back.

Face to face, fully *missionary* this time, all the parts of him she wished to touch were within reach. When he broke the kiss, she said, "I like keeping you naked. So little fuss."

Khalid's lips quirked on one side. "But it makes it hard to hide what I'm feeling."

Casey grinned back. "*Very* hard." She lifted her hips to grind his cock against her pubic bone. Her hands glided along his shoulders, feeling muscles flex and ripple as he held himself above her.

His smile dimmed. "We have much to accomplish today. And we will part."

"I know." She'd agree for now. Later...well, she'd play it by ear.

His hips lifted and the blunt tip of his cock pressed against her folds. They parted as he slid forward, seating himself deep inside her.

They stared at one another, sharing a moment of happiness.

Casey drew a deep breath. "I wish—"

"Me, too. We have this," he whispered, then he began to stroke inside her, slow, lazy glides that heated her core.

Casey caressed him tenderly, molding the muscles of his shoulders and back, growing slick with sweat as he thrust harder. Her breaths grew ragged, and toward the end, when his eyes closed and his whole body tensed, she sobbed and leaned up to kiss his neck and chin, anything she could reach with her mouth. Knowing this might be the last time, she treasured each exquisite minute—until she too was overcome and let the darkness sweep over her.

*****

With her hands filled with shopping bags, Casey made one last stop at a quaint, limestone grocery store. The old plank floor and the smells of animal fodder and sausages clipped with old-fashioned clothespins filled the air.

A television blared from behind the counter as she set down bottled water, cheese, bread and summer sausage.

"...the Halcyon Institute burned to the ground, along with seventeen staff and physicians, as firefighters fought to keep the blaze from spreading to surrounding fields. Although the exact cause is still unknown, an official who wished to keep his identity unknown speculated this might be the result of a terrorist act. According to our source, Halcyon's top secret military contracts may have been the target of militant extremists..."

Casey froze. With the attack on the southern border and Khalid's presence so near the medical facility, local authorities would be gunning for anyone whose appearance met their profile.

She paid for her purchases and hurried out

to the truck she'd parked at the side of the building. Although she'd been careful not to raise suspicion and had slicked back her hair into a non-descript knot, she knew her description might be in the hand of law enforcement officials at this moment.

She had to get to Khalid quickly. More importantly, she had to convince him to allow her to bring him in.

Chapter 5

As she pulled off the gravel road leading to the small wooded copse, she checked her rearview mirror one last time. Her palms were sweaty, her nerves a mess.

Khalid stepped out from behind a tree and walked toward her, his gaze alert.

Something of her alarm must have shown in her features, because his back stiffened and his glance swept the road behind her.

Resentment flared inside her. He'd placed his trust in her. She'd betrayed her agency for him. They were in this together now.

"Something has happened?" he asked, his voice carefully neutral, his gaze probing hers.

"There was an attack on Halcyon. It was burned to the ground. They suspect terrorist activity."

Khalid snorted. "So I'm a marked man? What's new?"

"Get dressed. We need to get to a phone."

"And who will you call, Casey McTaggert?"

"My boss. He'll know what to do."

To her dismay, he shook his head. "You must get to your phone and call. I must go where I am compelled to go."

He'd offered her a choice. He knew she could betray him.

Now, she stood at the crossroads, knowing she would lose everything she'd prized — her professional integrity, her exciting and important job. However, staring at him, she knew they'd be meaningless and her life empty if she didn't follow this through. Even though continuing down this path, with him, might kill her.

"I bought a map while I was out," she bit out. "Where's my briefcase?"Khalid read her decision in the tension in her shoulders and the upward tilt of her chin. While one part of him wanted her safe and untouched by the ugliness they were sure to meet down the road, another rejoiced.

He held out his hand for her packages and walked back to the Hummer, now parked beneath the corrugated tin stall. While she rummaged through her notes, he dressed in the blue jeans and t-shirt she'd bought him. His lips curved at the Texas Longhorn logo on the front of the burnt orange shirt. With his hair tied in a ponytail he might pass for a Hispanic student, at least from a distance.

She understood his tricks.

"The other shifters, the ones who have escaped our field agents, seem to be heading here," she said, pointing to the map.

He glanced over her shoulders and saw the green contours drawn to depict mountains just north of the location. He saw the name "Davis Mountains" and something inside him clicked. "I'm supposed to go here," he said, pointing toward a small-hatched area.

Her head jerked up. "That's a military post. A secret one. How do you know about it?" Suspicion showed in the hard glare she leveled on him. This was the Casey, the analyst.

He closed his eyes. "I have a picture—sand, mesquite trees and cactus, rough hills, a tall chain link fence with concertina wire strung across the top. I'm supposed to go there." When he opened his eyes, her pale brows were drawn.

"I don't understand. You see these things, but you don't know your purpose?"

Frustration made him cranky. "I was in a hospital. The one you know well," he said heatedly. "I heard the cries of other prisoners — all American. Something was done to me — perhaps to all of them — beside the DNA-splicing therapies that changed our bodies. I think they used brain-washing techniques to further a darker plan."

She nodded and refolded the map. "We'll head first to foothills. Let's see what we find there."

*****

The drive toward the Davis Mountains wore on both of them. The past hours had been spent in silence. The sense of connection they'd shared faded with the daylight, fading like the hope Casey held that somehow everything would turn out all right.

The closer they drew to their destination, the more rigid and scary Khalid grew. His hands fisted on his thighs, his face tautened into hard-edged fury that spelled trouble for anyone who crossed him.

In the distance, a lighted building and parking lot grew brighter and larger as they neared. If her suspicions were correct, they might find part of the puzzle here. The journeys of the soldiers who'd escaped the agency's net all converged in this vicinity.

"I'm going to stop for gas," she said, not mentioning what she suspected. No need to rile the tiger if she was dead wrong. "Maybe you should stretch your legs. Use the facilities."

He nodded and waited for her to draw up to the pumps. He stepped down from the cab and headed toward the convenience store to the left of a connecting bar with the name "Last Watering Hole" emblazoned across the top in bright red neon — a green neon prickly pear cactus at the side provided punctuation. As she unscrewed the gas cap, she watched him slowly approach the store. Suddenly, his back grew ramrod straight and his head pivoted toward the bar. His steps quickened. Casey dropped the cap on the pavement and circled the truck, intent on following him inside the bar.

He pushed through the old-fashioned swinging doors and disappeared inside. When they swung closed her hands were already there to brace against their outward swing. She peered over them, into the darkened interior. Light shone from behind the bar. Lamps on the booths lining the walls were dim, casting shadows on the few occupants.

As Khalid stepped further inside, growls — throaty, feline warnings erupted from one dark corner. Tall, broad-shouldered figures stepped into the light.

Khalid stood stock-still and his nostrils flared. He was scenting them. His neck appeared to bristle and a rumbling sound erupted from his throat.

Casey swept inside and stepped close.

"Get out of here, Casey," he said, over his shoulder, his attention never leaving the men warily approaching him.

"You can't shift now, Khalid. These guys are like you."

"You know this?" His head swung her way

and his gaze pinned her. "You brought me here because of them, didn't you? Do they work with you?"

"No! I swear I wasn't even sure they'd be here."

"But you didn't warn me." It was as though she watched a curtain lower over his face. His expression shuttered, closing her out.

While she recognized the mistake she'd made, she kept her focus on the present, quickly encroaching danger. She turned toward the men gathering closer. "I'm assuming you're Dylan Gomez, Kol Thorstein, and Ramon Osceola?"

That drew the men up short. Their attention turned from Khalid to her with a whiplash turn of their heads.

Her mouth suddenly grew dry as the desert outside. After all she was facing a pack of large, wild cats. "We need to talk." When they all tensed, looking as though they intended to pounce, she blurted out, "I think I know what's happening. Why you were drawn here."

A woman stepped around the three men. "We've already been talking, but I'm not sure it's safe to stay here now," she said staring at Khalid as though she knew him — and was afraid. "The news and all. His picture's been all over the TV."

"We go together," Khalid said. "Leave the woman behind," he said, lifting his chin toward the petite blonde.

The three looked at each other, and the one she knew was Kol Thorstein from his service bio photo stepped forward, menace emanating from every fiber of his being. "The woman goes with us. Where are you heading?"

Khalid glared back, not backing down. "I

think you know. We leave now." He turned on his heel and brushed past Casey without giving her a glance.

Heartsick and more than a little angry, she looked back at the others. "Like I said, I know a thing or two about what's happening here. I know about the experiments in that hospital. But it goes deeper."

"Why should we trust you—*and him?*"

"I think you know he's in a similar…state. Also a victim of a little genetic tampering, and he doesn't have a clue what he's doing here either."

"Then what the hell will we learn from him?"

"Not a damn thing."

Already operating like a single unit, the men narrowed their glances at her.

"He can't solve the mystery. But I have a few theories. But please, we need to go."

Ramon nodded slowly. "We'll come, but we won't go unarmed." His black eyes and taut expression issued a warning she couldn't mistake. *One false move and she'd be cat food!*

"Khalid has no weapons."

He snorted—something Casey was coming to recognize as a purely male form of communication. "He's a fucking tiger. He could rip us all to shreds."

"Into the truck, then?" she said, getting more anxious as the moments ticked by. "We don't have that far to go."

"I'll ride shotgun," Kol said, brushing past her just as rudely as Khalid had.

"Fine," Casey bit out, relieved the men would accompany them. But after this, she was swearing off men—and tigers and lions and bears!

*****

"She's a handful," the blond man said as he stared out the window.

Khalid bristled. He might be angry as hell with Casey, but she was his. "She's not for you."

"Hey, I wasn't saying…" Kol said, raising his free hand in mock surrender. "I have enough control not to jump the first set of female bones I see. Barely," he muttered the last word under his breath.

"Just so we understand each other."

"Loud and clear. It's not like I didn't smell your scent all over her."

Khalid gripped the steering wheel so hard it creaked. He eased off, reminding himself the man was just trying to get under his skin. "You were there. At the hospital."

"Yeah. I recognized your scent, too. Recognized the voice, too."

Khalid gave him a sharp glance.

"Your prayers. Five times a day. The singing kinda carried. Made me think the hospital might be in the Middle East."

"It wasn't."

"No, we figured that out." At Khalid's questioning glance, he added. "Hannah — the woman with us — she was one of the scientists working there. If you haven't guessed, that Halcyon facility that blew up this morning was it."

The steering wheel creaked again.

A short bark of laughter burst from Kol. "Yeah, I feel the same way. Wanted to light the fuse myself."

With one question answered, Khalid felt relief that finally he might be within reach of the last clues. Perhaps Casey was right. These men might help get to the bottom of the nightmares. "Do you have…dreams?"

"You mean do I see myself standing outside the fence of the new NORAD facility?" This time his glance held no animosity, just a question.

Khalid nodded, his throat tightening. "The same."

"Don't know what it means."

"Casey does, I think."

"She didn't clue you in?"

"No, she keeps secrets very well."

A knock sounded at the window at the back of the truck cab.

"She wants you to pull over at that rest stop," Kol said. "There!" He pointed to a blue sign at the side of the road.

Before he came to a full stop, the men in the back leapt from the truck bed. Khalid stepped out as Casey was helped down by two sets of male hands. He wanted to brush them all away, not let them touch her, but he held onto his anger, remembering how badly he'd misjudged them before. She might look at him with guileless eyes behind her silver-framed glasses, but she'd tricked *him* — The Tiger!

*****

Casey moved to the picnic benches set just out of the reach of lamplight and took a seat, facing away from the table and toward the men and woman who ringed her now. She gave them all a surly stare. "Jesus, I wish you guys wouldn't do that. I feel like I'm standing in front of the Inquisition."

"So tell us first how you know us," Ramon said, his voice an ominous mix of growling masculine frustration.

"I read your service files."

His large hands settled on his hips, which flexed his pecs and reminded her he wasn't any house cat. "Who are you with?"

"Um, I'm not sure you'd know. We're under the umbrella of the National Security Agency."

"A spook?" Kol asked, his posture no more encouraging than his "brother's".

"No, I'm just an analyst. I'm not field agent. I gather intelligence...and try to piece together...plots." She gave Khalid a wary glance, knowing they had never really gotten down to the brass tacks of what she did for a living. She cleared her throat. "For the past eight years, I've been gathering items specifically related to a man considered a Middle Eastern terrorist." She winced at her choice of words and gave Khalid an apologetic shrug, which directed all hostile eyes his way.

Khalid's expression grew deadly intent.

"Anything that 'felt' like it related to him, I kept," she said, speaking as if she wasn't talking about a man she'd taken as a lover and who wasn't standing five feet away. It was just easier.

"When he dropped off the face of the earth earlier this year," she continued, "I started searching for items a little farther afield. I'm guessing that's when he was picked up and transported to Hell Hospital—the Halcyon facility—although how they ever found him..."

"A round-up at a university," he muttered. "They didn't even know what they had."

"That explains it." She nodded, vowing to go back through the intelligence to find out which university and what branch of service or the government was responsible. They'd screwed up. That was, if she still had a job after all this.

"You were saying…" Dylan said, with an edge of irritation seeping into his voice.

"Yes, I was. Um, this is where it gets complicated. All this would seem unrelated. But I realized when I heard about the medical facility bombing…" She threw up her hands, frustrated she wasn't making herself clear. "Bear with me, I'm still assimilating. That medical facility was the cash cow for Senator Gonzalez on the House Armed Forces committee. His political well-being is directly tied to theirs. He sponsored legislation that funded their studies. He is in charge of the oversight investigation into allegations they've misused funds…for experiments that weren't approved."

They got it. Like light bulbs suddenly going off, they connected the dots, just like she finally had.

"Sonuvabitch!" Kol said, throwing a punch into the air. "The U.S. government paid for the research. The bastards at Halcyon decided to play God, and then when their hands were caught in the cookie jar, they blew the place up."

"But what about us?" Ramon asked.

"Along with the DNA-splicing," Khalid said, his voice dead even, "they conducted drug-induced brainwashing techniques. Nothing cutting edge there."

"But why?"

Khalid's gaze held hers. "They needed a scapegoat and several backups. You were all in line for the job—until they happened upon me."

Casey nodded. "You're perfect. You blow up the facility. Then you show up at NORAD to conduct an even worse attack, and they get to kill you and further the Senator's political agenda."

"Gonzalez opposed the peace talks." Khalid's head fell back and he drew a deep breath. *"Son-of-a-fucking-syphilis-ridden-goat!"*

First Kol, then Ramon and Dylan burst into laughter. Even Casey giggled.

When Khalid straightened, a sheepish grin stretched across his face. "So now we know why. Anyone have a guess as to how we put a stop to this?"

Chapter 6

Casey flipped Kol's cell phone closed. "That should do it. My boss will make the necessary phone calls to make sure the Department of Defense knows to back off. Until then we need to find a place to lay low."

"They expect us to continue to the Davis Mountains," Khalid said.

Kol shrugged. "So, we go the opposite direction?"

"Whatever we do, we need to move fast, because that call was likely traced," Casey said, wishing they were already miles from there.

"Can't we just sit tight and let them take us?" Hannah asked. When the men scowled her way, she shrugged. "If we turn ourselves in, we only have to sit in lock-up a short time while this is all sorted out."

Casey shook her head. "I wish it was that simple. The military's already seen what these guys can do. They aren't going to risk them turning into cats."

Ramon nodded. "It'll be strictly shoot to kill. And Hannah, you're on the short list, too. They blew up the rest of the staff at Halcyon to keep them from talking."

Hannah took a deep breath before nodding her agreement. "All right. We run."

They piled back into the truck. This time Khalid handed Casey up into the cab. His expression was no more inviting, but the fact he wanted her close by reassured her he was getting over his fury.

While he didn't speak, he also didn't object when her hand rested on his thigh as they pulled out of the rest stop and back onto the highway. Sitting beside him, breathing in his distinct male scent, brought her a calm she didn't expect. Casey even began to think this might work out—that there might be an end to their ordeal.

They drove without headlights to leave the last traceable signature, past the Last Watering Hole, heading southeast—away from the Davis Mountains, away from the southern NORAD headquarters.

Casey was dozing, her head falling against Khalid's shoulder, when a rumbling growl sounded from Khalid and Kol cursed under his breath. She straightened and saw that they approached a crossroad of a small state highway. In the distance, were the blue strobing lights of several police vehicles forming a roadblock.

"That's for us," Kol said, sitting on the other side of her.

"What do we do?" Casey asked, exhaustion making her mind feel sluggish and muzzy.

"Well, we can't stand and fight," Kol said. "We don't have a beef with these guys."

"Think they've seen us?" Casey's stomach plummeted.

Khalid stomped on the brakes and did a quick U-turn in the middle of the road, the truck's tires kicking up gravel from the shoulder.

"So much for subtle," Kol murmured.

Behind them, two police cruisers drew away from the roadblock.

"Fuck me! Khalid, step on it!"

Khalid pushed the old truck to its limit, but the police were gaining on them.

"We need to go off-road to make it harder for them to follow us," Kol said, his words firing like bullets.

"If we can just find a place to hide and hunker down until the agency gets the word out," Casey said, leaning forward to grip the dashboard.

Khalid shot her a glance. "Are you sure your people aren't willing to sacrifice us?" he said, his hands gripping the steering wheel so hard it groaned.

Casey gave him a bitter smile. "The one thing I know is that my agency looks for any chance to yank the administration's chain. Gonzalez is one of the VP's cronies. My guys are gonna have a field day with the intelligence you provide."

Suddenly, Khalid jerked the wheel to the right and headed across the desert toward a line of moon-silvered hills in the distance.

Casey glanced behind her. Those in the back of the truck held onto whatever they could to keep from being pitched over the side as the truck hit ever rock and hole on the desert floor.

The police vehicles didn't pursue, but Khalid continued toward the dark hills, shadowed by moonlight. A loud pop sounded and the truck lurched to one side.

"We blew a tire!" Kol shouted.

"We're not stopping to change it," Khalid said, from between gritted teeth.

Then they heard the sound they dreaded most—the whine of engines and the distinctive sound of whirring wings coming from the air above them.

Khalid brought the truck to an abrupt halt at the edge of an arroyo.

They all clambered out, sliding on their asses to the bottom of the dry creek bed. Once there, the men knelt in a circle in the dirt.

"We need to get into the hills," Ramon said, holding Hannah's hand. "If we can find a place to wait it out, we might buy some time."

"We may not have it," Khalid said. "Maybe we should leave the women behind. Hide them, then lead the helicopters away."

"No way," Hannah said, shouldering her way into the circle.

"I'm not staying behind." Casey grabbed Khalid's arm. "We stick together."

The men shared charged glances.

"We won't be able to shift," Kol said. "The women will never keep up."

"We stick together," Casey repeated. "And shifting is out of the question. Don't give them an excuse to shoot." A hundred awful scenarios played through her mind. No way was she letting the guys sacrifice themselves for her.

Hannah's chin lifted. "We're wasting time." Without waiting for the guys to make up their minds what to do, she took off, running through the bottom of the creek bed, away from the roar of the aircraft bearing down on them from above.

Casey followed on her heels, cursing under her breath as her pumps twisted in the gravel and sand. Khalid ran up beside her and grabbed her hand, pulling her along, steadying her.

When they reached the end of the arroyo, Dylan crawled up the side and signaled for them to follow. Under the cover of trees, they ran full out toward an outcrop of rocks.

Casey felt a sense of déjà vu. This had been how it all started. In the rocks, cowering from an unseen enemy. She wondered now who had been firing at them in the first place—she knew who had provided the intelligence to pinpoint Khalid's location, but she didn't know whom Halcyon had paid to take him out. If she lived past tonight, she'd see they roasted in hell.

They crested a rise and started over it, just as the first machine guns started to fire.

"There's a canyon! Get into the canyon," Ramon shouted.

Khalid nearly pulled her arm out of her socket as he forced her to run in a zigzag pattern. They weren't going to make it. The shots were coming too close. Then a bright light shone on them from above. Suddenly, the firing ceased. Casey didn't stop, didn't try to think. She followed blindly, the darkness inside the canyon walls an impenetrable cloak. Thankful for Khalid's superior night vision, she put one foot in front of the other, trusting he wouldn't let her fall. He pulled short and ducked behind a large boulder. He shoved her to the ground and pushed her close to the rock, then blanketed her body with his own.

Her heartbeat pounded so loud, it almost shut out the sounds happening beyond the entrance to the canyon. Men shouting, a dozen boot steps scraping over rocks. She didn't know where the others had gone, whether they'd been hit and might be lying wounded or dying on the canyon floor.

However, Khalid's solid body, pressed so close to hers reassured her. If this was how it all ended, at least she knew he still cared.

It took a moment to register the silence that

fell around them. Pregnant, menacing — now that she was no longer running for her life, Casey started to shake.

"Shhh," Khalid whispered a warning.

What in hell am I doing here? I'm going to get him killed. This was so far removed from her experience. The most dangerous thing she'd ever faced in her life was her morning commute.

"Shhh," he repeated, a hand sliding between the rock she faced to wrap around her middle.

A shallow sob tore from her throat.

Khalid's lips grazed her cheek, and then he slid his cheek alongside hers.

It was enough to still the scream threatening to erupt from inside her. She closed her eyes and leaned back against him, accepting his comfort in this cold, hard place.

"This is Captain Gunnar Sorensen," a familiar voice sounded over a loud speaker. "Send out Casey McTaggert."

She jerked against Khalid.

He remained still, not breathing behind her for all of a second, then moved away from her. "Go!" he whispered.

Casey rolled onto her back, peering into the darkness. She could see the outline of his body, lying beside her in the dirt. "I won't leave you."

"You're our only chance, Casey."

She knew he was right, but she was afraid to leave him, afraid this would be the last time she'd have a chance to say what she was in her heart. She reached for him, finding his face. Her palms cupped his cheeks and she leaned toward him. "Khalid Razeh, don't you do anything foolish — and don't you get yourself killed. I care about you. I believe in you. See this through?"

His lips found hers for a short, searing kiss. His hand clasped the back of her neck and he placed his forehead against hers. "I can't do this, Casey. Not unless you live." He kissed her hard, one last time and then let her go.

She climbed to her feet, still hugging the side of the boulder. "Captain Sorensen, I'm coming out," she shouted.

*****

The surrender of the shifters was almost an anti-climax. One by one, Kol, Dylan, and Ramon strode out of the canyon with their hands behind their heads. Hannah limped out behind Ramon, looking owl-eyed and frightened.

After they'd all been manacled and herded aboard a chopper, Casey fastened her harness. "I'm glad you're okay, Captain. I worried about you."

"I had a hell of a headache, but there was no way in hell I'd have missed the action tonight. Although I have to admit, it turned out a lot different than I'd planned." He gave her lopsided smile. "That's some story you have. Hope some of it's true. I'm breakin' all kinds rules here."

Casey leaned over him to peer into his hand-held link-up. He'd sent a message to his command to let them know about the change of plans. A message blinked, and he clicked to open it. *New orders. Bring them to NORAD. ASAP.*

He gave her a thumbs up, and she settled back for the ride. For once her stomach didn't feel the least bit queasy. She glanced back at the helicopter carrying the men and Hannah and finally let herself relax.

She'd have one hell of a debriefing once they landed. Then all hell would break lose.

Halcyon and Senator Gonzalez would be up on charges that would have Washington buzzing for months.

It wouldn't be an easy time for the shifters. Halcyon might not be their keepers any longer, but the military and intelligence community would all want a piece of them.

Khalid's fate was a little harder to predict. 'The Tiger' no longer had a viable cover in the field. But where could a former Middle Eastern operative be welcome? If she got a chance to make a suggestion, there was a burning need for someone with his experience and perspective right inside her agency's policy think tank. They'd need all the help they could get to achieve a working truce.

And after…well, maybe she'd finally get the chance to find out if a tiger could purr.